Black Gold

Stella LaRosa
Book 3

L.T. Ryan

with

Kristi Belcamino

For information contact:

contact@ltryan.com

https://LTRyan.com

https://www.instagram.com/ltryanauthor/

https://www.facebook.com/LTRyanAuthor

Prologue

Ocean Beach
San Francisco

The night sky was brilliant with stars.

The ferocious winds from earlier in the day had blown all the low hanging clouds inland toward the Oakland Hills.

Even though Stella had parked only a few blocks from a crowded, noisy, and well-lit San Francisco neighborhood, Ocean Boulevard was desolate, a world away from the vibrant city life. The dark sky and the even darker sea to her left stretched on forever.

In front of her, the road was cordoned off with yellow police tape, strung from a parking meter on one side to a stop sign on the other. It whipped and twisted in the strong winds, threatening to tear it off. A squad car with its lights off was parked diagonal in front of the flimsy plastic barricade.

When she pulled up and saw that the crime scene tape had been strung so far away from the actual scene, she began to suspect foul play. Otherwise, the tape might have been limited to a block or even just the parking lot at the beach. Stringing up tape that far away meant protecting evidence at a crime scene.

As Stella stepped out of her vehicle, the fierce wind pushed her back against the SUV's door, blowing the hair out of her face. Fighting the breeze lashing against her, she trained her gaze on the beach north of her, where a dead body had washed up on the white sand.

A football field away, red and blue strobe lights flashed across the beach. But between her and the yellow tape, was a cop. Nothing she couldn't handle with a little finesse.

As Stella drew closer to the flapping crime scene tape, she recognized the uniformed officer standing by the squad car.

Perfect.

"Hey, LaRosa," the woman shouted, her voice nearly drowned out by the sound of the howling wind.

Only family and close friends used Stella's real last name. To everyone else, she was Stella Collins.

Although she wasn't close to this cop, Sgt. Tommy Mazzoli, who was as close to family as a friend could be, had been the one to introduce them at his barbecue a few weeks earlier.

"Hey, Carol," she replied easily. "What's the story?"

"Beats me. With this wicked wind, it's probably some poor sap from Hawaii who got blown ashore."

Stella gave the obligatory laugh. Stella hadn't expected Carol to give her any real information. That was the job of the police department's public information officer.

Carol's job was to keep people—especially newspaper reporters—out of the crime scene. Which was not an option.

"Hey, I'm just going to take a walk on the beach," Stella said, stepping off the road and onto the sand. "Clear my head. You didn't see me, right?"

"I didn't see you. No idea how you got onto the beach, but it wasn't past me," Carol said in a gruff voice. "These aren't the droids you're looking for."

Stella smirked and veered off into the sand for several yards. She didn't want to get the retired Air Force lieutenant in trouble.

The day after the barbecue, Stella had teased Mazzy about Carol being attractive. He'd gotten pissy and wouldn't talk about it, which only meant one thing: He liked the no-nonsense gray-haired woman.

Stella liked her, too. Especially tonight.

Squinting against the sharp wind as she walked, Stella could distinguish a line of dark silhouettes near the crashing waves lapping at the shore. Beams of light bobbed next to them. Investigators shining their flashlights on the sand.

Above them, the famous Cliff House restaurant sat high on the bluff overlooking the dark beach and inky Pacific Ocean beyond. The windows glowed with golden warmth, a stark contrast to the dark, cold night.

The icy wind kicked up, whipping Stella's hair and pushing her along the stretch of shore. Her arms prickled with goosebumps, stinging from the gust against her skin. Why in the hell had she left her jacket in the car? She'd been in a hurry. It had taken her much longer than she'd wanted to drive across town.

Even so, only twenty minutes had passed since the information came across the police scanner at her desk.

Body washed up on shore on Ocean Beach.

While she was still in the newsroom, she ticked off the possibilities in her head. A dead body could mean a number of things. A jumper off the Golden Gate Bridge; a junkie who had overdosed; a tourist caught in a riptide during a nighttime dip. But why anyone would want to swim in the frigid ocean and paddle against this wind was beyond her.

But there was one more option Stella had to consider. A murder.

She'd packed up her belongings and told the night copy editors at the newspaper she would call if there was a story.

Now, nearly out of breath from fighting against the piercing wind, Stella finally reached the beach under the Cliff House.

The investigators were gathered several hundred yards away, near the churning surf. A line of police and emergency vehicles were parked on the road below the bluff.

Right when she arrived, two paramedics carried an empty gurney past her from the road, stepping over a small stone wall to the sand.

Stella paused to decide if she should follow them when she heard a sound.

A man clearing his throat behind her. A man she knew too well for her own good.

Damn it.

Detective Robert Griffin was a pretty boy. His cheekbones were chiseled, full lips adorned his face, and dark eyes peered from under his brows. She hated how good looking he was. It made things even worse.

As luck would have it, she'd managed to avoid him the past few months at all the crime scenes she'd reported on.

Her luck had apparently run out.

He let out an irritated sigh, his shoulders dipping. "I don't even want to know how you got past the crime scene tape."

Stella examined him. The death of the FBI agent he'd loved had taken its toll. The fine lines around his eyes had not been there before. Patches of gray lined his temples.

Stella ignored the ripple of guilt that ran through her.

"How are you?" she asked, her voice soft, softer than she'd spoken to anyone in a long time.

He exhaled, his eyes resting on the crashing waves, the invisible horizon. "I've been better."

There was nothing to say to that. He'd said he'd absolved her of her guilt in the FBI agent's death, but that didn't mean some small dark part of him didn't still blame her.

She cleared her throat and opted to change the subject. "You the point person here?" He often served as the public information officer in a pinch.

"Can't tell you anything. Yet."

"So, you are. Can you at least tell me if it's foul play?" A large gust of wind kicked up and she had to hold her hair back from her face to see his eyes.

"The head is missing, so I'm going to say yes."

Stella let out a low whistle and glanced over his shoulder at the uniformed cops heading their way. "Why would you tell me that?"

He cleared his throat and spoke in a low voice. "You asked me to confirm if the head was missing and when I said I couldn't comment, you took out those binoculars from your bag and saw for yourself."

"Right.," Stella scrambled in the tote bag at her side, retrieving the binoculars. She couldn't see anything in the dark, but at least he had a cover story. She shoved away the pain of him remembering this detail about her.

Griffin made a half-hearted attempt to stand in front of her as she held the binoculars up.

"You have to go wait in the parking lot with the other reporters." He pointed to the restaurant parking lot high above them. She glanced up and saw several TV station news trucks parked there.

A burly cop with freckles and a buzz cut got to them first. "Everything good here?"

"I'm going," Stella yelled, playing along. "I'll wait in the parking lot. Is that the media staging area, then?"

"Yes," Griffin said and turned to leave.

For a second, Stella watched him walk away. She caught a glimpse of a gun in a holster around his waist. He wore black slacks, a black button-down shirt, and black parka. Camouflaged against the dark beach. The all black was a good look for him. She remembered how hard the body beneath was. How once, while she was running her hands down his sides, she'd asked, "Is there an inch of you that isn't rock solid?"

"This way." The burly cop interrupted her memories and pointed toward the road that would lead to the parking lot.

She turned to go, but not before giving one last glance at the beach. Decapitated, huh?

Two hours later, Stella was sitting on a low wall in the restaurant parking lot eyeing the other reporters gathered for the press conference.

The coroner zipped up the body in a black bag and took it away thirty minutes after Stella had arrived.

When Griffin finally came to make a statement to the press, Stella hopped off her perch and joined the throng of reporters. She stepped to one side with her reporter's notebook and pen ready.

After the TV reporters put microphones on Griffin and asked him to hold up a white sheet of paper to check the white light, the press conference began.

Griffin cleared his throat and eyed the crowd of reporters. "At 2100 hours we received a call from a woman walking her dog that a body had washed up onto the shore here at Ocean Beach, about two blocks south of Fulton Street. When our officers arrived, they found a woman who appeared to be deceased. EMS arrived and pronounced the woman dead."

A woman?

"Our preliminary investigation indicates that she was killed somewhere else before the perpetrator brought her here."

That was different. Not washed up onto the shore. Why would anyone dump a body here, of all places?

The TV reporters began shouting their questions over one another, each fighting for their own story. As they liked to do.

The wind had picked up again, and Griffin's responses were nearly lost on the wind. Stella bowed over her reporter's notebook and tried to scribble down what he was saying, even though it was routine and she could've anticipated his answers.

One voice finally cut through the rest. "Detective, we heard the body was missing a head? Can you confirm that?"

Griffin's gaze shot to Stella. She widened her eyes in surprise and gave a barely imperceptible shake of her head. That info hadn't come from her. Someone else had tipped off the reporter.

"I cannot confirm anything at this point," Griffin responded. "That is all the information I can provide, since this is an active homicide investigation."

"We heard the victim was pregnant," another TV reporter said, a woman.

Stella stared at Griffin. His face had drained of color. He looked stricken, glanced at her for a second. Then he recovered.

Stella looked over at the reporter, wondering who she was and how she'd gotten that information. Someone had to have tipped her off. Someone in the police department.

"We are not able to comment on that information at this time," Griffin answered. "The coroner's office will release the victim's identity and cause of death after an autopsy and next of kin is notified."

It was all standard fare, and Stella barely took notes on it. The same thing was said at every homicide scene.

A petite woman with thick glasses and strawberry blonde hair spoke up. "I heard the woman was Columbian."

"We are unable to confirm that."

Stella's breath caught in her throat.

No. It couldn't be. It would be too much of a coincidence.

As much as she didn't want to believe it, Stella's gut roiled.

The whistleblower she was meeting tomorrow was Columbian.

1

Two Weeks Earlier

Stella LaRosa sat at her battered, ink-stained desk, her fingers drumming the rhythm of her thoughts against a half-empty coffee mug as she stared at her computer screen and the email she had clicked on.

The San Francisco Tribune newsroom buzzed with excitement around her: phones ringing, reporters speaking with urgency, the clatter of fingertips on keyboards. Laughter. Swearing. Groaning.

The air carried a whiff of stale coffee mixed with somebody's reheated broccoli casserole. Stella breathed it all in. This was home.

For the first time in a long time, a surge of excitement raced through her as she reread the subject line over and over.

Carter Barclay.

That name had haunted her for months. The mastermind of a string of crimes, he'd left behind a trail of dead bodies, including people she had cared about. He was never going to stop, unless she stopped him.

But she'd already tried and failed. Just one more thing her conscience nagged at her for, the ensuing guilt eating at her from the inside out.

Heart pounding, she continued to stare at the unopened email.

Looking furtively around the newsroom, she scanned for anyone keeping an eye on her. But the other reporters and editors were busy with their own computer screens. She turned back to her own and for a brief second, dread washed over her as her finger hovered above the cursor, ready to click open the email.

That's when she realized, her life was about to change.

It was about time.

For the last few months, the utter monotony of her life was only broken by the heartache she sometimes allowed herself to feel. Or rather, couldn't stop herself from feeling. For a long while, she'd tamped down the feelings by drinking herself numb, and often. Until it had nearly cost her job.

Now that she was on the wagon, all the festering guilt and loneliness and failure had nowhere to hide. She had to feel the feels, a vast majority of them caused by Carter Barclay.

It had begun two years back when she was working undercover. One of the missions she and the covert government team she worked with had gone sideways in the worst possible way. They had been set up. They had thought they were doing something good, but their actions had resulted in the deaths of several children at a party in Syria.

Although the children hadn't died at her hands alone, Stella had still been partly responsible.

Headway had recruited her to work intelligence for the band of assassins, but she'd soon found that she also had to kill to survive.

She'd only killed to save her teammates from certain death. She scoffed at the irony, since now, all her teammates were dead. Every single one of them. And memories, nightmares of the horrors just kept on coming in massive waves where she could barely reach the surface and catch her breath. After returning to the states, she'd been forced to kill the only man she had ever loved after finding out his real identity, his true mission. He'd been one of the monsters working for Barclay.

Not long after, an FBI agent—a woman Griffin had loved—had died saving Stella's life. That had been a hard pill to swallow. She hadn't killed Agent Carmen Rodriguez herself, but she couldn't shake the thought that if the two women had never met, the FBI agent would still be alive.

And the kicker? Carter Barclay had been behind all of it, yet was still walking around a free man. A disgustingly wealthy, powerful, free man.

It had been too much, those first weeks after Carmen's death, Griffin's sorrow. But instead of turning to alcohol to obliterate those dark shadows, Stella had instead decided to take to her bed for days, only waking to cover her night shifts at the newspaper. On her two days off, she'd sleep sometimes fifteen or twenty hours straight, with no help from a bottle of whiskey.

Hell yes, she was depressed. But she figured she had good reason to be.

Finally, she clicked the email open, her breath catching in her throat. Scanning the words for a long moment, unable to absorb or process the information it contained, she shook her head and read the short email again:

My name is Maria Perez. I am from Columbia. I am the director of my country's Department of Gene Expression and Development. My government is corrupt. They have contracted me to work for a Houston-based company owned by Carter Barclay. I know you know him and have written about him before. I don't trust anyone else. I have information about a cloning operation at this company. What I have to tell you must be said in person. I will be in California in two weeks. Text me at the number below. Use a burner phone. Tell no one. They won't hesitate to kill me if they know my plans. I will be in touch.

Stella stared at the subject line again. The thought of Barclay sent a sliver of apprehension down her back. The man was dangerous, and this woman was going to be a whistleblower in connection to his operation. Maria wasn't wrong. Barclay would kill anyone who tried to harm him or his businesses.

Stella shut down her computer, grabbed her belongings, and practically ran for the door.

"I'll be back!"

Her editor, Jack Garcia, hollered after her, getting her to slow for just a moment. “Anything good?”

Stella respected her editor, a no-nonsense newspaper man. He was short and wiry and reminded her of a terrier with his close-clipped goatee. He always wore a white dress shirt and loose tie as a nod to some long-forgotten formality from the golden days of newspaper. She wouldn’t be surprised if he wore a fedora to and from work.

But unlike the typical old school editors, he wasn’t usually gruff, but kind and supportive.

She was lucky to have him in her corner.

“I’ll let you know,” she replied, and slipped out the door seconds later.

Within the hour, she’d picked up a new stack of burner phones and activated one to message Maria on the number she’d provided.

Back in the newsroom, she picked up the burner phone a few times to see if she’d received a return call or text, but the phone remained silent on her desk..

Every day for a week, she’d carried that burner phone around with her.

And in the meantime, she began researching. At first it was surface-level digging: *Carter Barclay + Cloning.* Nothing. Then she did a deep dive into the cloning world. The last time she’d paid attention to it the news was about Dolly the sheep. The scientist who had cloned Dolly was now dead.

After a few more moments of the Dolly rabbit hole, she got back on track to looking into newer developments. And holy smokes, the science had flown past simply duplicating a barnyard animal. The technology had more recently been used to bring a species back from the dead. Using frozen genes, scientists had cloned a black-footed ferret, Jasmine, who had died thirty years before in 1988. They’d frozen her remains long before scientists understood the implications of what could be done with DNA technology. Fast-forward to 2018, and scientists had been able to create a genetic copy of Jasmine. A ferret they named Ridley.

These same scientists were now working to clone a woolly mammoth in the same way.

Unreal.

But there was something very unsettling about all this science. One thing in particular—the clone's temperament was unpredictable.

For instance, sweet Jasmine had been a beloved member of her family's household. She'd even slept curled up on the pillow of her owner, Sue Ann. Ridley, however, was another story. At ten days old, she bit off the finger of her handler. The ferret was wild, with none of the domesticated characteristics of Jasmine. The inability to predict a cloned animal's temperament would be an even larger problem if a woolly mammoth or dinosaur, were cloned. It could be something right out of the Jurassic Park movie, Stella thought as she read. If a ferret's temperament had turned unusually violent, what if cloned humans had the same propensity?

What was Carter Barclay up to? Surely nothing good. And apparently this woman wanted to tell Stella all about it. But when would she reach out?

Finally, thirteen long days after she'd received Maria's email, a text appeared on the burner phone.

It was six hours before the call about a body washing up on Ocean Beach.

I'm in San Francisco. Meet at Alcatraz Island tomorrow. 10 a.m. tour. A ticket will be waiting at the wharf with your name on it

2

Two Weeks Earlier
Athens

Carter Barclay stood back under a row of Tamarisk trees, nearly hidden, and watched the young man in a dark suit place a red rose on the gleaming black coffin. There were only a few mourners at the gravesite, but the funeral service at the massive gothic church had been packed.

As it should have been.

The graveside service was for family only, the bulletin said.

Barclay had paid for the right to be there. At least, that's what he told himself. He ordered his driver to wait at the foot of the cemetery. Once the hearse and two accompanying vehicles had entered, he waited another fifteen minutes before directing the driver up the hill. They parked behind the three vehicles, and Barclay made his way across the cemetery until he was within the length of a football field of the burial ceremony.

The spot was beautiful. The grave was at the top of a hill overlooking the Mediterranean Sea, the sun glittering in the waves. A cool breeze cut through the day's heat as he leaned against the shady tree. He wasn't hiding, but he also wasn't intruding.

He watched with distaste as the young man—his son—embraced another equally handsome man. His son's husband. An abomination.

Barclay had stalked the couple on social media. Both were attractive, intelligent, and successful young men. If he didn't know they were gay, he would have hired them in a second to work for his company. So, he had decided to set his prejudice aside.

It was time to finally acknowledge his son, embrace the boy, his blood, and the only one who had a chance of carrying the bloodline. The contract the boy's mother had signed said that, upon her death, Barclay would offer her son a job. Their son. And he would acknowledge the man as his own child. They would both pretend that Barclay had no knowledge of his son's existence previously.

In return, the woman would keep his son a secret until the day she died. Barclay would also pay for the best private schools for the boy. He had upheld his end of the bargain. The boy had been sent to an expensive and prestigious boarding school in England and then had a full-ride scholarship to Oxford University.

It was a sad fact that Barclay had never intended to fulfill the woman's final request, that he acknowledge their son's existence after her death and offer the kid a job.

However, the woman had hired an attorney who told Barclay if he didn't keep up his end of the bargain, a very incriminating video of him would be sent to the world media. The video would show him agreeing to meet Maria's terms—along with DNA proof that he had a son he was essentially abandoning.

Apparently, the video was already in some prominent journalist's hands, so killing the attorney wouldn't solve the issue.

Damn it. If Barclay had learned one thing over the years, it was that journalists were the only people who could not be bought. Journalists like Stella LaRosa. That one, she was out to take him down. He had no doubt about that.

It wouldn't destroy Barclay, but knowledge of his deal with Ariana and denying both her and their gay son would make him look bad.

Especially since he was on the board of half a dozen organizations for orphans and child welfare.

Although he was one of the richest men in the world, he had learned long ago that money didn't always buy respect, even though he thought it should. He had to earn that each and every day. His image was a carefully constructed one that Stella LaRosa was on a mission to tear down. He laughed. Nice try. She thought she was a formidable opponent in his world, but she was a pesky fly. Annoying, but ultimately harmless.

He had done the right thing staying out of the boy's life. He would have been a terrible father, having realized years ago that he wasn't cut out to raise a child. However, from a very young age, all the beautiful women he was attracted to—the most beautiful women in the world; the models, the actresses, the beauty queens—always ended up wanting kids. Whether they thought that was the key to getting a piece of his fortune or they really wanted to have his child, had never mattered.

Not long after he'd inherited his trust fund, he'd had a vasectomy to prevent any "accidents." So how had Ariana gotten pregnant?

At first, he'd laughed in her face, but she'd had a DNA test done. Showed him the results. The shock that flooded him was a sensation he hadn't experienced since his childhood. But he'd kept his cool, told her she must have fabricated the results. She'd given him all the documentation, proving the child she was carrying was, in fact, his. She'd threatened to go public with the knowledge unless he paid for her son to go to private schools. At the time, he hadn't wielded the power he did later on in life and had his attorney give her the hush money and the contract had been signed.

Of course he'd had the doctor who had done the vasectomy fired and run out of the medical profession. He'd had a second surgery and had been guaranteed this one was foolproof.

Over the years, he thought of Ariana every once in a while. She was quite a woman. But once he had denied his son, she never forgave him.

He didn't even really like her, but he did respect her. Is that why he felt something in his chest standing on the periphery of the graveside service? It was as if his heart seized. It felt like his heart was cramping. It was so odd, like a muscle cramp. Is that what a heart attack felt like? His hand flew up to his chest. Was he going into cardiac arrest? Across the world? On a Mediterranean island in the middle of nowhere? Was this how he was going to go? Lurking at a funeral as a man who didn't even know he was his son put a rose on the grave?

But the tension released. He wasn't dying.

Still, it was a reminder that he wouldn't live forever. Maybe having a son to inherit everything and carry on his name wasn't so bad after all.

3

PRESENT DAY
San Francisco

Standing near the ocean in the cold, windy night, Stella waited for Griffin to come back up to the parking lot on the bluff. The other reporters had already scrambled back to their vehicles to write and report their stories. Griffin had given them back their microphones and headed back down to the beach with two other police officers.

Stella remained in the parking lot, waiting. She had a much bigger story to flesh out. She needed to tell somebody. Somebody in law enforcement, somebody she could count on to be discreet.

Normally, she'd turn to Mazzoli, but he'd just left for Italy to visit his ailing grandmother.

So, it would have to be Griffin.

As she stood staring at the endless black sea beyond the surf, the strong wind gusts were like a hand pushing her on back, propelling her forward.

As she searched the beach for Griffin's silhouette, other figures stooped to the sand. She grabbed her binoculars. A man was scooping up the yellow crime scene markers. They were packing up the scene. She watched as the investigators filed off the beach.

Getting impatient, Stella decided to head back down to the beach. The worst they could do was yell at her for walking near a crime scene. She could just say she had to go that way to get to her car. That was true enough.

Griffin was one of the last ones to leave. He spotted Stella waiting on the boardwalk nearby and headed her way.

"Closed up the crime scene pretty quickly," Stella said as he drew closer.

"The waves washed any evidence away," he said tersely. "She was half submerged when the witness spotted her."

"Think that's why she was dumped here?"

Griffin shrugged. He looked up at the parking lot on the bluff and scowled. The other reporters were back out of their vehicles and had set up large lights for live footage with the beach in the background. The wind was whipping a TV reporter's hair around and threatening to topple a camera on a stand.

Stella laughed. "You really hate reporters, don't you?"

"Pretty much."

"All of them?" Her voice shook as she said it. Her whole body was shivering. The wind was still blustering and icy cold, seeping right through her clothes.

He ignored her question, his gaze on the distance as it seemed to be most often lately.

Stella cleared her throat. "When do you expect an ID?"

Shrugging, he nodded at her as she trembled against the gust. "You got a jacket or something?"

"Back in my car."

He sighed. "What do you want, Stella?"

Her breath caught at the sound her of name coming out of his mouth. He never called her that. Just like she never called him Robert. She was Collins. He was Griffin.

"I wanted to run something by you, *Robert*. Something I don't want to say over the phone. Can we take a walk down the beach?"

He stopped walking for a second and then nodded. "Stand by."

Leaving her side, he walked over to a cluster of cops near the line of parked cars on the side of the road. All of them looked over at Stella for a moment, then back at him. When he was finished, they all nodded and went back to their business. Griffin moved away from them and unlocked the passenger door of a navy Crown Victoria. He reached inside before slamming the door again. When he came back, he thrust something soft at her. A black hoodie.

Stella blinked. *Really? Crap.* If he started being nice to her now, she was going to lose it. It was easier to tamp down her feelings for him when he hated her.

Accepting the sweatshirt, she tugged it over her head. "Thanks."

"I've got five minutes," he said and started walking down the beach.

Stella speed-walked at his side to keep up with him, the wind blowing at her with more force now. "I think I know who the woman is," she said. "Nobody but you can know."

"Keep talking."

"So I—" Stella lost her footing in the deep, damp sand and fell flat on her face.

Griffin crouched down beside her, lifting her up by her upper arms. A chuckle was in his voice when he asked, "You okay?"

She scowled. A stinging pain shot up her leg. "I don't know. I think I cut myself."

Griffin kneeled by her and turned his phone flashlight on, aiming it at her leg. She lifted up her pant leg, tugging it up to her knee.

"Yep. You're bleeding."

"What?" Stella took out her own cell phone and aimed the flashlight behind her. She inhaled sharply. "Was there broken glass?"

"Good God! What is that?"

Alarmed, Stella looked up at Griffin and followed his gaze. A large chunk of cement protruded out of the sand. The object was in the shape of a cross. Griffin trained his phone flashlight on the cement to see the inscription of a name and dates deeply etched into the stone.

"Hot damn," Griffin said. "It's a tombstone."

"Okay, am I hallucinating?" Stella asked. "Did I actually hit my head instead of my leg?"

Griffin laughed. "Never thought I'd see the day. I'd only heard about this happening."

"What?" Stella snapped, losing her patience. "You heard about tombstones growing out of the sand of Ocean Beach near where decapitated bodies are appearing?"

Griffin held his hand out and pulled Stella upright.

"Do you want to go get your leg checked out?"

She shook her head.

They began to walk. As they did, he shone his light in a broad arc around them.

"Look!" he said. "There's another one."

He pointed a few yards away toward the water.

"Jesus."

"It's a thing. Every ten years or so, the sand blows away and the tombstones start popping up."

"That makes zero sense."

"In the early 1920s and 1930s, the city closed its cemeteries and relocated thousands of bodies to Colma."

Stella knew about the City of the Dead. Colma, south of San Francisco, had thousands upon thousands of bodies buried in its soil. The saying was that there were more dead people in that city than alive.

Griffin went on. "They repurposed all the old headstones. For fill, for breakwaters, to line gutters, build roads, create a seawall. And they actually took giant crypts and dumped them in the bay."

"Why on earth are they coming up out of the sand like something out of Poltergeist?"

"Every once in a while, when the weather gets crazy, and the wind is insane, it kicks up the sand and shifts it—and they surface. But the funny thing is, it's only happened a few times in recent history. Once in 1977 and once in 2012."

"So normally all these tombstones are just hanging out a few feet down under the sand on this beach? What does the city do about it when they start popping up?"

"Last time it happened? Nothing." Griffin shrugged. "The wind blows the sand around and they get buried again."

Stella stared at him a long moment, the blood on her leg drying quickly from the frozen wind. "How do you know so much?"

Again, he shrugged. "Born and raised here."

One of the police officers back at the parking lot shouted Griffin's name.

"Five minutes!" he shouted back, sounding annoyed.

"About what I wanted to tell you," Stella said. "That woman back there."

"You said you think you know who she is? Without a head, it's going to be even tougher to do an I.D. Could take a while longer to confirm. And there's been none on her body yet."

Stella nodded before speaking. "A woman reached out to me a few weeks ago. A whistleblower." Stella paused. "From Barclay's camp."

She waited for the reaction that name would bring.

Griffin gave it in the form of a low whistle.

Stella continued. "She had information about Barclay and she was coming to the city to tell me in person. I got a text today that she had arrived in town. We were supposed to meet tomorrow. Her name is Maria Perez. She's Columbian."

Griffin pulled up to a stop. "Jesus!"

"Which has me wondering... why did that other reporter ask if the woman was Columbian?"

Griffin swore. "Because there's a leak in the department."

"How would you guys know if the person was Columbian without some ID on her?"

"Because she has a tattoo in the shape of Columbia with the colors of the country's flag on the back of her neck." He paused for a moment. "Carmen had one, too."

Stella inhaled sharply. All she could hear was the keening sound that Griffin made when he saw Carmen's dead body. She shook her head to clear it.

"Carmen was from Columbia?"

"Her father was."

"There is a chance this is my whistleblower, then. She said if Barclay found out what she was doing, he wouldn't hesitate to kill her.

"It certainly is one hell of a coincidence."

Stella nodded, fixing her gaze on the ocean beyond. "That's what I'm thinking."

4

ATHENS

Patrick Barclay knelt in the dirt in front of his mother's coffin with the blazing hot sun pounding down on his back making small rivulets of sweat drip down onto his black suit.

The cemetery sat perched atop a sun-warmed hill overlooking the sprawling city of Athens, its whitewashed gravestones blindingly white in the sun. The hill was dotted with ancient olive trees, providing dark patches of shade if the burial spot was lucky enough to fall under one of the twisted trees.

Above the cluster of black-clothed mourners gathered around the grave near Patrick, the clear blue sky stretched endlessly only to meet the sea in the distance on one side. There was a breathtaking view of the Parthenon on the other.

The bustling metropolis of Athens lay far below, its busy city hum far from the serene cemetery.

One by one everybody left, leaving Patrick alone.

The only person who remained graveside was his partner, Theo, who stood back several feet to allow Patrick to say his final goodbyes in private. Patrick sensed his presence, and it was reassuring.

The tears flowed freely from Patrick's eyelashes, dripping on top of the yellow flower petals covering the white casket. His mother had loved yellow. She always said it was such a cheery color.

That's who his mother had been; cheerfulness personified.

No matter how tough things had gotten over the years, she'd always remained optimistic.

When she'd scrimped to buy him things that other kids had, he hadn't realized that it was connected to her eating rice and beans day in and day out. She said that the scholarships that allowed him to attend the world's finest schools were a gift he shouldn't squander.

And he had listened, becoming one of the best students in his class. For her.

For as long as he could remember, all he'd wanted was to make his mother proud.

He hoped that he had.

Drying his tears, he stood up, only a little wobbly.

Theo took his hand and walked with him to the car in silence. The tears erupted again when he reached the vehicle, realizing he was leaving his mother here, alone. As he was about to slide into the open door of the black sedan, someone called his name.

Patrick used the back of his palm to swipe at his tears.

Theo hopped inside the vehicle and paused. "Who is that?" he asked.

Patrick followed Theo's gaze to a man standing near a black livery car. "No clue. I'm sure it's someone who knew my mother."

The man was large, at least six-foot-five. He wore jeans, a cowboy-cut shirt, and shiny cowboy boots. A New York Yankees cap was pulled so low, his eyes were hidden.

"Is he American?" Patrick asked, turning back to his husband.

Theo gave a long sigh. "It's *that* guy."

"You know him?"

"No. but I saw him over by the trees during the service, lurking like a creeper."

"Theo!" Patrick said in a scolding voice, but he was also laughing.

"Get in the car," Theo said. "I'll deal with him. I'll tell him you are exhausted and not up to speaking to anybody else today. The minister specifically asked people at the funeral to respect your privacy and that the graveside service was close family only."

"It's okay." Patrick smiled at his protective husband. "You wait in the air conditioning in the car. I'll only be a few minutes."

The man had waited a respectable ways away, standing by his own black car. He took off his hat and held it in his hands. His gray hair was slicked back. He was still too far away for Patrick to see his expression.

As Patrick walked closer, the man stuck out his hand. "I'm so sorry about your loss. Your mother was a magnificent woman."

The man's blue eyes were startling, disconcerting against his tan and weathered face.

"Thank you," Patrick said, shaking his hand. "And you are?"

"Carter Barclay."

The billionaire?

Patrick was taken aback.

The older man's expression grew solemn. "It appears we have a lot to talk about. I received a letter upon your mother's death with some information affecting both of us."

Patrick frowned. He wasn't sure where this man was going. This American billionaire who apparently had known his mother.

"I don't mean to be rude," Patrick said, his tone turning hard, "but could you get to the point? I've had a long day."

Barclay chuckled, twisting the cap in his hands. "I appreciate a man who cuts to the chase."

Patrick simply nodded, hoping the man would spit it out.

The older man sighed and said, "It seems that I'm your father."

* * *

Theo must have seen the distress Patrick was in, the blood that had drained from his face. Patrick's ever-protective husband had leaped out of the car and was now standing at his side.

"What's going on here?" he asked, slightly out of breath.

Patrick gestured to Barclay. "This man is my father, or claims to be."

His biological father had supposedly disappeared after his mother had told him she was pregnant. But someone like Carter Barclay couldn't just disappear.

Patrick's head was spinning. What was going on? Why hadn't his mother said anything? He had held her hand as she'd taken her final breaths. She'd never acted like she had anything left to share. Knowing his father's identity had never been a concern for Patrick. His mother had been enough of a parent for him. She'd been both mother and father. She had been, as this man had said, "a magnificent woman."

But she was more than that. She was the best mother anyone could have asked for.

Theo frowned. "Sir, no offense, but this isn't a great time to break this sort of news. Give me your card and we'll be in touch tomorrow."

For a second, Patrick saw something flash across Barclay's face. A mix between cockiness and rage. Patrick got the feeling that nobody spoke to him that way. That he had conversations when and where he wanted them.

But as soon as the look had crossed his face, it was gone. Barclay smiled and handed Theo a card.

"Of course. Forgive me."

Theo put his arm around Patrick as they made their way back to the car. By the time they were settled in and Patrick turned to look back at the man and his black car, both were gone.

* * *

The next day, after their loved ones had left town and the two men were home alone in their simple white stucco house, they collapsed on the bed for a nap. A few hours later, they awoke with their two cats curled up on the quilt beside them. Patrick gave them each a scratch on the head and picked up his phone from the side table.

"Might as well get this over with," he murmured.

Swinging his legs from the bed, he retrieved Barclay's card from the top of the dark oak dresser where Theo had put his wallet and keys.

"It's Patrick. Barclay," he said awkwardly when the other man answered.

"Did you ever wonder why you had your last name? That it was different from your mothers?"

"No. She told me it was a common American name. Told me that my father was a common American man."

"Ouch," Theo mouthed.

Patrick tried to ignore him.

"I guess I deserve that," Carter Barclay said. "I think that's what I liked about your mom. I met her while she was backpacking through Europe after she graduated from college. I was a few years older and was living on a yacht in Cannes. She was not impressed by me at all. Maybe the only woman I've ever met who didn't care about my money. It was intoxicating."

"Yeah, she always saw past all that."

"She was never a typical American, I think that's why she decided to settle in Greece, don't you?"

"She definitely preferred a simple life," Patrick said.

"Well, anyway, I apologize for invading your life right now. I know I should have been in touch earlier. I just didn't know if your mother would have wanted me to interfere. As soon as I heard about her passing, I came here to meet you in person because I have a proposition to make."

By the time Patrick hung up thirty minutes later, he still had more questions than answers.

"If I heard your end of the conversation correctly, it sounds like he wants you to move to Texas to work for him?" Theo said and shook his head. "He pops up after thirty years and suddenly wants to be your dad and give you a job? Wants you to drop everything and move across the world?"

Patrick nodded.

"And you told him you'll think about it? Without even talking to me first?" The hurt in Theo's voice was undeniable.

"I'm sorry," Patrick said. "But, I have to tell you something. I didn't get that job."

Theo's eyes widened. "Oh my God. I thought you were a shoo-in?"

"Me too."

"Did we even pay this month's rent, then? I thought you were getting an advance?"

Patrick sighed and shook his head, unable to meet his husband's eyes.

"So we're going to be homeless?"

"I think we're going to have to move. We just can't afford this place on your salary," Patrick said.

"Does that mean we can't afford to become parents, either?" Theo asked.

"I don't know," Patrick said. "That's why I'm really considering accepting this job. It would solve so many of our problems. We could have money to adopt. We would have a place to live. In America."

"What did he offer you, Patrick?"

"A lot. More than a lot. He wants to give me a $250,000 signing bonus, a house in Houston, and two cars. We can use the bonus for the adoption."

"You've got to be joking," Theo said, and frowned. "What's the catch?"

Patrick shrugged. "Apparently nothing. I guess that's what happens when you are one of the richest men in the world and you find out you have a son."

5

STELLA'S WORDS HUNG IN THE SILENT NIGHT. IN THE NEAR distance, the moonlight swathed a path over the water, and beyond was nothing but pitch black.

She paused walking and turned to Griffin, waiting for him to reply.

"Listen," he said, raking a hand through his windblown hair to keep it out of his eyes. "I have to play by the rules here."

"I know. But I didn't have to share what I just did. We can help each other out."

He took a breath and looked back at her. "Here's what I can do. Once identity is confirmed, you're my first call."

Stella looked up at his face, which was still half in shadow. He avoided her eyes. "That's it?" she asked.

"Yes."

"If she doesn't show for our meet tomorrow, I'll have my answer."

"I'll be in touch," was all he said.

That was as much as he was going to give. "Okay."

"Griffin!" One of the cops behind them shouted. He half-turned.

"Go on. My car is right there."

The crime scene tape had been taken down and Carol had left. The road was eerily deserted.

"Are you sure?"

"Of course." She didn't need anybody to keep her safe. Especially not him.

That day in the hospital room, she'd been the one who had saved his life, after all.

She had killed the man she'd loved to save Griffin. You'd think that would count for something.

"I won't leave until I see your car leave here, okay?"

"It's fine, Griffin."

At her words, he nodded and turned, half-jogging up the beach.

Stella turned toward her car. The biting wind stung her face. Despite her brave words and thoughts, a sense of foreboding trickled down her spine. The feeling she was being watched returned.

She swiveled her head. Besides Griffin, there was nobody for as far as she could see.

Hurrying against the icy wind, she was glad for the hoodie Griffin had loaned her. Sometimes she hated how much of a good guy he was. It made it worse.

He was the good guy. She was the bad one.

Their potential love story had been doomed from the start. A non-starter.

But as she crawled into her car and cranked the heater, Stella dipped her nose into the sweatshirt opening and inhaled deeply. As much as she tried not to admit it, deep down inside, she knew she was in love with the detective.

* * *

Even though Stella was home in her cozy apartment, settled on the couch with the heater on and a blanket over her legs, the chill she'd caught on the beach remained deep in her bones. She kept Griffin's hoodie on as she wrote up a story for the paper, warming her more by the second.

At least, that's what she told herself was the reason for keeping it on.

Every once in a while, she bent forward and inhaled. The man smelled good. His spicy cologne reminded her of the nights they had spent together.

She set her laptop on the coffee table and picked up the burner phone to check the messages. As soon as she'd gotten home from the beach, she'd unearthed the burner phone and sent a quick message to Maria. *Confirming tomorrow's meet.*

There was no response.

After staring at the phone a few seconds, she set it back down.

In writing her story, she kept to the facts that Griffin had provided. A woman's body was found on Ocean Beach Thursday night. The preliminary investigation showed that the woman had likely been killed elsewhere and brought near the shoreline on Ocean Beach. Of course, she'd wanted to use the word "dumped" but as a journalist, she was supposed to remain as neutral as possible. So far, the story was pithy and short.

She monitored the TV stations' websites to see if they would be brazen—or irresponsible—enough to report that the woman had been pregnant and decapitated. To her relief, they didn't sink that low. But Stella knew damn well they were putting all their resources behind trying to verify that information.

She had Griffin and Mazzy as sources, but the TV reporters had their own.

Stella wouldn't be surprised if somebody in the coroner's office leaked more details to TV stations before morning.

Thinking of the woman being pregnant and missing her head made Stella's heart race. She'd been so busy writing her story she hadn't thought of the implications of those details.

If the woman did end up being Maria Perez, then she'd been murdered because she was going to talk to Stella. There was no other reason. It had to have been why.

The Columbian woman had to have been silenced to prevent her from telling Stella damning information about Carter Barclay.

Not only did Stella feel a wave of guilt and terror, but her heart sank into her stomach.

Without the whistleblower, Stella was back where she had been two weeks before, knowing a monster still walked the earth because she had been unable to convince authorities of his wrongdoing. When this woman had contacted Stella out of the blue, that despair had faded and her hope had grown wings.

That hope was once again starting to shrivel.

* * *

Stella woke early the next morning despite being up late. Grabbing her phone, she looked for a text from Griffin. Nothing. She reached for the burner phone that had Maria's number on it. Nothing there, either.

Before getting out of bed, she checked the TV stations' websites again to see if they had confirmed any additional information.

None had.

It was maddening. A pit of worry had formed in her stomach.

Picking up the burner phone again, Stella decided to text Maria again. It was plausible that the Columbian woman on the beach had nothing to do with the whistleblower.

We still on for today?

There was still no reply. It didn't mean anything. Not yet.

Just to be safe, she wrote more. *I'll be there for sure.*

And she would be.

The only thing to do was get her ticket for the 10 a.m. tour to Alcatraz and see what happened.

Meanwhile, she emailed Josh Griswold, the daytime cops reporter at the newspaper. *If you don't mind, I'll continue to follow the Ocean Beach body. But maybe we want to put the new intern on another story: tombstones on Ocean Beach. Some weird phenomenon that I'm sure we've written about in the archives.*

Feeling like she'd done her due diligence in her responsibilities to the paper, she hit send and decided to do some digging while she waited to go to the wharf to catch the boat to Alcatraz. She pulled out her Headway laptop and, using an encrypted IP, logged onto the Dark

Web as the Black Rose, her former code name for the secret government program.

Once online, she searched for any connection between Carter Barclay, Houston, and Maria Perez from Columbia.

At first, she couldn't find anything.

Then she found the name of Barclay's company in Houston.

ImmortalGen.

A press release said that the company was bringing in a Columbian scientist to work on its cloning project.

She clicked on the company's website. The screen filled with an eerie, glowing blue page. The page was blank. No text. No icons. Nothing. Stella moved her cursor around the page, randomly at first and then methodically, clicking as she went. Nothing happened.

There had to be a secret way to access the website.

She hit the space bar. Then the enter tab. Then a few other combinations of keys.

Still nothing.

She glanced at the time. She needed to get ready to go and, hopefully, meet Maria Perez, alive and well.

Wearing dark jeans, Griffin's hoodie, a black jacket, and boots, Stella told herself she was wearing the hoodie for good luck. She also donned a baseball cap and dark sunglasses. If the woman was a whistleblower, it would be dangerous for her to be seen with a San Francisco reporter, so Stella would show up incognito.

Deep down inside, Stella knew there would be no meeting. But she had to know for sure.

* * *

The ticket was waiting at the wharf's office as promised.

Stella had arrived early and searched the faces in the crowd on Pier 33, those waiting to take the tour over to Alcatraz Island.

She had met the eyes of a petite, heavier woman with dark skin and features, but she quickly looked away and a man her height joined her.

When they announced boarding for the small boat, Stella hesitated.

There was nobody who looked like they could be Maria Perez. There were parents with children and a few elderly couples. But not a single woman by herself.

Even so, Stella would go on the tour. Just in case.

There had been an 8 a.m. tour, so maybe Maria Perez was already on the island, having taken the early tour and stayed.

The big knot of dread that had formed in Stella's gut told her otherwise.

Maria Perez was not on Alcatraz Island. The Columbian woman was on a cold metal slab in the San Francisco morgue.

But she had to know for sure.

6

THE COLDNESS OF ALCATRAZ ISLAND SEEPED DEEP INTO Stella's bones.

It wasn't just the certainty that she was there to meet—or rather, not meet—a dead woman.

It was the knowledge that this island held years of pain and torture and death.

Which begged the question of why Maria had wanted to meet here in the first place.

When she'd first stepped off the boat, Stella joined dozens of other tourists waiting at the foot of a steep hill. The tourists were then shepherded to an area near a bookstore and giftshop. A state park ranger shouted at the crowd, warning them that the hike to the prison at the top of the hill was long and steep.

After climbing to the main prison yard, people began splitting off from the main group.

Stella hung back in case Maria was somewhere in the crowd waiting to approach her. When nobody did, Stella decided to explore the prison on a self-guided tour.

On her way to the prison block entrance, her phone rang.

Her heart raced for a second, her hand reaching inside her bag to grab the phone she hoped was ringing. But it wasn't the burner phone. She followed the buzzing sensation and lifted the phone out of her purse. It was her personal cell.

And it was her mother calling.

"Hi, Mama?"

"Stella, are you already working?"

Stella glanced around at the tourists surrounding her. "Sort of."

"I won't keep you. I just wanted to make sure you were coming to Sunday dinner. We're going to celebrate your brother's birthday."

Stella waited a beat. "Is Uncle Dominic going to be there?"

Her mother didn't answer. The tension rose within her.

"Mama, I can't be around him. You know that."

"I'm trying to understand and respect that you and your uncle don't get along. God knows I'm trying, Stella, but you can't avoid your entire family because of one argument."

"It's not one argument." But Stella said it in a meek voice. It was futile to argue with her mother. No matter what she said, her mother would insist Stella forgive her uncle and come to the family celebration. Her mother was Italian. Blood was thicker than water. *La Famiglia e Tutto.*

Again, her mother was silent. This time for longer than was comfortable. Stella decided to wait her out.

"I didn't want to tell you this," her mother said, her voice hitching. "But your uncle is sick. He is really ill. We're not sure he's going to make it."

Stella's heart sank. "Oh my God, Mama. Why haven't you told me?"

"He's been keeping it a secret for months. I'll tell you more later, but he's on the list for a transplant."

"A transplant? Of what?"

"His liver."

Stella shook her head. Dominic's lifetime of unhealthy habits had caught up with him. He could die. Call her cold-hearted, but she didn't care.

Plus, she wasn't sure it was even true. Her mother, an absolute saint, was also a little dramatic and not above twisting a narrative to make her daughter more inclined to showing up. This may or may not have been one of those times. But ultimately, Stella didn't want to hear about it. At least not right then.

Her mother's voice was suddenly chipper, as if the matter was settled. "So we'll see you there?"

"We'll see," Stella replied and hung up.

Her uncle was the patriarch of the family. He was her mother's brother, and her mother defended him no matter what. Stella's father wasn't much better. He might not defend her uncle, but he didn't stand up to the other man, either. His livelihood depended on staying in Dominic's good graces.

Although Dominic was the head of a mafia family, her father worked for one of his legitimate businesses. At least, Stella hoped so.

Her uncle had been harassing Stella to join the family business from the minute she'd graduated from high school. As a child, Stella had found her other aunt and uncle dead, victims of a mob hit from an opposing family. She'd hadn't spoken for months afterward. Only when she grew a bit older did she understand that her family was involved in organized crime and that her aunt and uncle had been slain because of it. From that moment on, she'd vowed to never join the family business.

Still, her uncle was persistent. He'd even had her arrested for a murder she didn't commit once to try to coerce her into joining forces with him. Later, he said he'd get her off the hook if she changed her mind. But Stella would rather go to prison for life than work for Dominic. She did go in for a little while. But, realizing having her in prison wouldn't help his cause, Dominic had had her released.

An awful man, while she didn't wish him dead—mostly for her mother's sake—she also wouldn't be crying at his funeral.

Now, as Stella scowled at the ground, she realized she was in front of the prison block entrance. A tall, gangly park worker handed her a set of headphones.

The entrance to the prison was through a large communal shower room. As Stella entered, a deep chill descended on her. This large room had never seen the light of day.

The self-guided tour through her headset included discussion about the history of the island, as well as stories told by former prisoners and guards of what life was like here.

Half-listening, Stella scanned the other tourists for Maria Perez as she joined a group making its way past prison cells that contained everyday items such as checker boards and books and pillows.

Stella glanced at the cells but was more interested in the people around her. She lingered behind as people walked on, giving Maria a chance to approach her—if the woman was on the island.

After an hour, nobody had come up to her or even caught her eye, except for an elderly man who winked at her. She scowled in response.

Finally, she gave up. She'd given the whistleblower plenty of time and several opportunities to approach her.

After the tour group had left and Stella was worried she'd miss the ferry back, she began walking back toward the entrance and took a wrong turn. She was alone inside an unidentified portion of the prison. The area looked abandoned. The walls began to narrow, and the ceiling hung lower.

As she walked, she came across yellow caution tape strung up blocking access to several doorways. There was also a warning sign saying the area was dangerous and unstable.

Panic washed over her. Stella had claustrophobia, but it usually only cropped up in confined spaces. This was fairly open air, but she was freaking out. She tried to calm herself by doing some deep breathing, but every fiber of her being wanted to run.

Turning around, she couldn't see the door she had come in. Everything looked the same. As she spun around, she saw an exit sign. Was that the way she had come in?

She just didn't know which direction to head. What if she ran, and it took her deeper into the bowels of the prison? What if she got locked in here overnight?

She took out her phone. No bars. No service. Crap.

On some level, she knew her disorientation was a direct result of her panic attack. But she couldn't stop it. Her heart was racing and the hair on the back of her neck was standing up. It was that same unnerving feeling she'd had on the beach the night before. She tried to convince herself it was because of all the evil the room had contained over the years.

Hearing a sound behind her, she glanced back in time to see a flash of someone ducking into an alcove.

"Hello?" she called, her wobbly voice echoing in the cold room. "Is someone there?"

The Edison bulbs, strung along a low wire, dimmed several watts. Another sound echoed behind her. Icy fear crawled across her scalp and before she realized what she was doing, she was sprinting, terror propelling her away from the sound.

There was only one place to go, down a narrower hallway. Running through it to a larger space with the same dim lighting, she exited the narrow hallway, and turned around to see if someone had been chasing her, but the space was empty.

Across this room, crumbling with chunks of stone on the ground and construction tools, she saw another red exit sign. She ran toward it. As she did, a man emerged from the other side, and she screamed. He wore a red vest like the tour guides.

"The ferry is waiting for you. We do head counts so people don't get lost like you did. That's why it's important to stay with your group," he said and turned back toward the open door. "This place has a maze of unchartered tunnels and passageways. You could have been down here for days. Not to mention that it's dangerous because of the rot and decay of the structure. We've had entire floors collapse from cracked concrete before."

Stella nodded as he kept talking and led her into a brightly lit hallway.

She followed him, heart pounding.

"You see, the exposure to saltwater and lack of maintenance in some areas doesn't bode well for lost tourists."

"I get it," Stella said and couldn't help but turn around to see if anybody else was lurking in the shadows. She could've sworn someone else had been behind her. Or had it just been her panic attack?

Emerging back into the daylight, Stella tried to calm her heartrate as she headed down to the dock where the ferry was waiting for her.

Not wanting anyone to overhear her conversation and not convinced that she wasn't being followed, Stella waited to call Griffin.

During her walk back to her car, she wove in and out of several tourist shops to make sure she wasn't being tailed. Stepping into a store selling San Francisco chocolates, she pretended to examine the wares, while she was looking out the window. Another time, she went in and tried on a hat while watching the street through the mirror. Once she was sure she wasn't being followed, she doubled back around to her car and locked her doors before calling the detective.

"Still waiting on an ID," he said upon answering.

Stella sighed. She didn't need an ID. "She never showed."

"Crap."

"Have they done the autopsy?"

"Yes. She wasn't pregnant." There was something in his voice—a strange hitch. Stella wasn't sure why this detail was important to include.

"Anything else?"

"We're working on it," he said, sounding distracted.

"Do you think it's Maria Perez?"

"Huh?" he said. Other voices surrounded him in the background.

"Griffin, I texted Maria's phone this morning telling her I would be at the meeting at Alcatraz and I never heard back from her, but while I was there I'm pretty sure someone was following me."

He waited a beat before answering.

"We haven't found a phone for the body yet. Be careful, Collins."

And then he hung up.

Back to Collins, huh? Fine. He'd sounded so strange.

That's when she remembered. She'd heard a rumor the previous week that Carmen had been pregnant when she'd been killed. Stella's hand flew up to her mouth and she gasped. It would have been Griffin's baby.

Stella had dismissed the rumor but now thinking of Griffin's reaction to saying the word "pregnant," she realized it was most likely true.

It was even more reason for Griffin to mourn the FBI agent's death.

And maybe even more reason for him to blame Stella.

7

McSweeney's Bar
Houston

Carlos Mendoza ordered another draft beer and stared at the black screen of his phone. He'd called Maria again and she still wasn't answering. He swore softly. Damn it. He'd warned her to mind her own business. But of course, she hadn't listened.

The week before, she'd stopped by his desk and slipped him a piece of paper. *McSweeney's. 8 p.m. Today.*

When he'd arrived, she'd been sitting at the bar alone.

Wearing jeans and a plaid button-down shirt, her thick black hair was pulled tightly back in a ponytail. Her head was bent over a beer. He examined her profile until she noticed him and gave him a nod. She was a good looking woman. Solid. Fine wrinkles around her eyes and mouth belying the years she'd lived. No wedding ring. Slightly crooked teeth, which made her endearing to him. But what he liked most about her was her intelligence and matter-of-fact honesty.

He'd known it wasn't a date. She had seemed too serious for that.

"Maria," he greeted.

"Carlos." She stared straight ahead as he slid onto the stool beside her. "Thanks for coming."

"Of course. What's going on?"

They'd complained about work conditions in the past, how they'd felt like token employees. Throughout the entire ImmortalGen company, they hadn't seen any other people of color. He figured their conversation would be about that. Maybe she was experiencing out-and-out racism. The thought made his blood boil. She'd ordered him a beer and then pivoted, turning on her stool to face him, scanning the room. He followed her gaze. The bar was nearly empty, save for a few truckers and a couple in a dark corner having an affair.

McSweeney's was near a truck stop thirty minutes outside of town. Nobody came here unless they were passing through or having a clandestine meeting..

"There's some bad stuff going down at our workplace," she said, searching his eyes.

Holding her gaze, he nodded. "Beyond overt racism?"

She gave a small chuckle. "I actually wish it was that level of evil."

He sat up straighter.

"Best case scenario is it's unethical. Worst case scenario, it's downright out of a horror movie."

Carlos tipped his glass and finished his beer, slamming the glass down on the counter. She watched as he scooted his bar stool back.

"I don't want to know a damn thing about what you're getting yourself into," he said. But he didn't mean it.

Maria saw right through him. She reached out and placed a hand on his sleeve.

"I don't know who else to turn to."

He paused for a moment, but didn't move her hand. "You got any family back in Columbia? Any parents or siblings? Kids?"

She met his eyes. "No one left but me."

"Same here."

"So what do you think? Can you help me?"

Damn it. He sighed, knowing he could never resist a plea from a good person trying to do the right thing. It was how he'd gotten into gangs in the first place. After a gang member had robbed and knocked down the elderly grandmother who'd raised him, he'd joined forces with the opposing gang. He'd killed the guy. He had no shame about it.

But it landed him in juvie until he turned twenty-one. And survival in a juvenile hall meant being the toughest gang member there. His large size gave him an immediate advantage.

After a few stints in prison for robbery and assault—only on other gang members, never on civilians—he was ready to throw in the towel. But you don't leave a gang. Or if you do, you leave in a casket.

Finally, he gave the head of the gang his life savings in exchange for his freedom from the gang.

He took a swig of his beer. Now, his life was simple. He worked as a data input specialist for ImmortalGen. Had a few friends there. Occasionally he'd stop by the taqueria in his neighborhood and get a tostada, even though he really just wanted tacos, but the lettuce on the tostada wouldn't hurt any. Then back at home, he would crack open a beer and watch the game for a few hours before going to bed. Once a month or so, he would meet up with some friends to play a little poker.

For the past ten years, he'd lived a peaceful life. No drama. No crazy girlfriends. Nobody wanted him dead. Anymore. His gang had let him go and all the old rival gang members he'd known had either forgiven him or grown too old to give a shit anymore.

"So, can I trust you?"

He gave her a long, annoyed look and she laughed.

Maria ordered them two more beers and took a long draught.

"I'm afraid to tell you too much." Taking a manila envelope out of her bag, she slid it toward him. "I hate even asking you to do this, but please take this and promise me you won't open it unless..."

She'd glanced around furtively before taking her hand off the envelope, barely moving her lips when she spoke again.

"Hide this somewhere safe. If something happens to me, open it."

"You sure?"

"Sure about what?"

"That I can't talk you out of it?"

Maria quirked a corner of her mouth up. "You are a good man. And

I'm sorry, because even meeting you here may have put you in danger. I just didn't know where else to turn."

"Maria, we're good." He placed his palm on top of her hand. "You came to the right guy. I'm not afraid of anyone."

She shook her head. "They will kill you in a heartbeat and leave your body to rot."

He looked her dead in the eye. "I've lived a good life."

Maria stared at him for a long moment before nodding once. "I'll see you here next week. Same time."

"I sure hope so."

After that night at the bar, when he'd realized that she was determined to expose Carter Barclay's operations, he had taken precautions. He had used connections from his former life to get her a fake ID. She'd been able to fly under an alias and book her hotel under the same name, Julie Dawson.

Someone had found out her plans.

That was the only explanation for her silence.

He'd told her to text him when she landed in San Francisco. Then again when she checked into the hotel. And after she got back from dinner. That's when she'd gone radio silent.

Sometime after checking into her hotel room, something had happened.

Something bad.

Picking up his phone again, he saw his text to her remained unanswered.

At the last minute, he clicked onto the *San Francisco Tribune's* webpage.

There it was, at the top. *Woman's body found on Ocean Beach. Identity unknown.*

His hand went to his eyes, rubbing them as he shook his head. *Damn it.*

It wasn't fair. She was a good woman trying to do the right thing. And she'd been killed for it. No use going to California now.

Now it was his turn to keep his end of the bargain. It was the last thing he wanted to do, but Maria had left specific instructions. *If something happens to me, open it.*

His life was simple and routine, just the way he liked it.

But all that was about to change. Sliding a twenty across the bar, he pushed back his stool and sighed.

His ex-wife would say he was a fool, but what else was new?

* * *

Back in his apartment, Carlos grabbed a beer and settled on his couch, a sturdy gray one with enough room to hold a friend or two during Sunday night football games.

Here, in his apartment, it was easy to see just who Carlos was: a simple man who only wanted a comfortable place to sit and pass the hours when the work day was over.

The old, scratched coffee table in front of the couch was like an old friend and a good place for Carlos to put up his feet after a long day. Today, he did just that and began to open the envelope that Maria had given him.

He stared at the thumb drive that fell out of the ripped end of the envelope.

That, and a slip of paper with an email address, was all that was inside. The email address was StellaCollins@SanFranciscoTribune.com.

Maria wanted him to email the contents of the thumb drive to this reporter.

So be it.

Logging onto his computer that sat on the desk in a corner of his living room, he stuck the thumb drive in smoothly and started to download the contents into a neat little file on his computer.

Easing back as the contents took their time to load, he wondered what information was on this device. Once the download was complete, he opened his email and typed in the reporter's address. For the subject line, he wrote, "Maria." Then he hit upload on the file. He still hadn't checked it to see what information it contained.

It took a long time for the file to upload. He worried it would be too large to send.

His senses went on high alert when a loud noise came from outside.

Somebody was outside his place.

The neighbor's dog began to bark, confirming the sound he'd heard.

The noise had come from the back door. Grabbing a baseball bat from a corner behind the kitchen door, he began to creep toward the back of the house.

He glanced over at the computer. The file had loaded.

He sidled over and hit send, watching as the email seemed to take forever to send.

He was about to reach for the thumb drive when he heard a noise and froze. But it was too late, someone was behind him. A cold, sharp blade pressed against his throat. White hot pain seared through him as a warmth trickled down his neck.

Keeping his eyes on the computer monitor, he smiled once the email went through.

It was the last thing he ever did.

8

Houston

Nestled in his office in his sprawling ranch house, Carter Barclay settled into his leather lounge chair, set his steaming cup of coffee on the table next to him, and perused the headlines on his iPad. He had a Google search set to alert him to any mention of his name.

He reviewed all the mentions of himself every morning for fun and never found anything of concern. He paid too much money to keep his reputation intact.

One of his assistants prepared a crib sheet of world headlines for him to review every day. Many years ago, he had learned that the president of the United States was given a daily briefing of world events each day, and Barclay hired someone to provide him something similar.

No matter that the President's Daily Brief was actually a sheet containing highly classified and secret national security information, Barclay liked to think his was similar. He did have a few covert operators who provided similar information.

Every morning as he sat and reviewed the briefing he'd been

provided, taking luxurious sips from his ritualistic coffee, Barclay mused about his next big goal: becoming president himself.

It could happen.

It wouldn't be the first time a billionaire had leveraged his wealth and fame into a successful run for the highest office in the land.

It had been another reason he'd sucked up to his son rather than let the chips fall as they may.

At least, no easily uncovered secrets.

All he had to do was curry favor with all the uncertain kingmakers in the country and world. And his new earth-shattering project at ImmortalGen would secure that.

There would be a line once the product was ready.

He would have the most powerful people in the world at his beck and call.

He was almost there.

After his daily scanning, he gave the iPad back to his assistant and hopped inside his walk-in shower. The designer of his downtown penthouse had called it a "wet room." Tiled all in black stone that had cost him an arm and a leg.

He also had a sauna and a plunge pool that was filled with freezing water, but it was too much of a pain in the butt to do any of that. Even though he heard people like Tony Robbins did something similar. Or was it Elon Musk? Whatever, he didn't have time for that new age crap.

He had work to do.

Right then, it was stopping a bunch of nosey busy bodies from trying to destroy his plans to create a business that would give him—and others—immortality.

9

THE WOMAN HAD BEEN MURDERED IN CHINA TOWN.

Griffin had tipped Stella off before the official press release went out.

He'd called her during her drive from Fisherman's Wharf, on her way to begin her night shift at the paper.

When she walked into the newsroom, Garcia wasn't at his desk. Neither was Josh. A quick glance at the conference room showed the two men inside. She paused, meeting Garcia's eye. He gave her a slight nod but didn't wave her in. Moving on, she headed to her desk. She didn't want to act cocky, but she knew more than they did. She'd get settled in at her desk and then go knock on the conference room door to share her information about where the woman was murdered.

Logging on, she saw the press release Griffin had released a few minutes after calling her, saying that detectives had discovered a crime scene without a body in a motel room in China Town. They believed it was connected to the body found on Ocean Beach but were still analyzing blood samples to see if they matched.

That was the official word.

But when Griffin had called Stella during her drive, he'd given her all the exclusive gory details.

"Collins?"

"Griffin?" she'd replied.

"I wanted you to hear it first."

"It's Maria?"

"Still waiting for positive ID. We are working with the Columbian government. Barclay's organization won't return calls."

"Figures."

"But we figured out where she was killed. There's a room in a China Town motel. The maid went in today and I'm not sure she's stopped screaming yet."

"Good God."

"Yeah, it's bad. I went down there. Blood bath. Floors, walls, even some of the ceiling soaked in blood."

"Consistent with a decapitation?"

"Only thing I think could cause that much blood. She took a while to bleed out. In the middle of the damn bed. Mattress soaked clear through."

Stella sighed and shook her head. "What kind of sicko does something like that? And also, did no one hear anything?"

"Our theory is that she was sleeping when someone came in and sliced her throat, then cut off her head. They found her discarded nightgown on the floor."

"How could you do something like that silently? I mean wouldn't you need something like a power tool?"

She cringed. You couldn't exactly hack through a neck with a knife.

"We think it was done with a machete."

Stella's breath caught in her throat, rendering her speechless at the next red light.

"Below the motel was a martial arts weapons store. The owner said a machete was missing, and the lock had been forced. We dusted for prints. Not a thing. A professional job."

A rush of icy cold ran down Stella's spine. "Where's the head?"

"No clue. Probably in the bottom of the ocean by now."

"So if you haven't identified her yet, that means no fingerprints on file, right?"

"Right. The Columbian government has the prints. We should be hearing back from them soon." He paused. "Hopefully. It's not like our government and theirs are on good terms."

She glanced back at the conference room. Garcia and Josh had pulled the blinds so she couldn't spy on them through the window. She cursed silently to herself and closed out of Griffin's email, scanning the others she'd received. Most were routine. Press releases about things she didn't care about and didn't cover on her beat; statistics on the most politically active senior citizens; a fast-food restaurant debuting cheesy pretzels; a county meeting on property taxes.

But one email caught her eye.

The subject line was Maria.

Her breathing stilled. Hand shaking, she opened it. The sender was a man named Carlos Mendoza.

Maria Perez is my friend. She told me if I didn't hear from her to send you this file. It's encrypted. She seemed to think you'd be able to open it. I haven't heard from her. I hope whatever this contains was worth it. She seemed to think it was.

Jesus.

Picking up her phone she texted Griffin. *We need to talk.*

Then she stared at the attached file.

Quickly, she replied to the email. *Thank you. Can you please call me at this number?*

She listed the number for one of her burner phones.

Now to figure out what the file contained.

Stella had dabbled here and there with rudimentary hacking as the Black Rose, but her skills were limited. This encrypted file escaped her abilities.

She could hire a hacker, but she risked the person seeing whatever the file contained. But she didn't have a choice.

Stella logged onto the Dark Web through a VPN so nobody could trace her to the newspaper. As Black Rose, she reached out to the best hacker she knew.

. . .

BL4D3 had a great reputation in the hacking world. He charged six figures, but Stella had worked with him once a very long time ago, when government was footing the bill. She would see if he would do her a solid once, hopefully for free. He'd told her that he'd hacked into the wrong person's account—an assassin who worked for a sheik. The assassin apparently had found the kid's home address and was going to kill him.

Stella had saved his butt.

A few days later, BL4D3 had messaged her. "I owe you. The guy said this was my one-time pass. Next time I'm dead."

Now, Stella messaged him.

He instantly replied.

"Black Rose."

"BL4D3."

"What's new?"

"I need a solid."

"I'm your guy."

"Thanks. It's an encrypted file."

"No sweat."

"The contents are risky. The woman who made it lost her head."

"Damn. Literally?"

"Literally."

"Okay then."

"You in?"

Stella stared at the computer screen, waiting. Finally, three dots appeared. He was typing.

"Of course."

"Can I upload it here?"

"Yes. But I won't be able to get to it for a few days. I've got a big paying gig I need to get done first."

"What will it take to make this one a priority?"

He was slow to reply again.

"I'll try my best."

Then his active status disappeared, and a small "upload" button appeared. Stella uploaded the file. It took a good fifteen minutes. Once it showed as uploaded, the screen went black.

Stella logged off the Dark Web.

Then she decided to do some Google searching.

Once again, she typed in Barclay's name and "news."

A hit.

The San Francisco Pulse, a magazine documenting the activities of the city's rich and famous, had a picture of Barclay plastered on its website.

The bastard was in town.

The headline above the photo and accompanying article read, "Political Fundraiser for Mayor Draws Luminaries to Cliff House."

The photo showed Barclay in a white cowboy cut suit, sitting at a candlelit table with two other men in suits and two older women in sequined dresses. The table before them held crystal dishes with caviar, silver baskets with sourdough bread, and platters of lobster, crab, and scallops drenched in butter.

Stella's heart pounded against her chest. She didn't know who the women were, but she definitely knew the men. The photo caption confirmed it.

"Philanthropist Carter Barclay joins Mayor Tyler Bradshaw, Mrs. Mayor Hennessey Bradshaw, Police Chief Darryl Mattson, and his wife, Donna Mattson, at the fundraiser dinner for Bradshaw."

Barclay sat in the middle of the couples. Even at a fancy dinner where the other men wore tuxedos, Barclay was still a cowboy. He was leaning forward and to one side, and his jacket had gaped open enough for Stella to spot the black strap of a gun holster. His piercing blue eyes were set against his tan, weathered face. Even in photographs, his gaze was icy cold.

The dinner was held at the Cliff House the night Maria's body was found. And Barclay had a stunning front row seat at the crime scene.

He'd had Maria killed and didn't even hide his presence in town that night. His smarmy smile seemed to jump through the screen at Stella, as if he were saying, "I can do whatever I want. Like I told you."

What an arrogant creep.

After searching a bit more and not finding anything else on Barclay's activities, she messaged Griffin a link to the article. He still hadn't called her back. He wouldn't be surprised about Barclay.

Stella turned back to her browser and punched in the name Carlos Mendoza + ImmortalGen. She wanted to see if she could find a phone number. She had been surprised the man had emailed her with his real name and email address. Wasn't he afraid?

A Houston newspaper article instantly appeared.

On the front page of the local section.

Man found dead in his apartment. Murder believed to be gang related.

Stella skimmed the article. Mendoza, a fifteen-year employee at ImmortalGen, was found dead in his apartment the night before, the apparent victim of gang violence. The article said Mendoza, a former gang member, had a prison record. They suspected he may have dipped back into that lifestyle.

Rage began to rise inside of Stella.

10

"COLLINS!" GARCIA CALLED FROM ACROSS THE NEWSROOM, startling Stella.

It was late and everyone but her, Garcia, a few guys in sports, and a handful of copyeditors had gone home for the night. As bodies had left, the newsroom had grown chilly and quiet. Outside the windows, San Francisco was lit up in all its glory. Skyscrapers dotted with lights. Wispy white clouds hanging in the black sky. In the distance, the Golden Gate bridge with dots of red taillights and white headlights swimming on its surface.

Stella looked up. Garcia was standing up at his desk facing her, making a chopping sign with his two palms.

"Chop chop!"

"Yo, what's up?"

"Where's my story?"

"Give me ten minutes."

She looked down, hoping he would sit down and relax.

"Slug it Body25."

"Got it."

"Also, paper's tight tonight. Keep it to twelve inches."

"Will do."

Stella opened a file and gave it the name Body25. Then she sat back and stared at the blank page. Sometimes that first line was the toughest to write. As a journalist, she knew the two most important parts of an article were the first line and the last.

But if you didn't draw the reader in by the first line, you didn't need to worry about the last one.

She was relieved Garcia had said it only needed to be 12 inches. It would be easier to write if it were short. The information from her first story would take up all the backstory of about ten inches. Perfect.

Her hands on the keyboard, she decided that the lede of the story didn't need any fancy writing. In this case, it was enough to let the facts speak for themselves. She wrote the first sentence and then re-read it.

A woman found decapitated on Ocean Beach Tuesday night was slain in a China Town hotel and dumped on the beach.

Ouch. She deleted the word dumped.

A woman found decapitated on Ocean Beach Tuesday Night was murdered in a China Town hotel, police said.

The killer then left the body on the beach where a man walking his dog came across it and called police.

Nope. She couldn't say that. She didn't know for sure that the killer was the one who had taken the body to the beach. He might have just chopped off the head and had some goon dump the body.

She looked at her notes and then rewrote the second sentence to include a few more details:

The body was left on Ocean Beach just south of The Cliff House Restaurant. A man walking his dog called police at about 11 p.m. when he spotted it.

It was a start.

Ten minutes later, she had a story about the woman on the beach who'd been murdered in a China Town hotel. She left the gory details out of course.

After turning in her story, Stella packed up for the night. Hesitating before leaving, she had to talk to Garcia about her plans. While she had been looking into Barclay's company, she saw they were hiring an executive secretary, and it gave her an idea.

Maybe that was a way inside the company. Or even just the building itself if she could nab an interview. Further research led her to an announcement that ImmortalGen would be a prominent organization at an industry trade show in Houston in two days. It was perfect.

Walking past Garcia's desk, she paused until he looked up.

"Okay. Paper has been put to bed." He shut his computer down and turned to face Stella. "What's up?"

She did not hold back, spilling the information in a verbal tumble. "My source told me the woman was decapitated with a machete that had been stolen from a knife shop."

Garcia's face plummeted and stared at her for a moment before muttering, "Jesus."

"There's something else, something important." Garcia met her eyes. She exhaled loudly. "Do you trust me?"

He nodded solemnly.

"That woman ... I think she was in town to meet with me."

Garcia's eyes widened in surprise.

"If she is who I think, then she is—was a whistleblower. And everyone who knows an inch of whatever she did has ended up murdered like her."

"Hmm. This sounds a lot bigger than a gang murder or revenge killing.

"I think it is," she said.

"What do you need from me?" he asked.

"I think I need to go to Texas. For a while."

Stella waited as Garcia stroked his goatee, always a sign he was thinking. Then he nodded, almost as if he were convincing himself. "Just expense whatever you need."

"Thanks."

Stella turned to leave before he called her name again. "Collins?"

She paused.

"Be careful, okay?"

She smiled, nodded, and left.

* * *

The next morning, Stella made a double espresso and sat on her couch with her laptop. She sipped her coffee and searched for airline tickets to Houston and found one for the following day. It was a red eye and would get her to Houston the next morning. It would work out great. She'd get there in time to attend the trade show.

She hauled a suitcase down from a top shelf and began to pack. She threw in three burner phones still in their packaging. Eyeing her gun, she wished she could take it with her, but she'd have to turn to the Dark Web for one.

Logging on as the Black rose, she reached out to an old contact who sold illegal items and arranged for some weapons to be waiting for her in Texas. The seller told her there would be a 13-inch Italian stiletto switchblade and a Glock model 42 waiting for her in a gas station bathroom in Houston between 11 and 11:15 am the next day. It was a tight meet up, but it would have to do. She'd have to head straight there when she got off the plane.

The seller said there would be eyes on her—likely a sharpshooter or some heavies around the corner—so as soon as she picked up the weapons and approved of them, she was to send the payment that moment. She wouldn't even consider trying to mess with guys who sold weapons. That'd be signing her death warrant.

After arranging her plane and plans for a hotel room near the ImmortalGen headquarters—all under a false name—Stella eyed her suitcase.

She would need a disguise. In an old box that had held her belongings when she came back from Europe, she found some items she'd used as a disguise on an op where she infiltrated a factory in Istanbul: dumpy oversized clothes, a wig, and thick fake glasses.

Her suitcase was packed, her plans were made, and she felt woefully unprepared for the trip. It was because of who she was after.

Carter Barclay had more money than God and for some reason he liked to spend it on hiring the world's best assassins to do his dirty work. He'd gone through two elite assassins trying to kill Stella before. They had both failed. If he found out she was going after him again, he'd only hire the best of the best. That meant Stella had to be able to fend off someone who was likely twice her size and had probably twice as much experience.

That meant daily runs and workouts, including time in the gym and martial arts.

It was a little late to train for a showdown right then, but still she had a lot of energy to burn, so she went for a run. It was not pretty. She ran three miles before she was bent over, hands on her knees, panting. But it was a start.

Along with being on the wagon, she was trying to get back in shape. When she was working for Headway overseas, she trained with the others on her team: daily sit-ups, pullups, pushups, running, and martial arts. She wanted to be back in that fighting form. She had a feeling she was going to *need* to be back in fighting form.

After her run, she took a shower, but she couldn't shake the restlessness streaming through her limbs. In the past, she had tamped down feelings like this with alcohol or sex or smoking. But no more. Instead, she cleaned her apartment.

It was mostly picking up clothing, emptying anything in her refrigerator that would spoil, and starting a last load of dishes. When she was done, she surveyed her work.

With her blackout curtains drawn and her dark furniture, the place was cave-like. Her apartment was small and nondescript. The most interesting thing was the expensive Italian espresso machine on the counter. Everything else was put away. No pictures on end tables. No books out in the open. No art on her walls. For some reason, hanging something up, even a photograph, made it seem too permanent. Too intimate. Too hard to leave behind. For that reason, she kept her place furnished like a high-end hotel room. Sparse of personal touches but luxurious with the best sheets, towels, and furniture.

The apartment was her sanctuary. And yet it was empty.

Surveying it one last time, standing in the doorway, she pushed down a wave of sadness and closed the door.

She heard her neighbor Billy on the stairs, followed by a woman's giggle. Stella had turned to Billy for mindless sex in the past. It had been a while since she'd cut him out of her life. She hadn't been touched since then. Her body ached for someone to touch it.

Unbidden, a memory of her and Griffin making love surfaced. They had more than just a physical connection. But with Billy, it was just pure lust. The difference between those connections was striking. Lust on its own faded quickly. Lust plus an emotional and intellectual connection grew exponentially.

The last time she'd had sex with Billy, she'd been bored.

The last time she'd had sex with Griffin had been the best she'd ever had.

She shook her head. That ship had sailed.

As she drove to the newsroom, Stella decided she would wait to feel that connection again before jumping into bed with someone else.

Walking into the newsroom, she immediately drew up short when her gaze reached the conference room windows. Griffin sat in the enclosed room along with Garcia, the police chief, and the publisher, Patricia Sontag.

Nearly six feet tall and model-slim, Sontag always wore tailored suits that cost a fortune and today was no exception. Her reddish bob was slicked back behind her ears, and her thin lips were painted a similar burnished red. Her air of confidence and nonchalance intrigued Stella. But the woman was also the devil, working for the hedge fund that owned the paper and seemed intent on running it out of business.

Garcia made eye contact with Stella through the glass and motioned for her to join them.

Her face warmed. Whatever was going on would not be good.

11

GARCIA MET HER AT THE DOOR, HOLDING IT OPEN FOR HER. "Admit nothing."

Two short words of warning.

The men stood briefly as she entered, then sat back down as Stella did.

"Thanks for joining us, Stella," Garcia said.

"Sure," she said, avoiding Griffin's eyes. "What's going on?"

Sontag cleared her throat. "We called this meeting because the chief here received some intel that someone on the department was slipping you information about this week's murder."

Stella burst into laughter. The chief scowled.

"I wish," Stella said lightly. "If someone had been tipping me off, our newspaper would have a much better story than we do now."

The publisher frowned. "How do you mean?"

"I'd have a scoop. Remember those, Garcia?" Stella turned toward him and smirked. Then she turned back to the publisher and police chief. "Once upon a time we used to get those, before every story was put online immediately after we wrote it. If I had a source—if I *were* being tipped off by someone in the department or anywhere else—my story wouldn't be the same as every other story the local media had, would it?"

The chief scratched his head and tugged at his collar. He seemed to be growing uncomfortable. Then he cleared his throat. "It's no secret that you and Detective Griffin are close."

"*Were* close," Stella said quickly, hoping her face wouldn't grow red by the second. Her neck was feeling a little warm already.

"When I first started at the paper we were friends. We are no longer."

Stella avoided Griffin's eyes.

"It's true," Griffin acknowledged, avoiding Stella's gaze in return. "We had a falling out after I began seeing Special Agent Rodriguez."

His voice cracked a little. Stella wondered what that sentence cost him emotionally.

The chief gawked at him. "You were seeing her?"

Griffin let out a lifeless laugh. "Your sources have failed you. FBI Special Agent Carmen Rodriguez and I were an item." He paused, looking down at the table. "We were talking about getting married."

It was as if a knife had been plunged through Stella's heart. She finally looked up at Griffin, fighting to keep her expression neutral.

The chief waved his hand as if Griffin's confession meant nothing. An incredibly heartless gesture, considering Rodriguez, the woman he had planned to marry, was dead.

"For full transparency," the chief said, "I need to know if you and this reporter had a physical affair in the past."

Griffin cleared his throat, his gaze still cast down. "Yes."

"Before I was a reporter," Stella said. "We met when I first came back to town—before I was hired by the *Tribune*. As soon as I was hired, we agreed to just be friends."

"Is that so, Detective?" the chief asked.

Stella silently begged him to back her story. She was terrified that he'd been about to spill everything and confess to sleeping with Stella while she'd been a reporter, which would have possibly resulted in his own discipline—and hers. Now, if he argued, he would be calling Stella a liar and getting her in trouble. He would willingly take any punishment involved for his own discretion to stop her from getting in trouble. She was banking on his integrity and willingness to protect her reputation. Guy was too honest for his own good.

"Yes," Griffin said finally. "She didn't know I was a police officer, and I didn't know she had become a reporter until we saw each other at the press conference for the murder of Mark Bellamy." He looked over at Stella. "I think we were both surprised."

Stella nodded, her face warming rapidly now.

Griffin was not a liar, but he was also no dummy.

Garcia stood. "Listen, I think we've established that our reporter has acted with integrity here. We've got a paper to fill so if you don't have any more questions, chief?"

Both Stella and Griffin stood as well. The chief and publisher remained seated.

There was an awkward pause before Sontag stood.

"I'm not sure we have established that," she said, "but I'm also not sure anything else can be done today." She straightened her suit jacket, smoothing it down her torso. She fixed her piercing gaze on Stella. "But if I hear that you are receiving information under the table, we will be forced to take action."

To Stella's surprise, Garcia whirled and scowled, holding up a palm to her. "Who do you work for here? The police chief, or the newspaper? Our job, Ms. Sontag, is to print the truth. To shine a light on the darkness, and disseminate justice to the public."

The publisher's face drained of color.

Garcia turned and walked out. Stella followed him, keeping her eyes in front of her. She resisted the urge to look back at Griffin, who still stood in a silent standoff with his superior.

Sitting down at her desk and logging on, Stella kept her eyes trained on her computer monitor, but out of the corner of her eye, she could see the chief, Griffin, and the publisher stop at Garcia's desk. The three of them exchanged words with him. Garcia was still standing his ground, even seated with his hands folded over his stomach.

A few minutes later, they were gone.

Stella stomped over to her editor.

He pushed back his chair as she arrived and made a face. "I know."

"Are we forever going to be controlled by a hedge fund with a publisher who doesn't know the first thing about journalism?"

Garcia sighed. "I hope not, but I don't know what to tell you. Our best bet is to fly under the radar, agree to whatever they want, then still do our own thing."

Relief filled Stella. "Okay."

When Stella had first started, Garcia had held her back, saying the publisher didn't want her to do this or do that. But in the time she'd been there, he'd found his backbone again.

He cleared his throat. "With that said, I need a cover story for you going to Texas. Can you say you're researching the oil industry?"

"Too obvious." Stella put a finger on her chin as she thought. "I don't even want them to know I'm out of town. How about I'm just taking a personal leave?"

"You can't get paid for personal leave, Collins."

"Understood."

12

A FEW HOURS LATER, STELLA LOGGED OFF HER COMPUTER.

She'd written several short stories, including one about a motorcyclist who crashed and died on the Bay Bridge after doing wheelies. Other motorists were cheering him on and videotaping his stunt until he smacked into the back of a semi-truck.

After filing that story, she packed up to leave.

Garcia was in the news meeting, so she didn't stop to say bye on her way out. She decided not to write him a note either; he would remember when he saw her empty desk.

Stella hurried out of the newsroom and to her car. Traffic to the airport was often horrendous, and she was already leaving ten minutes later than she'd planned.

Tommy Mazzoli was already out at the curb when she pulled up. She would recognize him anywhere with his thick head of curly hair and gigantic Mario Brothers mustache. A true Italian man, if there ever was one. He had a worn leather duffel bag slung over one shoulder. Stella put the car in park and unlocked the doors. Before she opened her door to greet him, he threw his duffle in the back seat and hopped into the passenger's side with a big grin.

She smiled back at the older man. "You travel light, *paesano*."

"What? I just need some clean underwear and socks, right?"

"Right," she chuckled and rolled her eyes.

"I'm beat. I need to stop and get an espresso before the party."

Stella put the car in drive and headed away from the airport. "Party?"

Keeping his gaze out the window, he replied. "Didn't I tell you? We're stopping by a retirement party before we go to my place."

"You didn't tell me." Stella glanced at him, but he still wouldn't make eye contact. "I think I can drop you off at home first."

"Nah, it's on the way. You should go. Get a chance to meet some more of my cop buddies. It's a small private party. None of the crooked cops allowed."

"I don't think so," Stella said. "I'm leaving town in the morning. I need to get ready."

It wasn't a total lie, but she also wasn't up to socializing. The thought of hobnobbing with a bunch of cops made her nauseated.

"Where you going?" he asked, finally looking her way.

"Just to visit a friend."

"Bull. I can tell when you lie from a mile away."

Stella cursed under her breath. She regretted mentioning she was leaving town. "I can't tell you."

"Stella LaRosa!"

"It's a long story."

Mazzoli glanced at his watch. "We got twenty minutes at least. The party is in the Sunset district."

Stella sighed. "Fine."

And then she told him everything.

He let out a low whistle.

"You weren't going to tell me this? You need someone to know these things. What if it goes sideways? You keep in touch with me every morning and every night, you understand?"

"Okay." Even though she hadn't wanted to tell Mazzoli since everyone who knew about the whistleblower ended up dead, she was relieved that he had made her confess what was going on.

As they wound through the twisty streets of San Francisco in the golden light of the sunset, Stella kept her eyes on the road and counted on Mazzy to give her directions.

Finally, after getting stuck in traffic on Market Street, they went up a steep hill in a neighborhood with narrow streets.

"Turn left," he said, leaning forward. "We're almost there."

They pulled down a street of old Victorians and plenty of parking—a rarity for San Francisco. Stella pressed the brake pedal to slow her speed on the residential street.

Mazzoli pointed off to the right. "It's that light blue one right there."

Stella put on her blinker and veered next to the curb. "Shouldn't we have brought wine or something?"

He leaned over and retrieved his bag from the back. "That's what the duty-free shop at the airport is for." He winked and withdrew a bottle of scotch. "This is Mickey's favorite."

"Mickey who? I should probably know the name of the guy whose party I'm crashing."

"You ain't crashing," he replied. "You're my date."

Stella cocked an eyebrow. "Carol won't like that."

To her delight, Mazzoli shut his mouth.

She continued to tease him as they walked up the front steps. "You're embarrassed, aren't you?"

"No."

"Yes you are!"

Her smile faded as she saw a car door open and Griffin got out.

Great. Twice in one day was two times too many.

To her surprise, Mazzoli went over to Griffin and gave him a big hug.

"Missed you, man," he said.

Griffin returned the sentiment and clapped the big man on the back.

Missed you? Stella thought they barely knew each other.

She approached behind Mazzoli. "I didn't know you guys were such good friends?"

"After I was shot and Griffin was in the hospital," Mazzoli said, facing her. "Started meeting for coffee a few times a week after his release."

Stella furrowed her brows. She couldn't stop them from being friends even if it was awkward for her.

"Did you call me earlier?" Griffin asked Stella as he walked up.

"Yeah. Not sure if you saw, but there's a picture in the local magazine showing Barclay, the chief, and the mayor at a fundraiser," she paused. "At the Cliff House restaurant."

His head swiveled toward her and his eyes grew wide.

"Any guesses on what night that was?"

"You've got to be kidding?"

Stella shook her head.

During moments like this, it seemed almost as if they were friends again.

But then it always got weird. There was an awkward silence that Mazzy interrupted.

"Come on," the older cop said. "We're already late."

Stella and Griffin glanced at one another before the three of them crossed the street.

They walked up the sidewalk leading to the house. The party was in the large backyard, so the trio filed out back and down a set of steps.

A small group was gathered around a stone patio with a dining table and grill off to one side.

Spotting Carol, Stella took off toward the other woman standing near the pool. She was holding a beer can and talking to another woman about her age. Stella introduced herself, and Mazzoli appeared with his own beer can. And Griffin trailed up behind him. Stella stopped herself from rolling her eyes. Then, to her surprise, Mazzoli slung his arm around Carol's shoulders. Despite herself, Stella made eye contact with Griffin whose eyes widened. Damn. Talk about a public reveal of their relationship! And even though she knew she would regret it, she smiled at Griffin who smiled back. Both loved Mazzoli and were happy for him. At last, they had found common ground.

But the comradery didn't last long. Mazzoli and Carol wandered off to get hamburgers off the grill. That left Stella and Griffin alone. Stella was too tired to deal with the emotional toll of talking to Griffin any more in a non-professional setting.

She needed to get out of there, stat.

"I'm beat," she said. "You know Mazzoli is going to shut this party down. I can't do it tonight. Can you give him a ride home if I leave?"

Griffin looked surprised. "Yeah, sure."

"I've got his duffel bag in my car. Can I put that in yours first?"

"No problem."

He followed her back through the house and out to the street. Stella handed Griffin the duffel bag and threw it in his car. Then he shut the door and stood there, staring at her. She stared back at him.

Finally, he cleared his throat. "I love fall in the city."

The sun was setting, and the sky was a brilliant deep navy with stars just starting to appear in the east. To the west, behind the house, the horizon was tinged with orange and pink and red. Heat rose from the pavement but was met by a cool ocean breeze that smelled of salt.

It was the perfect San Francisco night.

"Doesn't get much better than this," she replied.

When he leaned towards her, Stella's heart stopped. Was he going to kiss her? His fingers tucked a strand of hair behind her ear. He was only inches away. "I don't hate you."

"Could've fooled me."

"I was falling in love with you."

"But?"

"But you ghosted."

Stella pressed her lips together and nodded. He was right. She had.

"You're not going to say anything?"

"No. I did disappear. Because..." *I was falling in love with you too.* "I knew it would never work out."

Both were true.

His eyes sparkled with the fading sunlight and streetlamps. "You never even gave us a chance."

She hesitated, wishing it could be different. But it still wouldn't work. And she couldn't risk that kind of hurt. Not again.

Her voice turned cold when she said, "It's too late now."

His expression hardened, and he pulled away from her, only responding with a "yep," before walking back to the house.

Standing next to his car, she watched him walk away. Any warmth from the moment they had shared was gone. In its place was the hollow chill of regret and bitterness.

* * *

Stella found herself a while later parked at the entrance to the cemetery, restless and filled with sorrow. The sunset had somehow revived itself from its seemingly imminent demise and the sky had lightened and become streaked with lavender, pink, and orange, the horizon tinged with a deep red. She left her car and made her way over to a grave she had gotten to know quite well over the past weeks.

In another life, she and Agent Carmen Rodriguez would have been friends. In another life, Stella would have been a mother and housewife in the suburbs. Carmen would have still been alive, married to Griffin, having his children.

But this was the only life Stella had, and it was only thanks to Carmen.

As she mounted a hill toward the grave, trudging through the grass, Stella drew up short. Someone was at the grave.

Leery in the past of stumbling upon Griffin, she was always on the lookout for his car parked near the bottom of the hill. Once, she'd seen it as she pulled in and she'd turned around and left.

But there had been no other cars parked in the small lot.

This was a petite woman with dark, curly hair pulled back. The woman stood facing the gravestone. She wore a black trench coat and high-heels below bare legs. Her shoulders were slight and shaking, as if she were weeping. Then the woman shifted her head and Stella caught a glimpse of her profile. A cold chill raced down Stella's spine. Carmen.

But Carmen was dead. Stella had seen her get murdered.

As if she sensed Stella, the woman turned.

Stella lifted a hand halfway, almost to reassure the woman not to be afraid.

The woman had tears pouring down her face. Swiping at them, she smiled.

Stella swallowed her trepidation and continued walking.

By the time she got there, the woman had dried her tears. Up close, the resemblance between this woman and Carmen was striking. Not identical twins, but definitely blood relatives.

"I'm Stella Collins," she said, offering her hand.

The woman gave a small smile. "I know who you are."

Of course she did. Stella took a step back. She was dismayed that she was disturbing a family member during an intimate moment of mourning. And this woman might have, like Griffin, held Stella responsible for Carmen's death.

"Don't leave," the woman said. "Please."

Stella nodded and stayed planted where she was.

"I'm Ana."

"I'm so sorry about your loss."

"Thank you." Ana dabbed at her nose. "Do you come here often?"

Stella came at least once a week, most often bearing flowers to replace the dead ones. She'd spend a few minutes picking up dead leaves that had blown onto the grave and rearranging the fresh flowers in a vase that stuck out of the ground. Then she'd leave without a word to her dead almost-friend.

"The guy at the office told me you come every week and bring flowers."

Stella swallowed and nodded. *Damn.*

Ana smiled, clearly sensing Stella's sheepishness. "Thank you."

Uncomfortable, Stella looked away. How could she admit it was guilt that motivated her?

The two women stood in silence for a few seconds before Ana broke it. "I have to get back to the office. I've only been there a week, so I am still getting situated, but I hope we can grab coffee soon. I've got some business to discuss with you."

"Business?" Stella blinked, confused.

Ana laughed and opened her trench coat. An FBI badge encased in a leather lanyard holder flashed.

"Oh my God." The words slipped out before Stella could help it. "You're with the FBI?"

"I'm not taking her place," Ana said, stepping forward with wide eyes. "I asked for the transfer so I could follow up on Carmen's cases. I've been working in Austin for the past few years."

Stella was rendered speechless. It took her a few seconds to find her next question. "Are you identical twins?"

"No. I'm five years younger." Ana took a step away. "I was serious. Do you want to grab coffee? I am meeting with most of the media during my first two weeks. I'm going to be the public information officer."

"I would, but ... I'm actually leaving town for a while."

Disappointment filled Ana's face. "I was especially looking forward to talking to you. I know...you were with her that night."

Stella closed her eyes and shook her head. "Did you talk to Detective Griffin about it?"

"Of course."

Stella nodded and took a deep breath. "We can get together when I get back, if that's okay?"

"Sure," Ana said.

Stella turned to leave. But she had only taken a few steps when Ana spoke again.

"I know it wasn't your fault. I know my sister better than anyone else. She would put her life on the line to save someone else's. She's done it before." Ana gave a small, sad laugh. "I know how stubborn she was and nobody could have talked her into—or out of—doing anything. *Anything*. So her death is on her."

Stella gave a very slow nod and turned to glance at the woman past her shoulder. "Thank you. That means more than I can say," she whispered.

Then she hurriedly walked away. She couldn't turn around. She couldn't let Ana see the tears streaming down her face.

13

I WAS FALLING IN LOVE WITH YOU.

Damn it. Griffin's words echoed in her head.

She was furious he had told her that. That had been the last thing she'd wanted to hear. They'd never had a chance. They would never be together. So what had been the point of telling her that?

Stella scowled as she pulled her suitcase through the airport terminal, heading toward her gate. She absentmindedly wove through the crowd, lost in her thoughts.

He ruined everything. Why did Griffin have to wear his heart on his sleeve like that? She shook her head. How could they ever be friends now? She was angry, clutching the handle of her suitcase with a grip that could kill.

But anger always hid another emotion. Sadness, regret, fear. But right now, she wasn't going to dig deeper for the true feeling. Not on this matter.

Instead, she focused on her task at hand. Taking Carter Barclay down.

When she'd gotten to the airport, it'd still been dark out. Dressed in her wig, frumpy clothes and oversized glasses, she looked like a different woman. She looked like the woman on her passport, Rose St. James.

She then found a seat at her gate and took out her Headway laptop. The computer had a built-in VPN that made it invisible on the web. At least, that's what she was banking on. Once upon a time, somebody had tracked the Headway laptops. When the program had been disbanded, she assumed that had gone away. Otherwise, over the past two years, there might have been a few times the government could have found her and taken her out.

There was an email from Mazzoli. Strange. He wasn't a big tech guy. The subject line was titled, "Question."

She opened it.

Sorry for the email but I didn't get a chance to ask you in person last night and Carol made me send this as soon as I got home because it's too long for text and you're probably asleep right now and I don't want to disturb your beauty sleep.

Frowning, Stella realized her heart was pounding, and she raced to read on.

But here's the deal–Carol and I are getting married.

Stella gasped and then quickly looked around. Nobody in the seats around her reacted. She drew her eyes back to the screen.

We are planning on a thing for family around Thanksgiving when everyone is in town, but we wanted to make it official now. At City Hall. Next Tuesday. Carol and I want you to be a witness.

Tears pricked Stella's eyes.

She picked up the phone and dialed.

As soon as Mazzoli answered, she shouted, "Yes! Yes! I'd be honored. Congratulations!"

"Geez, Stella. It's five in the morning."

"I'm so excited for you."

He chuckled softly. "I wanted to tell you before you left town."

"I'll be there. For sure."

"Great. Can I go back to sleep now?" He used his fake grumbling voice. He tried to come off like such a tough guy, but he was the biggest teddy bear.

"Sweet dreams," she said and hung up.

Stella couldn't stop smiling, despite the strange looks from the other tired travelers, likely itching to get a nap on the early flight.

Mazzoli was getting married! To a great woman.

Her smile faded. She'd promised him she'd be there. She better make sure she was. She'd fly back from Texas for the ceremony, even if she had to turn around and go back afterward.

An announcement was made and boarding began.

The industry trade show was in six hours. She'd have time to get a rental car, pick up the gun and knife, and head to the show. From there, she'd have to wing it.

* * *

The weapons pick up went seamlessly. She was there early, but the weapons were already in place wrapped in heavy duty plastic bags in the tank of the gas station toilet. As soon as she unwrapped the gun, she wired the money as instructed.

She didn't even bother trying to spot the sharpshooter, figuring the more she kept her head down the better. She was also glad she had the disguise. Meeting people from the Dark Web in person could be treacherous. It was better they had no idea what she really looked like. She wouldn't put it past them to use some type of facial recognition to identify her.

From there, she drove a very circuitous route to the trade show, dipping on and off the freeway and through neighborhoods to ensure she wasn't being followed. At one point, she stopped in the empty parking lot of a park and dug a dealer plate out of her duffel bag. She strung it up from the trunk so it covered her real license plates and then continued driving, hoping nobody would notice the difference between the front and back plates.

The parking lot of the conference center was packed. Stella parked at the far end and made her way to the front door.

. . .

The Genomics Expo trade show was held in a large outbuilding at the Astrodome complex. Dozens of people streamed toward the entrance with Stella. She slipped into a group and tailed behind them as they entered.

Rows of booths lined the space, most with large tables of wares and banners advertising their specialties. Some shared information about seed cloning. Stella paused at another focused on tissue culture. A small brochure said tissue culture was growing tissues, cells, or organs from a plant or animal. Organs.

The last time Stella had faced Barclay it was over his role in having people killed to harvest their organs as part of a depraved competition among his billionaire friends. Everyone had been arrested except for him. Of course.

And then when she had provided proof that he was behind a plot to assassinate the president, someone way up the line had swept it under the rug.

He was untouchable.

Until now. Stella would not rest until he was stopped.

Some booths were for gene companies that researched immunology, oncology, viruses and allergies. Selling items such as antibodies, tissues, gene expression. Stella didn't know what half of it meant or how those items would be used by researchers.

She kept walking, looking for ImmortalGen's booth.

Genomics and cloning worked hand in hand. Cloning involved making identical copies of cells or DNA. For research purposes. Allegedly.

Then at the end of one aisle, she saw it. ImmortalGen took up one entire corner of the large outbuilding. At least eight spaces. Every other company had one space, two at the most.

A large banner hung on the wall behind the booth. In it was the largest photo of Carter Barclay that Stella had yet to see. The caption read, "We care about more than just this state's black gold. We care about your future and that of your great, great grandchildren. See what we are doing now with ImmortalGen. Here today and better tomorrow."

Stella reread the lines.

This state's black gold.

Oil.

Interesting, Stella thought. Nothing good had come from Barclay's fortune in oil. Calling it black gold was like putting lipstick on a pig.

Stella paused. Half a dozen employees were dressed in black polos with the gold ImmortalGen logo on the left side. People crowded the tables. The employees were animated and eager, with wide smiles.

It was by far the most popular booth at the trade show.

As Stella wove her way through the crowd and grew closer, she saw people clamoring for small, deep blue vials with rubber tops displayed artistically in neat stands. Every time a row of the vials emptied, a young woman with a strawberry blonde ponytail crouched beneath the table and came back up with more to fill the empty spots.

Eventually, the customers in front of her grabbed their vials and left. Finally, Stella made it to the front. A small sign on the table read, "Free Genome Sequence. Our testing will compile your risk factors for disease, scan for inherited disorders, and provide you with your own unique genetic fingerprint."

Another sign read, "If you take a vial and submit a DNA sample, our company is offering the first 100 people a free report and analysis."

The nearest man in front of her made eye contact and said, "Hi!"

Stella almost took a step back. The man looked like a model. He could be advertising fancy underwear on a Times Square billboard. That's when Stella noticed everyone working the booth was young and extraordinarily good looking.

"I'm new here," Stella said, pointing down. "What are those?"

"Be sure to grab an envelope to send it back to us,"the blonde said as she stood, grinning, hands filled with vials. "It's prepaid postage."

Up close, this woman looked like the actress Florence Pugh.

"Huh," Stella said, trying to hide her surprise. "Why are you—I mean why is your company doing this ... for free?"

The young man flashed his megawatt smile. "It's a way of

promoting our services. Eventually, we will be selling this service, but you can be one of our early adopters."

Early adopters.

This didn't sit right. Stella's skin was crawling. Barclay's company was collecting at least a hundred DNA samples from strangers, likely more.

It couldn't be for any good reason. Not if Barclay was involved.

One of the other young men in the booth began speaking into a microphone. Stella glanced behind her and noticed the crowd had picked up, vibrating at the sight of the blue vials.

"Thanks for joining us here today," the man said, voice slightly robotic from the microphone. "I know you all have been patiently waiting, but we now are ready to hear from Patrick Barclay."

Stella froze at the name.

Another man stepped out from behind a curtain. His short brown hair was graying at the temples. His black polo was tight around his torso and showcased his well-toned biceps. Under other circumstances, Stella would have thought him attractive, but he looked average around the young people with movie star looks surrounding him.

Who was he?

"Thanks so much for coming out today. My father and I are very excited about the possibilities for preventing disease and curing others, such as cancer. Thank you for being a part of this groundbreaking research."

He droned on about some more scientific stuff, but Stella was lost in her thoughts.

My father.

Carter Barclay had a son.

14

In all her hours of research on the man, she'd never heard of Barclay having offspring.

After a few seconds, she realized Patrick had stopped speaking, the crowd had thinned, and he was staring at her.

He'd said something.

"I'm sorry?" she replied.

"Did you have any questions?"

Stella nodded and gave a slow smile. "More than you can imagine."

He grinned back.

"I was going to go grab a coffee near the concession booths. Can I buy you one as well?"

"That would be great," she said.

Coming out from behind the booth, he stuck out his head. "Patrick Barclay."

For a second, she opened her mouth opened to say Stella LaRosa, then quickly remembered to give her fake name. "Rose St. James."

He led the way in the direction of the concession stand. "What brings you to the trade show today, Ms. St. James?"

"Call me Rose."

"Rose it is."

"I heard that your company was hiring. I don't know much about what you do, but I just moved to Houston, and I need a job. I worked for the past ten years as an executive assistant, so I know how to keep an office organized."

On the airplane, Stella had written up a fake resume that would make her uber qualified for the executive secretary position. She'd planned to ask where to send it, but this was even better.

"How convenient," he said, his eyes slightly narrowing. "The position is for my assistant. Did you know that?"

The surprise on Stella's face was real and her cheeks grew warm.

"No, I did not," she said, her laughter filled with nerves. "I'm actually a little embarrassed. Gosh, that makes me seem stalkerish."

He laughed out loud. "I can tell that you aren't a stalker. Maybe you are just someone in the right place at the right time?"

"I'm definitely lucky that way."

He had no idea.

"Why don't you shoot me your resume?"

"I can text it right now if you like."

After exchanging phone numbers, Stella texted him her resume and he scanned it as she watched.

"I like it. I'm not sure how all this hiring stuff works since I'm new, but I've always gone by my gut instincts. The formal hiring process could take a few months, I was told. But I really do need help now. Like yesterday. I'd like to offer you the job as a temporary position and then we can see if it's a good fit for both of us before we do the official hiring process? How does that sound? If you're interested, I'd love for you to start tomorrow."

Stella stopped walking. "I'm interested."

"Great. The job will be pretty boring. At first, you'll basically just help me set up my office and organize my life in this new job."

"Tell me more."

They were at the coffee booth then. After ordering two black coffees, he added cream and sugar to his.

Patrick moved toward the wall and Stella followed, leaning against it to face him. "It's a long story," he said, "but my dad owns the company."

Stella waited for him to continue. If she'd learned anything as a reporter, it was that people always filled silence on their own if you were patient. Often, some of the most telling details came after this beat of awkward silence.

"My mother died two weeks ago. He showed up at the funeral and claimed me. I'd never made the connection between his last name and mine. Probably should have. My mom raised me in Greece and Barclay isn't a Greek name."

Stella noticed that he had quickly skipped over the mother dying part.

"I'm so sorry for your loss."

"Thank you." He looked down at his cup, suddenly interested in the lid. "She was the best mother anyone could have."

"That's great," she said, a sad smile crossing her lips. "I'm just wondering why you said your father, 'claimed' you?"

Chuckling, he glanced up at her. "It sort of feels like that, I guess. Sorry if I'm oversharing, but I'm still processing so much of it."

Stella held her breath, her next question bait. "What do you think of your father?"

"Not sure," he replied, shaking his head. "I haven't been able to spend much time with him. It's been a whirlwind, mourning my mother, handling her affairs, then packing up my life in Greece to settle in here and now working for my father."

"How's that been?" Stella asked before taking a sip of her drink. "Working for him?"

"Tomorrow's my first day. I'll let you know."

"So we'll start together then?"

"That's what I was hoping."

When he smiled at her she couldn't help but smile back. Guilt lingered at the thought of her plan. Essentially, she would be using him to infiltrate his father's organization. So far, he seemed nothing like his father.

"What time do I start?" Stella asked.

"Are you an early riser?"

"Yes," she lied.

"I like to get there about seven. Will that work?"

Please, no. "Perfect."

"Okay then." He took a deep breath and nodded. "I better get back to the booth."

"See you in the morning."

15

SAN FRANCISCO

The powers that be had given Ana her sister's old desk in the San Francisco bureau. When Ana walked in, the desk had not been cleaned out, per se. Instead, a cardboard box containing all of Carmen's personal items rested on top of it.

Her supervisor, Supervisory Special Agent Martha Craig, had rushed over in embarrassment and grabbed the box just as Ana pulled out a framed photograph. Tears sprung to Ana's eyes when she saw the picture. The photograph was of a family trip to Washington, D.C. taken on the steps of the Lincoln Memorial. Younger versions of Ana and Carmen flanked her parents who were grinning broadly. They were so proud of Carmen having completed FBI training at Quantico. The ceremony had been the weekend before, and the four of them had extended the celebration into a trip to the nation's capital.

Her intelligent and curious parents were enthralled by the museums in D.C. and spent each day touring the Smithsonian, Library of Congress, National Air and Space Museum, National Gallery of Art, and walked the National Mall among other places.

Despite a few crabby incidents from the fiery and volatile Carmen, the trip had been a resounding success and had permanently cemented beautiful memories.

Now, all three of them were gone. Ana was the only one left from her small family.

She was an orphan in the world.

While she still had gobs of aunties and uncles and cousins, it wasn't the same as having your big sister and Mami and Papi at family gatherings.

"I'm so sorry," Martha told her, withdrawing her hand. "I didn't know that would be there. I thought..."

"You thought someone would've picked it up?" Ana said with a sad smile. "Well ... I'm that someone."

"Would you like another desk? I can find room near the printer?"

"No," Ana said and gave a sweet smile. "I'd love to use Carmen's desk."

And she meant it.

The desk faced floor-to-ceiling windows with a view of the Bay Bridge and the Oakland Hills beyond.

Martha caught her gaze and laughed nervously. "The view is pretty good."

Ana nodded, then turned her head and pointed at a large gray cabinet in the corner. "Her files? Are they still in this cabinet?"

"Yes, only her personal items were removed. All FBI business is still intact."

Ana hid her wince. It was habit now. People were so careful to talk about the dead and yet, the strangest comments often stung the most.

Now, a few months later, the desk had become her own. She had retrieved the framed photo and given it a prominent position. Sometimes she wondered if Carmen had also placed it on the far right corner. Of course, she'd never ask but wondered when people stopped by to talk to her if they would know.

Looking out at the glittering lights of the Oakland Hills, Ana realized it had grown dark and the office behind her had emptied. Ana placed an order for some roses to take to Carmen's grave. Thinking of the cemetery made her think of running into Stella LaRosa.

It had been strange, yet healing, to talk to the woman. For some reason, she had the strangest feeling that they were going to be friends. Ana had premonitions like that.

Her *abuela* had always said she saw and knew things before they happened.

If that was true, why hadn't she seen Carmen's death? If she had, she might have been able to stop it. Same with her parents. What was the use in being able to know things before they happened if you couldn't save the lives of the people you loved?

She shut her laptop and sighed, looking at the mess on her desk. She was too tired to try to straighten it. It was more than just a few minutes of work. It would take at least thirty minutes to get the mess picked up in an organized manner.

Instinctively, she knew Carmen's desk had never looked like this. Not even for a moment.

Carmen was organized, efficient. A force of nature.

Ana was a messy procrastinator and liked to stay in the background.

Ana had never minded living in her sister's shadow. Her parents had categorized the sisters, put them into separate boxes, from a young age. Whether that had been right or wrong to do that to them, Ana didn't know.

Carmen was feisty, stubborn, and smart.

Ana was sweet, quiet, and creative.

At least according to their mother and father.

But Ana had a fire burning within that she tamped down so Carmen could be the center of attention. Ana held it in, opting instead to sit back and observe. She saw where her sister succeeded, where she failed. And she took it all in, quietly, from the sidelines.

Because their parents had never considered Ana smart, they hadn't pushed her to go to college like they had Carmen. In some ways, in their traditional family, Carmen had taken on the son role. It had been up to her to strike out in the world and find success. It had put pressure on Carmen, leading her to struggle with perfectionism and briefly flirting with an eating disorder.

After four years at Stanford, she'd applied for the FBI and worked her way up until she was qualified to be the Special Agent in Charge in San Francisco—the closest office to her parents' house.

Sadly, her parents had both passed by then, only a few years before she'd made it.

While Carmen had dealt with her grief by working harder and hitting her stride as an FBI agent, Ana had taken the opposite route.

Although she had also gone to college, San Francisco State, she had become an EMT. She'd worked nights and enrolled in the police academy during the day. When she'd finished the police academy, she'd been hired as a police officer for a small East Bay agency.

It'd been in that role that she had dealt with her grief in an unproductive way.

She'd fallen for one of the gang members she'd arrested.

Angel Ruiz had been the most beautiful boy she had ever seen. The 24-year-old had been a few years younger than her, yet more man than any of her exes.

His charisma had been off the charts. When she'd burst into the drug house, her police department-issued Glock .22-caliber pointing in his face, he had put his hands up. Then gave her a sexy smile.

"Damn *mamacita*," he'd said. "If I would've known they were sending *you* to arrest me, I would've turned myself in a long time ago."

"Put your goddamn hands in the air!" she'd screamed, angry that she was flustered by his black eyes and sideways grin that lit up the room.

"Easy, I'll go anywhere you say, *mi amor*.

"You're going to a six-by-six cell where you belong, *chico*. You're wasting my time. Let's go."

After cuffing him and trying not to notice how hard his forearms were, she directed him outside.

"Do I get to ride with you? I just want to get to know you, baby. Even if it's just a short car ride. I promise I'll be on my best behavior. I'm really not that bad a guy."

Ignoring him, she nodded at a local police officer who pushed Angel toward the back of his squad. He yelled over his shoulder, "I'll never forget you, my beautiful FBI agent."

That night, lying in bed in the dark, the adrenaline from the stake out and arrest wearing off, Ana had found herself tossing and turning in the dark, nearly wild with desire thinking about that punk gang member. He had an animal magnetism about him. Up until then, she'd seriously wondered if she would ever be wildly attracted to any man. Most bored her. Most didn't excite her physically. But something about this man made her want to have sex with him immediately.

A month later, when he had apparently been sprung on some lame technicality, he'd showed up at her apartment with a dozen red roses. He'd been wearing a dark suit over a tight, black t-shirt, shiny shoes, and his black hair was slicked back.

She waited a beat, watching him through the peephole, and then sighed, opening the door.

He'd promised he was done with a life of crime and got a job as an electrician's apprentice, working long hours with the goal of becoming a journeyman in two years.

He'd wooed her and behaved more like a gentleman than any other man had in her whole damn life. She'd fallen for it. Fallen for him.

When she got pregnant and miscarried, he cried with her. When her roommates started acting weird, he moved her into the house he'd inherited from his parents. It was a three-bedroom in a safe neighborhood in Pleasanton, in the East Bay of San Francisco.

One day, she'd been searching for the first aid kit in the cupboard under the sink. A piece of plywood against the back wall fell down.

Behind it, she found a secret compartment he'd carved into the wall.

Her heart had sunk deep into her core.

Inside were bags full of meth and heroin.

Eyeballing the plastic-wrapped bundles, she estimated two-hundred-thousand dollars' worth of methamphetamine and seventy-five worth of heroin.

That bastard.

She was a police officer. He had brought drugs into their home.

When she'd confronted him about it and told him she was leaving, he went crazy.

She packed a bag and hid it in her car. But he came home early from work and threatened to hunt her down and kill her if she left him. He said she'd never be safe and he would not rest until he found her. She'd be with him, or she'd be dead.

When she tried to leave, he grabbed her and beat her until she was lying on the floor unable to move.

"I'm going to go get some beer," he'd said, towering over her. "You better be here when I get back."

As soon as he'd walked out the door, she'd crawled to the phone and called the lieutenant in vice.

Within the hour, Angel was arrested.

Within the year, he was serving a life sentence in prison.

This time, he hadn't been able to pull the strings, to make the charges go away.

For a few years, he'd called constantly, but she'd never accepted. He'd written her letters that appeared in her mailbox at the police department daily. After reading the first and becoming physically ill over his threats to hunt her down and kill her, she'd never read another.

Finally, one of the secretaries at the police department had noticed the overflowing mailbox and offered to intercept the letters and box them up for Ana in case they could be used as evidence one day.

After her sister had died, she'd accepted the job offer at the San Francisco FBI transferring from Austin. Something deep down inside her made her want to carry on what Carmen had started. They had always been so different, according to her parents, but with Carmen's death, Ana realized they were more alike than she had ever allowed herself to believe.

Now, she was settling into the role. Going over the cases her sister had left. Getting her bearings, learning the ropes, trying not to even think for a second she could be as good as Carmen had been at the job.

It was growing late, and the sky outside of her window had grown dark. Lights were starting to turn on in the buildings around her, small squares of cheeriness illuminating empty offices.

Her inbox was almost empty.

There were a few briefs for her to file and then some mail.

She flipped through the mail. Most of it was junk.

But then there was a small plain envelope.

Without a return address. That sixth sense kicked in. A wave of apprehension rippled down her back.

Heart racing, she took her sword-shaped letter opener and ripped it open.

The words were typed.

I know what you did.

16

IMMORTALGEN TOOK UP AT LEAST FOUR CITY BLOCKS ON A stretch of industrial land ten miles north of the Houston city limits. The compound was surrounded by a tall electric fence bordered by tall trees set so close together it was difficult to see anything past them. Rolls of barbed wire topped the fence along with security cameras every ten feet. Stella also spotted small cameras with laser beams at both the bottom and tops of the fence. Security at ImmortalGen was no joke.

A line of cars waited to gain entrance at a guarded gate. When it was Stella's turn, the guard asked her name. She gave her fake one, and he asked for two forms of ID.

She took out her fake passport and fake driver's license. The man disappeared into the guard house for a few seconds and then came back. He handed her back her documents.

"You're going to the main building. Park in the underground parking and when you take the elevator to the lobby, check in at the desk."

Driving through, she followed the signs for the underground parking lot, and surveyed the buildings looming ahead. The compound was composed of three large glass buildings. The main building was several stories taller than the other two flanking it. The three structures were connected by skyways at the fourth level.

The elevator door opened on the lobby level, revealing stations of metal detectors and x-ray machines like an airport security checkpoint. A man sat at the front desk, watching her. She headed his way. They did not exchange pleasantries.

He took her photo and issued her a magnetic pass. "This will get you in and out of this building for today. Your boss will have to arrange your clearance into the other buildings. Your office is on the tenth floor."

"Thank you," Stella said.

After sending her tote bag through the x-ray machine and passing through the metal detector, Stella took another elevator to the tenth floor. There were eleven floors in total. She wondered if Carter Barclay had the penthouse office.

Of course he did.

Before the elevator reached the tenth floor, she hit the button for the fourth floor, which led to the skyways. When she poked her head out onto the fourth floor, she saw directional signs. On one side, a skyway led to the manufacturing facility. On the other, it led to a laboratory. Underneath the word were red letters. Security Clearance Required.

A keypad beside the door would gain her entry if she had the right badge. Stella wondered how hard it would be to get one.

Back in the elevator, she stepped out on the tenth floor into a large lobby with gray leather couches and large green plants. The one door in the space immediately opened, and Patrick Barclay came out grinning.

"You found it!"

"Impressive."

"I know, right?"

"Is the penthouse your father's office?" she asked casually.

Patrick frowned. "Yeah. But I don't think he's around much, honestly. He's often over at his other business—the oil company."

She was happy to hear that Carter Barclay wasn't around much. Her disguise was good, but if he saw through it, she would be in danger.

Changing the subject, she asked, "Is this my desk?"

He nodded and walked toward the door, opening it. "I'll show you my office."

The large corner office's back wall was made up entirely of windows. Connected to a conference room, an open door on one side of the office revealed a bedroom.

He gave her a look and went to close it. "Weird, right? Like who would want to sleep here? But the shower could come in handy. There's a gym in the basement."

"Does the penthouse have a bedroom suite, as well, you think?" Stella asked to bring the conversation back to Carter Barclay.

"I'd have to go there to find out," Patrick said. "I actually haven't seen my dad since I moved."

That was strange.

"Interesting," she said.

"Right now he's in D.C. Has a house there. He does a lot of lobbying, so I guess it comes in handy. What we're working on requires a lot of government regulation on the stem cell research."

"Why's that?"

"It's so cutting edge that nothing like this has ever been done before. The regulations need to be in place to prevent corruption."

This answer was vague, but Stella suspected he wasn't trying to dodge the question. He didn't actually know. It was his first day on the job, after all.

"Luckily, I don't have to know a ton about that," he added. "My job is really marketing." "The samples being collected at the trade show? What can you tell me about that?"

"From what I was told, by volunteering to submit samples, they will get a gene sequence and analysis with information that could save someone's life. Say someone doesn't even know they are at risk for a particular type of cancer. With the genetic fingerprint, they can pay for extra screening. It's all very by-the-book. We had the samples stored in custom temperature-controlled cases and transported by an armored truck back to our labs here. One of the adjoining buildings is filled with research laboratories. It's very hush-hush, what goes on in there.

Top secret stuff, like I could tell you but I'd have to kill you kind of stuff."

Stella's mouth grew dry. But he was making a joke. He couldn't possibly know. He seemed way too nice to be involved in any of the violent crime his father perpetrated. She thought about what he had said.

"Armored truck? Like what you use to transport cash?"

He held his hands up in a surrender position. "I also thought it was a bit much, but whatever."

It was a bit much. Something wasn't adding up.

The office itself was a mess, filled with boxes, remains of his breakfast on the desk. A laptop and a to-go cup of coffee.

She pointed to the boxes. "What's in these?"

"All the files from my predecessor. His office was on the fifth floor. He seemed to have left in a hurry. I opened one box and it had a family photo on top. I don't think he actually packed the boxes himself or he wouldn't have left it, would he?"

He was almost musing to himself, so Stella didn't answer.

"I wish I could have met him and learned a little bit about his position."

How convenient, Stella thought. Carter Barclay wanted to offer his estranged son a job after a sudden opening.

"Is he still alive?" Stella asked, surprised at her own question. "I mean maybe he had a heart attack or something?"

Or Carter Barclay killed him, too.

"Don't know. I didn't ask."

Patrick Barclay was sweet and kind. Naïve and innocent.

Stella picked up a photo from his desk. It was the only thing besides the laptop, coffee, and a phone. It was him with a dark-haired woman, smile lines around her eyes. They had their arms around each other and the crystal blue of the Mediterranean in the background. "Your mother is beautiful."

Patrick smiled. "A saint."

Stella set the photo down and asked, "Did you grow up in Greece?"

"I did. My mother moved there before I was born. She had dual citizenship: American and Greek." he said. "When I was ten, my mother sent me to boarding school in England. She said that the education our island offered would not be enough. At first I was heartbroken, but now I understand. She struggled financially. I'm not sure she could've supported me. She worked as a housekeeper for wealthy residents. I had a full-ride scholarship with food, tuition, boarding. I think it was the only way we could survive."

Except that your father is one of the richest men in the world.

The fact was left unspoken but hung in the air between them.

Reaching over, Stella grabbed a box cutter and sliced through the tape at the top of one. "Why don't we get this place organized?"

"Oh thank God. I can't think with how it is now. Sometimes I'm so disorganized. That's why I think we'll make a good team."

She smiled at him, beginning to unpack the contents. "I'll take care of it. Just do what you need to do."

"Right now, just meetings."

He had grabbed a briefcase off the chair and paused at the door. "You good for now?"

"I'm perfect. When will you be back?"

"I'm not sure, but if I'm still gone by five, don't stay a second after, okay?"

Stella nodded. "Got it."

He walked out and Stella was relieved he hadn't grabbed his laptop.

After waiting about fifteen minutes, she closed the office door and flipped open the lid of the laptop. It was password protected. Damn it.

17

Houston

Deep in the bowels of his Texas ranch house, Carter Barclay stood in front of the bookshelf and pushed one particular, special, book further back on the bookshelf. When he did so, the entire unit swung open, revealing his secret room inside the basement bunker.

The basement was an exact replica of the ground floor of the home, down to the large windows, which he kept covered with ruby velvet curtains. He only brought people in here with blindfolds, allowing them to remove the covers once inside the replica.

If a nosy houseguest happened to pull back the heavy fabric, he would see a black privacy film on the window, which was easy enough to explain. He didn't want any prying eyes. Didn't trust that high-flying drones wouldn't zoom in on his windows and see him inside. Or worse, drones equipped with weapons that could fire a sniper bullet through the walls of his house. The AR-1 drone can carry and fire an assault rifle.

Either way, most guests were thrilled to simply be in his company. He was known as an extremely private man when it came to his home. Even presidents and foreign leaders viewed it as an honor to be invited to his compound.

Besides the duplicate underground bunker, the compound stretched for miles as a working ecosystem. He could drop out of the world and live for twenty years without needing a damn thing from the outside.

That was what he had planned. He'd consulted the world's experts on prepping and then had the bunker built. He'd heard at least one other person in the world, Shirley McClain, had done something similar.

But the room behind the bookshelf was his private sanctum. He had brought some of his most trusted colleagues there once to show them his collection. They were all either dead or in prison now. Those in prison were too afraid of him to talk. At least, that's what he was counting on.

He stepped inside the room, bordered by the backlit black walls. Jars of body parts were displayed: a hovering slice of a face; an oversized heart suspended in liquid; a fetus curled up like a tiny bean. His heart began to pound with excitement.

He moved toward his favorite piece. A slice of skin containing a phoenix tattoo.

So close.

The jar didn't contain Stella LaRosa's phoenix tattoo. Hers would have taken a fish tank since it spanned her back from shoulder to shoulder and then dipped down to her lower back, right where the spine indents before the hips swelled out. He'd been sent a photo of her back once when she had gone swimming in a gym pool in the city, unaware that CCTV was capturing her every move.

He found he was becoming aroused imagining her tattoo.

Not attracted to her, per se. He was attracted to wielding power over her.

That attraction was much greater than just sexual lust.

Carter Barclay had spent the past three years fantasizing about watching the life drain from Stella LaRosa's eyes. To watch her spark ebb and glassy eyes turn dull.

It was the ultimate victory.

He turned to the wall that held a bank of computer monitors. Three large ones each contained twelve live video feeds. Yet none of them showed LaRosa.

She'd gone off the grid.

All her usual haunts yielded nothing.

He had cameras hidden everywhere. In her car, apartment, the newsroom, her gym, then some CCTV feeds around San Francisco set to scan for her through facial recognition.

She'd disappeared two days ago.

The last video of her showed her packing a suitcase and walking out of her apartment.

That was the only flaw in his surveillance system. If she took public transportation, he couldn't track her.

The first thing he did was reach out to his tech guy who tapped into the CCTV system to see if she had bought an airplane or train ticket. He also searched Homeland Security and FTA records for her boarding a flight.

Nothing came back.

Then he told the man to search CTC feeds at the airport and train stations using facial recognition. Nothing again.

Maybe she had rented a car? He directed his guy to search feeds at every rental car lot in the Bay Area.

Zilch.

Nobody could just disappear. The only way she had escaped detection was if someone had picked her up and driven her some place. Or if she had used a different identity for her travels.

18

The next morning, Stella showed up at ImmortalGen with two hot coffees a few minutes before 7.

She'd barely made a dent in unpacking the stack of boxes. When she walked in, she found Patrick sitting at his large walnut desk, except now it was covered with files. Unopened boxes, ones from yesterday and ones she hadn't seen before, were piled waist-high on each side of him.

He looked up and smiled nodding at a wall of halfway-filled book-cases. Stella's main handiwork from yesterday.

"You made some good progress. Thank you for organizing them by subject and alphabetical order. That will be the most helpful to me.

Stella nodded and walked towards him. "I love organizing. We'll have this office whipped into shape in no time."

She thrust a coffee at him. It was the same he'd ordered at the show —dark roast with two containers of creamer and one packet of sugar.

"Thank you!" He reached for his wallet. "What do I owe you?"

She waved him off. "My treat."

He set the wallet down. "Then lunch is on me."

Stella couldn't believe how nice her new boss was. He was the complete opposite of his awful father. No wonder they had been estranged.

Patrick gestured at the boxes flanking the large desk in the center of the room.

"These are all the company's invoices since the beginning of time, apparently. I'm not sure what to do with them. Ideally, once they are organized, I'd like you to digitize them. Hauling all this financial information around in boxes is archaic. And frankly, stupid."

"I got this," Stella said, grabbing a box cutter off his desk and sliding it across the nearest box. "You worry about whatever else you need to do."

By 1 in the afternoon, Stella had all the boxes unpacked and organized. Stella got started, unpacking and organizing, getting files put away by date and ready for her to scan and digitize.

"When the scanner arrives tomorrow, can you just put them directly on my work laptop?" He pointed to a pink post-it note on the corner of the desk. "My password is on there."

Stella hid her surprise at the open invitation to his privacy. Had it really been that easy?

"Of course."

He blushed and pointed to a stack of post-it notes sticking together. "And that's my calendar right now. Think you can put it on a Google calendar with reminder notifications and all that?"

"Easy peasy."

Stella got to work and Patrick spent the rest of the morning in his private lobby on phone calls. Once, someone had come into the outer office and called his name. Stella had frozen, thinking it was Carter Barclay, but it was just someone from human resources.

As they discussed hiring documents, Patrick poked his head in. "Rose, will you come out here for a second?"

Patrick stood with a man in a brown suit with a brown and gold striped tie. He was stocky and had thinning hair brushed over to one side.

"Rose, this is the head of human resources, Mark Hanners. Mr. Hanners, this is my assistant Rose St. James. We need to get her officially onboard. I hired her as a temporary worker at the trade show. But I'd like to bring her on permanently."

Stella was surprised.

Seeing the look on her face, Patrick added. "That is, if you're interested?"

"Oh yes, thank you," Stella said.

A look of irritation flashed across the older man's face. "That's not usually how it's done here, with all due respect. We have to do background checks and get references."

Patrick kept his voice even when he said, "I'm sure we can skip all that since my father owns the place."

Good. He did have a backbone, after all.

"Nice to meet you." Stella watched as the man stuck out his hand as if her touch was distasteful. She shook it as firmly as she could, crushing his fat sweaty hand a little and he tried to pull away before she was done. Then he took a step back.

"Rose will swing by your office at the end of the week to get all the official documents signed," Patrick said.

Hanners stood for a few seconds as if he had something to say, then left without a word. Stella had watched his face. He hadn't liked having Stella working without all the official documents signed, but he also had been afraid to stand up to the owner's son.

The longer she delayed filling out any paperwork the better. A background check was not going to fly. And references? Not so much.

She only had a few days, maybe another week at most to find out what she needed and get back to California.

However, it would be nice to get access into that HR office and find out personnel information. On the two dead ImmortalGen employees: Maria Perez, and also Carlos Mendoza. She'd find out where Mr. Hanners parked and make sure he was gone for the day one day this week before she helped herself to his office.

After Hanners had walked out, Stella acted surprised and said, "I need an access badge, don't I? The guard said today was the last day he would let me in the building without one."

"Oh, no problem. I actually have two. You can have one." It was unbelievable good luck. He handed her a black fob on a key ring.

"That way, you can also park in the executive garage."

"Wow," she said, taking the fob. "Thanks."

His phone beeped. He looked down at it and frowned.

"Hey, I know I said I wanted to buy you lunch, but can you take a raincheck? Big Papa apparently needs to see me."

Stella's heart raced at the mention of his father. "No, that's fine. Is he meeting you here?"

Patrick scoffed. "Of course not. Why would he go slumming? I'm going to *his* office. In the penthouse."

Stella laughed, then secretly hoped that Patrick would be gone for the rest of the afternoon. It would give her time to snoop.

"I'm actually not that hungry," she said. "Maybe I'll stay and work through lunch?"

"Sure. I can have something delivered if you like?"

"I'll just pop down to the cafeteria later."

He looked down at his phone again. His response was distracted. "Sounds good."

As soon as he walked out and closed the door, Stella sat down at his desk and logged onto the internet, then logged onto her own email. She'd stored information in her drafts file on how to access the Dark Web from any computer in the world, with the use of a VPN to keep her IP address secret. Once she did, she reached out to the BL4D3.

"Anything on that encrypted file?" she wrote. "Also, send me an email to this address so that when I open it and click on a link it will give me access to all the files remotely."

It was Hacker 101. And she'd be the one to click on the file and then download the means that would allow her to remotely access the computer. Usually it had to be done in real time, but there could be a delay of an hour or so. Hopefully, BL4D3 would get this message before Patrick came back. Unfortunately, she lost track of time and was still sitting at his desk with his laptop open when Patrick came back to the office.

She looked up and felt her face get hot.

"What are you doing?" he asked, his eyebrows knitting together as he reached for his cell phone.

19

Ana sank back into her chair and re-read the note.

I know what you did.

It had happened a long time ago.

Few people knew about it.

Angel was one of them. Carmen had been the other.

Looking up from the note, her gaze traveled to the wall in front of her. It had to be him.

But how was he writing to her from prison with an unmarked envelope?

All prison correspondence was heavily scanned and had the return address. Ana's face turned to ice.

She had spent so many sleepless nights questioning what it was about herself that had allowed her to fall for such a creep. She had a good childhood and knew she was loved. Unlike so many women she'd worked with over the years, she had not fallen for a criminal because she had lacked love as a child or doubted her self worth. Ultimately, the conclusion she came to was that he had been the only man who had been able to help her escape her mind and enjoy her body. It was shameful that all her sense flew from her head and her body had taken over. Only when she finally got away from him had she realized what had happened.

The other realization she'd had was that she had fallen in love with the potential of him. She had wanted to change him, to save him from his previous hard life. She had loved a specter created in her own mind and ignored anything that conflicted with that.

Unbidden, a memory came flashing back.

They were on the beach in Venice. The moon was low in the sky, lighting up the ocean before them. The swath of sand glowed beneath their feet.

They sat on a scratchy blanket Angel had pulled out of the back of his souped-up Mustang. He retrieved a bottle of red wine and two glasses. Their legs stretched out in front of them and full glasses of wine in hand, they watched the silvery reflection of the moon bounce off the rolling waves. A backdrop as they drank the wine and shared dreams.

Angel's were grandiose. Buy a beach house, a Ferrari, and spend his time as a day trader.

Ana's were simpler. She wanted to get married, have three children, and drop to part-time with the police department so she could be home when the kids got home from school. She wasn't sure how it would work. Maybe it would involve working overnights. She could leave for work when Angel and the kids were in bed, then be home to send them off to school and greet them in the afternoon. It sounded perfect. Except for finding time to sleep. She'd have to sleep while they were at school.

"What about me, *mi vida*? When will I see you?"

"Are you already jealous of our unborn children?" she teased him.

His body stiffened, and he grew silent, staring out at the ocean. A wave of unease rolled down her back. Lately, he had been a little prickly. He wasn't great at being teased. Part of her felt bad, but the other part of her wanted to tell him to grow up.

Ana had grown up with her parents gently teasing one another—never taking it too far or hurtful, of course, yet they had still been able to laugh or smile.

Angel had rarely done either if she teased him.

Finally, he turned to her and she saw his white teeth in the near dark as he smiled at her.

"You won't have to work when you're married to me," he told her, looping his arm over her shoulders and drawing her close to kiss the top of her head. "I want to provide. I want to support you."

"I don't need a big house on the beach or a Ferrari to be happy like you do," she said, gentle concern in her voice. "I only need you."

His tone grew hard and his jaw tightened. "I will have those things. It's not a question. It is my destiny."

Ana internally winced. Sometimes he seemed like such a child. Of course, everyone said they wanted a beach house and a Ferrari. But most knew deep down that wasn't an option.

"Maybe we don't want the same things..." she said.

"Nonsense, *mi amor*. You let me make the money. You have the babies and do whatever you want. If you want to work, you should. If you don't, you shouldn't. I just don't think you should be a police officer. Not when you are the mother of my children."

Ana drew back from his embrace. She loved her job. Loved the adrenaline rush, her coworkers. Putting the bad guys away and working on the side of justice. In that respect, she and Angel were lifetimes apart.

Her job could be dangerous, that much was true. She wasn't a large woman, and he'd expressed concern before about her dealing with some pretty bad suspects.

"I'm not sure I would want to leave law enforcement," she replied. "If you are worried about my safety, maybe I could just work in the jail or something."

"*Dios mio*!" he said angrily and stood. Sand flew into her eyes, and she reached up to wipe them off.

"No woman of mine is going to work in a jail. To be around that *filth* every day and then come home to my babies. No way." He turned to face her, towering over her. "I put my foot down there, Ana. It's not going to happen. We get married. You quit your job. Sit at home and pet the cat all day, I don't care, but you will leave law enforcement."

Anger flared within her. But she sat there, biting her tongue.

"*Comprendo?*"

She remained silent, tears forming, but she wasn't sure whether from anger or sadness.

He yanked at the blanket she sat on so forcibly that she tumbled off to one side, scratching her legs as it scraped across them.

Then he was walking away, swearing and kicking up sand as he marched back to the car. She heard the Mustang's engine start up, a loud growl that pierced the night.

And then he was gone.

The beach was empty. The road alongside the beach was empty. It was close to 2 in the morning. Her phone and house keys were in the small bag at her side, but that was it. He'd driven them both here. She shivered against the salty wind as she looked around. Down the beach was a parking lot with large orange lights.

Standing up, Ana swiped at her tears and wiped away the sand stuck to her body. She slid her sandals off, looped her bag onto her shoulder, and ran toward the parking lot. She hated Angel. Hated him with a fury. How dare he dictate what she do? She would never ever marry him. Never. He was a bully. A chauvinist.

How dare he leave her alone on a beach in the middle of the night?

Once she made it to the parking lot, she slipped her sandals back on and called for a ride share. She wasn't going back home to him. She didn't have enough money for a hotel.

At the last second, she texted a girlfriend she hadn't really talked to since she'd started seeing Angel.

I need a place to stay tonight.

Within seconds, there was a reply. It was terse. But that was to be expected. Ana had basically disappeared. But their friendship went back years. She knew she could count on having a place to sleep that night.

The front door will be unlocked. I'll leave a pillow and blanket on the couch.

An hour later, she settled onto her friend's couch, the borrowed sweatpants warm against her legs. Her friend had already gone to bed.

Just as her eyes began to close, Angel began to blow up her phone.

Her heartrate spiked when she scrolled through the plethora of messages.

At first, he apologized and said he was worried about her and begged her to come home. Then he began to threaten her, eventually saying he would kill her if he ever saw her again.

Finally, she muted his texts and fell asleep.

This continued for the next three days. The front desk at the police station knew not to give out information even though Angel had bombarded them with calls and visits. When Ana showed up for her shifts, she was waved into the gated police lot by the guard and tried not to look over at the Mustang parked across the street, or the man inside of it. When she walked from her car to the department door, she could feel Angel's eyes on her. He was stalking her, trying to intimidate her. She had abandoned all her belongings at his house just to avoid ever seeing him again, and yet here he was. Every day.

But he had quit calling. He'd quit texting. The front desk said he had stopped showing up.

Yet he still parked outside the gated lot each morning

After four more mornings of him waiting outside the gate, she stopped her car beside his and rolled down her window.

"What do you want, Angel?"

"For you to forgive me." She searched his face. He looked haggard, his eyes red. "I am a fool. I'm learning. I hate myself for leaving you on the beach. I have regretted it every second since it happened. I turned around and came back, but you were gone. I was frantic. I was desperate. I would die if anything ever happened to you."

"Oh yeah?" Ana arched an eyebrow. "I still have a text from you saying you wanted to kill me."

"That was me being angry."

"If you ever say anything like that to me again, I will disappear and you will never ever see me again."

"I promise, *mi amor*. I will treat you like my queen for the rest of your life. I've learned my lesson."

"You go to anger management counseling, and I'll come home."

"Deal. I will find someone today and make the appointment."

She stared at him for a long moment, her eyes never leaving his. "Also, if I want to be a police officer for the rest of my life, I will be. It's none of your damn business. If you don't like it, then we should end it now."

He nodded once, keeping her gaze. "Understood."

She watched him carefully for signs of anger, but all she saw was meekness.

"Text me after your first counseling session and I'll think about coming home."

He nodded.

She drove off.

By the weekend, she had gone home.

And then it was good. Really good.

For a while.

About a month later was when she'd found the drugs and he beat her up.

Now, thinking back, she felt sorry for the young woman she had been, who had put up with Angel's nonsense. She tried to be compassionate to her younger self instead of regretful.

But her mistake didn't seem to want to go away.

He was clearly back.

And still angry.

And now, possibly out of prison.

She opened her laptop. When she searched for his name under current prisoners at San Quentin, he didn't come up. She hopped over to the department of justice website and records.

Her breath hitched in her chest. Terror rose in her whole body.

He'd been released. A week ago. On parole.

20

After being caught sitting at his desk with his laptop open, Stella had to think fast. She told him she was working hard to get his calendar up to date. He bought it. Barely.

He told her that she'd done enough and he'd take over.

Worried that she'd aroused suspicion, Stella spent the next two days diligently unpacking his boxes until his office was spotless.

On the third day, when she walked in at seven with a coffee for Patrick, she stood in the doorway of his office looking around in approval.

Without all the clutter, she noticed just how luxurious the office space was. Tucked into the corner of ImmortalGen's glass-paneled headquarters, it was sophisticated and modern. The space was large yet efficient and had a masculine, minimalist style. The doors to the conference room and strange little bedroom were closed.

The floor-to-ceiling windows offered sweeping views of the downtown Houston skyline in the distance.

Patrick sat behind the walnut desk in the center of the room. The desk was empty save a computer, pad of paper, and water bottle.

"Hi Rose!" Patrick said in a welcoming voice, looking up from his computer.

She set the coffee down on his desk.

"Thanks! You spoil me. Tomorrow it's my treat," he said and turned back toward his computer screen.

She didn't answer and waited for him to look up.

"What's up?"

"I have something on my mind."

Closing the lid of his laptop, he gave her his full attention.

"I've heard some rumors about your dad, Patrick."

"I've heard them all, too, I bet," he said and smiled. "That he's a rich jerk who only cares about making money, yada yada."

"There may be a bit more," Stella said carefully.

"I get it. But honestly, Rose, he's been nothing but a good guy to me from the minute I got here."

Stella nodded, trying to keep her tone light. "How was your meeting with him yesterday?"

"It was good." His eyes were a little glassy now. "You can tell he's really trying to make up for lost time."

Stella wondered if he was going to cry.

She was pushing it to ask such a personal question, but she couldn't hold it back any longer. "So how do you feel about him?"

He looked at her for a moment. Finally, he smiled and said, "I'm hopeful."

Damn. How could she tell this kind, sincere, genuine man that his father was an utter monster? The wizard behind the curtain orchestrating vile murders across the world?

But she played along, nodding. "You think I should ignore the rumors, then?" she asked.

"Definitely."

Conversation over. Stella knew better than to push it any further.

Although she wanted to save Patrick from a terrible paternal relationship, she couldn't jeopardize the reason she was there.

That afternoon, Patrick asked her to take some documents up to his father's office. Stella hesitated to accept the task. If Carter was there, he'd see right through her disguise. That was not a confrontation Stella was ready for.

Regardless, she was determined to make friends with his personal secretary. Stella set out for his office, stepping into the elevator. A few floors up, the elevator came to a pause and doors opened. Carter stepped inside. Her heart began to race. This could be it. Would he throw her out or try to kill her?

Not knowing what to do, she gave him a small, shy smile. He responded with a tight-mouthed smile and looked away. She caught him rolling his eyes.

Wow. Her disguise worked. She looked so dowdy, he wouldn't even give her the time of day if she asked. Pompous jerk. But she was also relieved.

When the elevator stopped at the penthouse, he came out of his reverie and looked at her in surprise. "Did you miss your stop?"

His voice was ice cold.

Stella lifted the sheath of papers in her arms. "Just dropping something off with Mindy."

A slight frown passed over his face before he stepped out of the elevator, leaving her behind without another word. So much for women first.

He would've been the guy on the Titanic to shove the women and children off the lifeboat to make room for himself. Stella giggled, thinking this.

Stella stepped off the elevator and Carter Barclay was long gone, a heavy black door closing behind his figure. In front of the door was a large desk with a small woman sitting behind it.

That was her first introduction to Mindy, a voluptuous blonde who resembled Marilyn Monroe. Stella couldn't tell if Mindy's huge head of platinum blonde hair was a wig or not. She'd heard that Texas women had big hair, but this was ridiculous. The only thing bigger on Mindy were her breasts, which she was obviously proud of with her revealing top.

To her surprise, the woman gave her a genuine smile when Stella approached with the folder and introduced herself.

"Welcome!" Mindy said, her southern belle drawl accenting every word. "You're going to love working here. The Barclays are the best. Patrick seems so sweet, too."

The woman was blushing. She didn't know Patrick was gay.

"He's the best," Stella agreed. "Such a nice guy."

"And a billionaire!" Mindy added.

Aha. That made even more sense. The secretary's interest veered toward the monetary.

Stella leaned in closer across the desk. "I heard him saying he really likes women with blonde hair who know how to dress well and who understand what it's like to be married to a man with a job like his."

Mindy grinned and then quickly stifled it. "He really said that?"

Stella nodded. "He did. I can imagine his reluctance in finding a wife if someone doesn't understand the demands of his job. Like you completely understand what a job here is like, right? So you get it."

"I do," she said, pulling her shoulders back. "Why don't you join me and some of the other personal assistants for our weekly happy hour? It's tonight. I think you and I should be better friends."

"Really? That's so nice."

"Really. And honey, you've got potential," Mindy said, sizing Stella up. "But we're going to have to do something with your wardrobe, your hair, no offense, honey, and haven't you ever heard of contact lenses?"

Stella scoffed. "Excuse me?"

"Or buying clothes in the right size? Even that alone would make you look a million times better. We could get your hair blown out? I know the best gal for that!"

Stella tried to keep her face neutral. No blowing out the hideous wig she was wearing.

"You know, I better go back down to my office."

"I'll meet you at your desk at 5 p.m.," Mindy said and paused, her expression growing serious. "Does Patrick leave early?"

"Oh, not usually."

The big smile was back. "Great. See you then."

* * *

That night, Stella went out with the executive secretaries at ImmortalGen. They hunkered down at a bar nearby. A country western band was playing on a large stage and cowboys filled the venue..

The six secretaries were interchangeable. They all had big hair, big boobs, and big voices. And they drank their margarita pitchers like the beverage was their only source of survival.

After the first few rounds of Stella pretending to sip hers and refill it, nobody noticed when she kept pouring more for them and none for herself.

For the first half of the night, the women caught each other up on home life. Half were married and talked about how annoying their husbands were. The other half were single, at least two divorced, and talked about how awful men were.

Then Mindy turned to Stella. "Rosie here works for Carter's son!"

The women all exclaimed in unison.

"He's awfully good looking."

"Just a dream boat!"

"He is as fine as frog hair split four ways!" said a woman named Stephanie. Or was it Bethany?

They all waited for her to answer, eyes wide.

"He is very sweet," she finally said.

Mindy narrowed her eyes. "But don't you think he's cute as all get-out?"

"I do," she said, avoiding their beady gazes, "but I have a boyfriend back home. We're trying long distance." Quickly she added, "We're engaged."

One woman smiled and turned to her neighbor. "Plus, it is bad form to date your boss. Like illegal or something, right, sugar?"

"Yeah, you can't do that," the woman replied, pressing her hot pink lips together and taking a swig of her margarita.

"But nothing against someone *else* dating him," the first woman said.

Stella smiled. Were all these women dense? Had they never met a gay man before?

Texas, at least in this small pocket of it, maybe was a little less savvy about things like that.

Finally, after the women were sufficiently drunk, Stella grabbed the opportunity by the balls.

"My aunt told me about this job. Said her friend worked here, but I can't seem to find her." The women all stared at Stella intently through glassy slits of their eyes. "Her name is Maria Perez. Do you all know her? I'd like to buy her lunch to thank her for telling my aunt about the job opening."

One woman made a noncommittal noise. "Never heard of her."

"Me, either," another echoed.

A few others shook their heads.

"Sorry," Mindy said, slurring a little. "Can't help you."

But then one woman scrunched up her face. "I think I know who you mean," she said, "but it was sort of weird. I heard someone talking *about* her. They said she just disappeared. Stopped coming to work. But also, her apartment still had all her stuff still in it."

"Wait a minute," Mindy said, lifting a finger. "I heard the same thing. And then that guy in her same department was murdered!" She leaned in conspiratorially. Her cohorts followed suit. "The rumor I heard was that he killed her and hid her body and then someone in her family found out about it and killed *him*."

"Whoa," the redheaded woman said, lifting the straw to her mouth and taking a sip. "That's dark."

"I don't believe it," another woman said, sitting back. "He was a nice guy. He volunteered with kids or something."

Mindy clicked her tongue. "Once they get a taste of it, they don't stop."

"A taste of what?" Stella asked, unable to bite her tongue any longer.

Mindy turned to her and leaned in. "I heard a rumor he was a former gang member. I listen to those true crime stories. They say that once a killer does it once, they don't change. There's no going back. It's like they can't control themselves. They have to kill again and again."

Stella narrowed her eyes. "You said he was an ex-gang member, not a serial killer, right?"

"Same diff," Mindy said, shrugging her shoulders and taking a sip of her margarita.

Fury swarmed through Stella, but she needed to play nice. Rose St. James wasn't confrontational. She was there to gather information not teach ignorant women a thing or two.

"What department did they work in?" Stella asked. "Maybe I could go ask someone if they had contact information for her family. I'm sure my aunt would appreciate that."

"They worked over in research and development," another woman said. "You can take the fourth-floor skyway. Push the doorbell and tell them what you want, so they'll let you in. Security over there is tighter than a fiddle string."

Nothing she couldn't handle, Stella thought.

21

THAT NIGHT IN HER HOTEL ROOM, STELLA SAT DOWN AT THE small desk in the corner with the cheeseburger she'd bought across the street. The women she'd gone out drinking with apparently didn't believe in eating dinner.

Taking a big bite of the burger, she logged onto the Dark Web. BL4D3 had messaged her back.

Heart pounding, she clicked to open the message.

Cracked it.

She raced through the unencrypted files, eyes widening as secrets unpeeled with each click of her mouse. She sat back, stunned.

It was worse than what she had imagined. And she'd imagined something pretty damn bad.

Taking another bite of her burger and a sip of her soda, she read it all again, slower this time, and hovering the cursor over each line.

The first file was a cover letter explaining all the other files.

Stella read this letter a second time and swore out loud. BL4D3 now knew who the Black Rose really was. Damn it all. But she didn't have time to worry about that.

I am writing to you because I saw the article you wrote about Carter Barclay and his cohorts. Even though he somehow managed to escape punishment for his role in the organ collecting part (and probably every other evil deed he has done). I know that you know what he is really like. I can trust no one else.

Despite that article, Carter Barclay had somehow bought his freedom and innocence and was still a free man. His money convinced everyone of this. And she couldn't count on Patrick to believe the media over his own father.

However, even though Stella's articles hadn't stopped Barclay, they had led this woman to Stella.

Unfortunately, the woman hadn't realized that Barclay could kill in the blink of an eye.

Turning to Stella had cost Maria Perez her life.

I have found proof (enclosed in these files) that Barclay is funding and operating an illegal cloning operation. The goal of cloning is to harvest organs from the clones for his wealthy clients. The clones are people, but not people. They are an abomination. I have not seen them, only discovered pictures of them in a file (included).

Rather than be alive in the sense that we would expect a human to be, they are treated as medical specimens, kept in a comatose state in huge floating tanks. There are only three so far that have been viable as of this date.

This must be stopped. This goes against everything good and right. He is growing people in laboratories to make money. It is the evilest thing I have ever encountered in my life, and I grew up in the slums of Colombia, where horrible injustices happen daily.

Ms. LaRosa, please stop this. I am risking my life to get this information to you because I feel that it is that important. I have included all the proof I could obtain with my limited access. I'm flying out as soon as I finish this email. I am at the airport now. If you get this before you meet me, it's because they got me. If so, it's up to you to stop them.

Stella took a deep breath and clicked through the other files.

The first photo was blurry, but it showed a dark lab with several giant fishtank-type containers. Three ghostly white, hairless bodies were suspended in them. Two women. One man.

Stella's mouth went dry at the image, her appetite suddenly lost to the science fiction horror in front of her.

Then she opened the other files. Spreadsheets documenting the attempts to clone people. She scanned them carefully.

The oldest cloning attempt was dated twenty years earlier. Five thousand embryos had not survived cloning since then. The first had become viable a decade ago. They had implanted the cloned embryo into a woman they called Mary, the Original Mother. Her baby girl was born nine months later. They named her Eve, the Second. She survived two years in the lab in a medically induced coma. She ended up dying.

As she read on, the burger in Stella's stomach churned and threatened to exit her system. She couldn't even imagine.

Other "host" mothers were recruited to carry the cloned embryos.

Over the next few years, another dozen cloned children died. Then a girl was born and survived, and then another girl and then last, a boy. Eve, the Eighth. Jane, the Fifth, Samuel, the Third.

These were the three in the picture.

Another room apparently held three more clones of varying ages, a one-year-old, a five-year-old, and a seven-year-old.

Stella clicked on another document.

This was an email to a group called The Black Gold Team.

"We need to speed up our process as the success rate is still stuck at one percent. To do so, I propose another $5 million in funding where we can have our four scientists work around the clock, two at a time, while then two rest to relieve the others. We are very close to refining the success rate. We just need a little more time. We need $1 million in funding if we are going to get Friedrich Zimmerman away from Clonaid."

Schmidt: "Our clients are impatient. We need to harvest immediately. I've enclosed the list of organs needed. Once they receive the transplant, the remainder will be paid, and we can fund the additional research."

Johansen: "We risk losing the ability to study our successes if we fill this list. We must keep at least one of the specimens viable for research purposes. Please advise which organs are most crucial."

"We need every organ on two specimens. You may keep the third for research."

"Very well. Please coordinate a day when all recipients will be at the hospital in Mexico, and our team will transport the donor bodies there the day before. Any earlier and we risk premature death."

"The hospital is ours from midnight on October 12 to midnight October 13."

Today was October 6.

Stella sat back, stunned. How could something as earth shattering as human cloning have happened without the world knowing?

Then again, she hadn't specifically searched whether a human had been cloned.

Now, she did.

As early as 1998, South Korean scientists said they had made some progress in cloning a human embryo but had come across a roadblock that had set them back. In 2004, a paper was published in a respected scientific journal by South Korean researchers claiming a human embryo had been cloned in a test tube. The research paper was later retracted when no additional evidence was provided.

In 2002, a religious group called Clonaid held a news conference to announce they had successfully implanted a cloned embryo into a woman and that a baby had been born named Eve.

The group also claimed to have cloned twelve other embryos successfully. But when the world asked for proof in the form of DNA testing, the group had refused to provide it.

Stella clicked back to the memo and found a request for funding to hire scientists with Clonaid.

Quickly, she searched for information but found nothing.

She clicked over to the Dark Web and submitted a request with BL4D3. *Anything on Friedrich Zimmerman or a group called Clonaid? I'll pay you double your rate if you can expedite this.*

Back to her searching, Stella found that primates had been cloned, with scientists declaring, "The impossible has been made possible."

Two six-year-old cloned monkeys were alive and "happy and healthy," the article said.

It had taken her a few minutes after opening Maria's file for it to sink in, but Stella finally had to acknowledge that what she saw was not a hoax.

This was real.

Carter Barclay was cloning people to harvest their organs for profit.

At best, it was horrifically unethical. At worst, an illegal atrocity.

Stella searched and found there was no federal ban on cloning in the United States. Several states, however, had banned cloning on their own.

It was complicated.

Therapeutic cloning, where embryonic stem cells were used for medical research and therapy, was legal in many states that had banned reproductive cloning.

To Stella, none of that was relevant. Carter Barclay was keeping people in adult-sized test tubes, in medically induced comas, to murder them for their body parts.

All she could think about was whether these cloned people were really alive. What if they were taken out of their coma? Would they be like anyone else? Or would they be in a vegetative state? Had they even had a chance to live like real people?

The more she thought about it, the more instances of terribly horrific indignities were possible. Either way, there was no other way to look at what was going to happen in Mexico as anything less than murder.

The first transplants would take place in less than a week. And two of the three bodies she had seen in the photos would have their body parts and organs harvested, from their hearts to their eyeballs to their skin. And then they would be disposed of, like garbage.

And now, with Maria dead, Stella knew she might be the only one who could stop it.

22

Carter Barclay was out in the fields with his favorite stallion, Rogan. The black beast was fiery and fast but followed Barclay's orders. Nobody else was allowed to ride him. He used his riding crop to bring the beast to a gallop, charging across the fields. Patrick rode on a tamer horse behind them, trying to keep up.

When they reached the creek bed lined by willow trees, Carter brought Rogan up short. The horse's eyes were red and wild, and his mouth was rimmed with foam.

"Good boy."

He turned to face Patrick. The boy needed to learn to ride. He was leaning forward too much and holding onto Rush too tightly. His knees gripped the sides of the horse, rather than his inner thighs.

The young man was attractive, Carter would give him that. Too bad he had some sugar in his tank. Carter needed more heirs. He would encourage him to give his sperm to a donor so there would be a blood grandchild.

Blood. As Carter grew older, he realized there was no stronger tie.

He had already arranged for his DNA to be off limits for this. The thought of another one of him walking around on the earth after he died was the stuff of nightmares. There was, and would always be, only one Carter Barclay.

No, the way he wanted to be continued was through his son.

Carter had already made other plans in case Patrick refused to have a child. He had Patrick's DNA extracted after the drug screening process. Carter had ordered a blood draw to accompany the usual urine testing, saying it was company policy since he had lived overseas. Patrick was a smart man, but also a bit naïve.

He'd readily agreed.

Carter wouldn't hesitate to use the DNA sample to clone Patrick one day. So far, none of the previous clones had been able to live on their own without life support, but his scientists were getting closer every day.

The first had lived for a few minutes before her heart had stopped. She had been resuscitated and kept alive on life support for a few weeks, but after several cardiac arrests, her heart had given out.

The second could live with a breathing machine.

Ultimately, without life support machines, the specimens would not live longer than a year.

After a few of these failures, Carter had come up with a solution: that the specimens be kept in a medically induced coma hooked up to life support machines for the duration of their lives.

Now, his researchers thought they had come up with a cloned embryo that could survive on its own.

They were very close to seeing whether that was true.

The first four babies were slated to be born in the next few months. This time, they would stay with their mothers in the hospital and be under careful observation.

Carter was hopeful, because along with his organ transplant project, he was being pressured to go into the "baby selling business," as he liked to think about it.

But his wealthy friends who wanted children also wanted a guarantee that the babies wouldn't turn feral like those cloned animals.

Even though he had offered to give a few people babies for free as sort of guinea pigs, nobody was willing to do that. At least nobody in his circles.

However, he had men scouting out infertile couples in poor American ghettos. One of the new babies would leave the hospital and be given to a worthy couple for free. This couple would agree to be observed in exchange for the child. For field research.

Patrick had said something to him. He was staring at Carter intently.

"Sorry, son," Carter replied with a broad grin. "I missed that."

"I just said that if you want, I can take riding lessons. I'd like to get better so we can ride together." Patrick rubbed a hand on the back of his neck. "I feel like I'm holding you back today."

Carter waved him away, feigning patience. "Not at all, Patrick. It will take time. I'm not in a hurry. I'm just enjoying the afternoon with you."

The young man smiled. He was so simple. Sometimes that worried Carter. But it was for the best.

"I never realized what I was missing out on until I met you," Carter said, kneeing Rogan as he passed by. "Have you thought of having children?"

"Yeah. We're thinking of adopting."

"It sure would mean a lot to me if you considered a surrogate mother," Carter said over his shoulder. "I'd like our bloodline to continue."

He waited a beat. Patrick didn't answer.

He turned Rogan and met his son's eyes. "Is that something you'd be interested in? I'd be happy to front the costs and make sure the young lady carrying my grandchild is put up in the best accommodations and receives the best care. Consider it my gift to you."

Something flashed across his son's face. Something Carter didn't like. But it was gone.

"That's very generous," Patrick said in a solemn voice. "We are pretty set on adoption, but I'll check with Theo."

"Why adopt when you can have a child with your own DNA?"

Patrick shifted. "Mostly because there are so many kids already out there who need a home."

Carter winced.

His son needed to be more of a man. He should be the one making the decisions, not being wishy washy, asking his husband about whether it was okay. Being gay was fine. Hell, everyone was gay nowadays, but if Carter Barclay's son was going to be gay, then he better be the man in the relationship. Was that too much to ask?

Carter spurred Rogan, and the horse took off at a gallop.

"See you back at the barn," he shouted over his shoulder.

Wouldn't hurt to show Patrick what a real man acted like. A real man wasn't a pussy who waited around for those who were slower than him.

* * *

After dinner on the patio, filet mignon freshly cut from one of his own steers with roasted potatoes, fresh green beans from the garden, and a vintage wine selected from his cellar, Carter asked Patrick when he would be able to get to know Theo.

"I surely would like to get to know him a little better. He's not shy, is he?" Carter squinted a little. "I'm not a homophobe, or whatever they call them nowadays. What someone does in their bedroom is none of my business. I may be a Republican, but I'm not against the gays."

Patrick squirmed in his seat and downed a gulp of his wine. "Theo couldn't make it today because he had a zoom call with one of his clients."

"We do have internet service out here, you know. He could've gone into my office and done it there."

"Thanks," Patrick said, his lips forming a tight line. "I'll let him know for next time."

"What does he do again?"

"He's a teacher."

Carter raised his brows. "Teacher? How does that work on zoom?"

"He teaches international studies to students from across the world. Even when we were in Greece, he taught remotely. The pandemic changed everything."

"Sure did," Carter said. "I wasn't hurting in the financial department before, but when I invested in Pfizer in January 2020, it paid off, if I do say so myself."

Patrick smiled tightly. "You invested in Pfizer for the first time in January of 2020?"

"If you get to my level of wealth, son, you got people who keep you in the loop on things. When the shit started to hit the fan in China, I got a tip to invest in Pfizer and Moderna."

"Huh?" Patrick sat back in his seat. "Really? Is that legal?"

"Well, yeah. I mean the only thing we really knew was that those two were gonna be the ones tapped for a vaccine if the shit hit the fan, which as we all know, it did."

"It sure did."

Carter took a swig of his bourbon and glanced sideways at his son. Was the kid judging him? He put down his crystal tumbler and picked up the wine bottle, pouring more for them. No reason to let it go to waste. He had never opened a bottle of wine he didn't finish that same night. What was the use of that?

But a half hour later, when Patrick said he had to go, it didn't escape Carter that his son had barely sipped on the wine in his glass. Which meant that Carter had drank damn near the entire bottle. And countless fingers of bourbon, before and after dinner. No wonder he was feeling a little boozy.

Leaving everything on the patio as it was, he walked his son to the front door where a car waited to drive him back to the home which Carter had supplied.

When the red taillights had disappeared into the black night, Carter headed back in and down the secret elevator to the duplicate ranch house underground. From there, he went into his chambers and logged onto his computer.

He was greeted with a message from his hacker.

"Found her!" The note said. "Check out this footage."

Carter clicked on the link.

The drone footage was grainy but captured a park near the cemetery. Two women stood near a grave. One was unmistakably Stella

LaRosa. The other, a petite, dark-haired woman with dark skin, wasn't anybody he knew. Yet.

23

THE HOTEL SUITE WAS A SPACIOUS ONE-BEDROOM WITH AN attached living area with a sofa, coffee table, and flat-screen TV inside an armoire.

There was a small built-in kitchenette with a tiny refrigerator, microwave, and coffee maker.

The small café table could double as a workspace, complete with swivel chair and desk lamp.

The only thing Stella didn't like about it was that it was two separate rooms, which meant her bedroom was too far away from the entry. She had lodged a chair under the door handle, but she still slept uneasily, unsure how secure the room was.

At first when Stella woke at 3 a.m. she bolted up, worried she had heard a noise. But after checking both rooms, she realized she had been dreaming.

Unable to fall back asleep, she worked through her morning exercise routine: pushups, sit-ups, and some martial arts moves. It didn't help settle her mind.

Dressing in her usual dowdy costume, a baggy skirt, oversized sweater, and huge blazer, she wished she could take her gun inside. She'd have to find a way around those huge metal detectors in the lobby. In case things went sideways, she wanted a weapon. But her gun would set off alarms. However, she considered putting her switchblade in a special compartment of her boot that might help her slip it through the metal detector.

By 4:45 a.m., she was showing her new credentials at the guard house. The guard waved her through without taking her ID into the little shack.

The guard inside the building greeted her by name.

"Miss Rose, what on earth are you doing here at the crack of dawn, young lady?"

The guard was older, with gray at his temples and smile lines that crinkled in his dark skin.

"Trying to get a jump start on the day," she said. "Couldn't sleep."

"I hear you. It just gets worse when you get to my age."

"Stop. You're just a youngster."

He chuckled and then frowned when she stepped through the metal detector.

"Shoot," she said, lifting up her long skirt. "I forgot these are my steel-toed boots."

"You're fine," he replied, waving her through. "Have a good morning."

Guilt gnawed at Stella when she realized he would get in trouble if anyone discovered where she was headed. She also regretted not shoving the gun in her boot, since it had been easy enough to get away with the knife.

Once she was in the elevator, she pressed the button for the fourth floor. The elevator opened onto a long hall with two large doors. The skyway to the other building was to the right.

Holding her breath, she held her ID badge up to the scanner. She wasn't sure what sort of access Patrick Barclay's personal assistant would have, but he had given her his extra access pass. As the son of the owner, he should be able to go anywhere, right?

The light turned green and she quickly pushed the button for the door to slide open. The skyway lay before her, floor-to-ceiling windows still dim with the early morning. The building across the way was dark.

Hopefully this would go under the radar, but she still felt like a spotlight was shining on her as she walked across the skyway to the other building.

Then she was on the other side. Another door. Another green light. This time when she stepped through it, a series of lights turned on, startling her. They were simply motion-activated, she reassured herself.

This time, there was only one door. It was at the end of the small foyer.

"Research Lab. Security Clearance Needed."

This was where she would really find out how much Carter Barclay trusted his son.

Quickly, she walked to the other end and held her badge against the reader.

The light turned green. The door clicked, unlocked. Pressing it open, she stepped inside a small room. Stella groaned. There was another door to access the lab. This was ridiculous. But if what was inside matched the images she'd seen last night, the precautions were undoubtedly necessary for the company. She pressed her badge to the reader. This one did not turn green.

Her breath hitched.

Maybe Daddy didn't want his son to see the horrors that lay beyond.

Raised voices sounded on the other side of the door. Two people were arguing. And they were growing closer.

She darted back toward the other door and slipped through to the other side just as the lab's door handle turned.

Stella kicked her pace into a run, racing for the other door and back through the skyway to the safety of her own building.

Heart racing, she waited for the elevator.

She wiped the sweat on her brow. The arguing voices were quickly approaching from behind. The elevator still wasn't there. The seconds seemed to take hours. Shifting from foot to foot, Stella waited impatiently.

Then the door from the skyway swung open. She turned to see two men in lab coats. They were arguing animatedly but drew back when they saw Stella.

They glanced at each other, then one of them cleared his throat. "Can I help you?"

"Yes, please," Stella said, turning to face the men and turning on her best helpless damsel impression. "I got off on the wrong floor and can't remember which has the cafeteria. I've already tried two floors and they've both been wrong."

The other man eyed Stella suspiciously, but the first nodded.

"We're on our way to get coffee, too," he said, as the elevator opened. "The cafeteria is on the sixth floor."

"I'll just follow you there, then."

He gave a strange smile. "They can't make a girl guess where the coffee is if she hasn't even had any yet, right?"

The second one kept staring at her and asked, "How did you get the elevator to go to the fourth floor anyway?"

Stella shrugged. "Used my badge?"

"You shouldn't have clearance for that floor."

"Really?" she said. "I thought as the personal assistant to the owner's son I'd pretty much have clearance anywhere. I mean, I need to go wherever my boss needs me to, right?"

"Nobody should have clearance to the fourth floor," he said, his serious expression boring into her. "Not even the owner's son."

"Why's that?"

"Proprietary secrets," the first, nicer man said.

"Like I said, I just do whatever my boss needs."

The elevator opened. "Here's the cafeteria," the first man said.

She stepped out, but the men did not follow her. "Aren't you coming?"

"No, we're heading to the executive lounge," the crabby one said.

The first man smiled at her and the elevator door slid shut. Stella watched to see what floor it went to. She waited until the light above the elevator stopped at the eighth floor. After waiting a few minutes, she saw it descend back to the fourth floor. Only then did she summon an elevator and take it to the tenth floor.

Turning on the lights, she headed into Patrick's office.

Settling at his desk, she used the password for his laptop and began searching for anything that might indicate he knew about the cloning operation. She couldn't find a darn thing. She looked in every folder and area there was. In a sense, this was a relief. She truly believed that Patrick was a good guy who didn't know about his father's terrible wrongdoings. Just in case, though, she began copying the files on his hard drive to an external hard drive.

It was still in the process of backing up when Patrick's desk phone rang. Stella jumped, startled.

For a second, she debated picking it up, but then worried it might expose her.

She waited until the light lit up. A voicemail had been left. She pressed the button to listen to it.

Her face grew hot as she listened to the voice on the other end.

"We have some footage of your personal assistant that we need to speak to you about."

The gig was up.

* * *

By the time Patrick came to work that morning, she'd planted herself at her desk, preparing herself for him to confront her. The external hard drive was stuck into her boot shaft. She was apprehensive. As soon as he listened to his messages, it was game over.

"Good morning!" he said cheerfully.

"Good morning!" she replied, echoing his tone.

He disappeared into his office, closing his door, which was unusual. Maybe someone had tipped him off. After about fifteen minutes, she heard the voice on the answering machine.

Then the office door opened, and he appeared in the frame. His eyebrows were knit together. "Rose? I got a strange voice message."

"Oh yeah?" she said brightly, looking up.

"Were you here early trying to get into the fourth floor research wing?"

She met his eyes and nodded.

"Can you explain that to me?" His brows knit together. "Please don't lie."

She wanted to lie. She really did. But she couldn't lie to this earnest young man. She'd decided hours earlier to tell him the truth and let the chips fall as they may. Of course, it would mean her leaving as his assistant.

Unless he believed her and wanted to help her stop his father.

"This might sound crazy." She paused. "But my name isn't Rose. My name is Stella, and I'm an investigative journalist."

He watched her and waited, his eyebrows shooting up.

"I was contacted by a whistleblower who ended up murdered just a week after contacting me. Afterwards, I received proof of ImmortalGen involved in unethical cloning." She swallowed. "The clones' organs will be harvested for profit."

His mouth dropped open and he scrunched up his face even more.

He shook his head and blinked furiously. "What are you talking about? What proof could you possibly have?"

"I have the files. I can show you."

He gawked at her. "This company does stem cell research. We are working on technology that could save men like Christopher Reeves."

She sighed. He was so genuine and good-hearted. He was nothing like his father.

"That may be true," she said, "but it may only be a front for what is really going on. I'm sorry to be the one to tell you this. I know you are trying to develop a relationship with your father, but he's using this company to clone people illegally."

He shook his head and for the first time seemed to grow angry. His voice rose. "You don't know anything about him or anything about me."

"I'm sorry I lied. My real name is Stella LaRosa. Ask your dad about me."

"This is crazy. You're lying."

"I may be crazy, but I'm not lying—not anymore." Stella took a deep breath. "The first transplants are happening at a Mexican hospital. Next week."

Now he was growing agitated. A red flush had crept up his neck to his jaw.

"Did you go to the trade show to stalk me? To talk me into giving you a job?"

"No. It just worked out that way. I just thought by going there I could meet people and find out more about the job opening."

Patrick reached for his phone. "I'm calling security."

She stood, holding up her hands in surrender. "I'll leave on my own. But you are the only one who can stop this atrocity. Find out for yourself. Go see what's in the fourth-floor lab and look out for a transport truck headed to Mexico."

Looping her bag over her shoulder, she plucked her jacket off the back of her chair.

"Please just go," he said. His face was red, colored by a pained expression.

After punching the button for the elevator, she turned to face him. "When you realize I'm right, you can find me at the *San Francisco Tribune*. My email is on the paper's website."

She stepped into the elevator and met his eyes, full of pain, until the doors slid shut.

The entire ride down, Stella wondered whether he would call security and have her detained or arrested. She was banking on having planted the smallest sliver of doubt in his mind. If he thought there was a slight chance she was right, he might let her go free.

She stepped into the lobby and headed for the exit door, holding her breath.

Nobody looked at her. The security guards were engaged in lively conversation about the previous day's football game. She walked out and breathed a sigh of relief.

Now, to get into her car and out the gate.

Ten minutes later, she pulled onto the main road.

Her day had not gone as she had planned.

24

SITTING IN HIS PLUSH LEATHER CHAIR BEHIND HIS LARGE DESK, Carter Barclay watched on his computer monitor as the frumpy woman and his son engaged in heated conversation.

Carter had been alerted to someone trying to gain unauthorized access to the fourth-floor research lab using his son's access pass. But his son was not present in the footage. The video feed showed a woman. Then he tapped into the hidden cameras in his son's office.

The only problem was it didn't have sound. His son looked upset. He watched as the woman gathered her things and walked out. Had she quit or did Patrick fire her?

There was something slightly familiar about her gait as she walked. *Could it be—?*

No. He shook his head. That would be too much of a coincidence.

Switching feeds, he began watching the lobby. The elevator door opened, and the same woman stepped out. For a brief second, she looked up. He hit a "capture" button on the screen. He'd send this to his tech guy to run a facial recognition program.

He blew up the picture and stared at it for a long time.

It could be her.

It could be Stella LaRosa.

What were the odds?

Then he switched to the cameras at the gate. He rewound the footage until he saw her driving away. Again, he froze the image and captured the car and its license plate.

By looking at the license plate, his tech guy could find out who the vehicle was registered to. One way or another, Carter would find this woman and see just what she was doing trying to break into his lab. He sent his tech guy a message with the screenshots and was told he'd have answers within the hour.

In the meantime, he'd ask Patrick about it.

Picking up his phone, he dialed his son. As he did, he clicked back to the hidden camera in his son's office. Which reminded him, he'd ask his tech guy to send clips of all the office footage since that woman had been hired. He'd find out just what she'd been up to during her brief tenure as assistant.

He watched as Patrick paced his office and then glanced at his cell phone sitting on the desk. He stopped near his phone, looking down, obviously seeing that it was his father calling. But instead of picking it up, the young man shook his head.

Interesting.

Eyes narrowing, Carter watched as his son reached for the phone and then drew his hand back, hovering.

What the hell was going on?

The phone continued to ring.

Finally, the young man picked up the phone.

"Patrick Barclay."

"Hello, son."

Patrick was rigid as he spoke. "Good morning."

"Hey, I heard something weird this morning..." Carter trailed off giving his son a chance to tell him.

"Yes. I'm sorry. I just dealt with the situation."

Carter sat back. He was liking how his son was handling this already. But he wanted to know more.

"What was the situation, anyway? All I heard was that your

assistant made an unauthorized attempt to get into an area she didn't have clearance for. Was she lost? How did you deal with the situation?"

"I let her go."

"On what basis?"

"Oh!" his son sounded surprised. "I didn't realize that might be an issue."

"No issue." Carter responded calmly. "You can do whatever you want. You're my son."

He saw a smile cross the young man's face. The boy liked being called his son. Maybe he just enjoyed the power that came with being Carter Barclay's son. Either way, this would work out just fine.

"I didn't quite get to the bottom of it," Patrick continued, "but I think she got a job under false pretenses. I think she was a religious zealot. Opposed to our stem cell research and was sent as a plant to try to destroy our lab."

"Good Lord."

He watched on as Patrick held up a warning palm. "I don't have any proof, it was just a feeling I had. So I let her go."

"Good job, son. You did the right thing."

"Thank you."

"I won't worry about it any longer. I'm glad you handled it. I'll see you tonight at the dinner with the visiting researcher from South Africa?"

"Of course. 7 p.m. at La Travanti."

"Perfect."

Carter hung up and watched the screen to see what his son did.

His son leaned back in his chair. For a few seconds he seemed to be staring off into space. Then, the boy leaned forward, planting his elbows on his desk and put his head in his hands.

Carter's eyes narrowed. What the hell was that about?

25

STELLA LAROSA KNEW SHE WOULD HAVE TO SWITCH THINGS UP immediately. She would stay in town, but her car and motel were burned.

Packing up her things, she left the rental apartment, notifying the owner by email that she was going back home to New Jersey early, in case the woman was questioned by Barclay's team. Then she turned in her car and took the shuttle from the rental agency to the airport. If anyone was following her, they would think she was leaving town.

Once she got to the airport, she bought a ticket to Newark. Then she slipped into the airport bathroom and shed her disguise, stuffing her clothes, wig, and glasses into her duffle bag before donning an oversized hoodie, sunglasses, and a baseball cap.

Pulling the hat low and the hoodie up, she headed back out to the curb, keeping her head down. She took a cab to the opposite side of town from where she had been staying and rented a hotel room under another fake name. When they asked for an ID and credit card, she was able to provide both. One thing Headway had taught her: always have burner phones and at least three fake IDs.

After dumping her belongings in her new room, she walked to a rental car agency and rented another car, this time a sports car, under her new fake name.

During all of this, she kept on the baseball cap and sunglasses. It wouldn't do to have a CCT camera pick her up and recognize her face. If Patrick went to his dad and mentioned her name, the camera closest to her now would be the first place he would search.

Back in her hotel room, she used a VPN to log onto her newspaper email account, even though the Headway laptop was supposed to be off grid. There was nothing from Patrick. But there was something from Garcia.

Wanted to let you know they arrested someone in the murder of that woman. Some guy who said he was hired off the Dark Web to assassinate her. From Stockton. He confessed when he got caught with her head in a duffel bag on BART. An older woman sitting near him saw him unzip the bag and saw what was inside. She screamed and some big biker dude tackled the guy until the cops got there. This guy, he's one sick S.O.B. He could have got away with it, but he told detectives in Walnut Creek he was on his way to Ocean Beach. He said after reading our story about the washed-up tombstones he wanted to leave the head near them as an offering to his master or something.

"Disgusting," Stella wrote back. "But are you saying that our story led to his capture? That's sort of what I'm thinking." She laughed as she hit send. It wasn't funny. But it was. Sometimes gallows humor was the only thing that kept her from going off the deep end.

Before she logged off, she saw another email.

This one was from arodriguez@fbi.org. Ana. Carmen's sister.

Stella, it was nice to meet you. Would you have time to meet for coffee? Also, I found out some stuff about the woman who was decapitated. I thought you might be interested in sharing information if you had any. I know you covered the story.

Crap. No, Stella wouldn't want to share her information, but she was curious about what Ana had found. Still, she did want to meet the woman for coffee, but she wasn't sure how long she'd be in Texas.

I'm out of town for a bit but can reach out when I'm back. I don't know much more than what was in the paper but if you wouldn't mind sharing what you found out, I can keep it as background info?

Then at the last minute, she typed in her burner phone number to the email and said Ana could call her if she wanted.

She hit send.

After closing her laptop, Stella reached for the burner phone.

Stella knew she better touch base with her mom. She'd lied and told her she was doing some investigative project that was top secret and off the grid in Morocco, so she would only be able to call once a week.

Using the burner phone, she dialed her mother's cell.

"Hello?"

"Mama, it's me."

"Stella! I don't like not being able to reach you. What if something happened to you, I wouldn't even know."

"You'd find out."

"When? When would I find out?"

"I'm sorry."

What she wanted to say was she was more worried about something happening to her mother and her not knowing.

Stella always worried about her mother. The woman was in great shape, but that didn't stop Stella from being concerned. Her mother was the most important person in Stella's world.

"How are you?" Stella asked.

"I'm fine. Your uncle is not."

Stella hoped her mother couldn't tell she was rolling her eyes across the country. "What's going on?"

"He's in the hospital. That's what I wanted to tell you. But I couldn't even call you."

"What happened?"

"The same thing, but now it's bad. He is on the list for a liver transplant. He said there is one coming through next week, but he has to fly to Mexico. Have you ever heard of such a thing? I told him he's signing his death certificate. Why would he go to another country when we have some of the best doctors in the world?"

Her mother kept talking, but Stella wasn't listening.

Her uncle was going to get one of the organs that Carter Barclay was selling.

She tuned back in.

"What city in Mexico, Mama?"

"I don't know!"

"Can you do me a favor and find out? I can do some digging and check out how safe the program is."

Wincing as she said it, she loathed lying to her mother, but this might be what she needed to stop the transplants, or at least find out more information about them to get someone else to stop them.

Sitting back, Stella thought about it. And it seemed obvious. Her uncle had always been very strange about Stella's investigation into Carter Barclay. As the leader of a powerful organized crime family, Dominic LaRosa had connections that were impressive at best and terrifying at worst.

Her uncle was working with, or at least running in the same secretive uber wealthy inner circles that her mortal enemy was in. All these years, her uncle had been in touch with Carter Barclay.

This was terrifying.

Her mother's voice brought her back to the present.

"I will call you later," she said. "I am taking some soup over there later today. The hospital food is awful. Plus, he needs some of my good bread. He's not eating, and his strength is fading."

"Okay, Mama, just let me know what you find out. But don't tell him I asked you. He doesn't need to know we are questioning his decisions, right?"

Her mother paused before answering, and Stella held her breath.

"I don't like keeping secrets, but you're right. If you find anything really bad, we'll have your dad talk to him."

"Sounds good. Love you Mama."

"I love you, Stella."

Stella hung up.

If needed, she would use her uncle to infiltrate the operation. She would be his escort to the Mexican hospital. But that was a last resort.

If she had her way, the operation would be shut down way before cloned bodies and people awaiting organs crossed the border.

Exposing the cloning and organ transplant operation would be incredibly dangerous and would possibly ruin him and his business. And might even cost her uncle his life.

It was what she had to do.

26

Carter Barclay sat back in his leather chair and grinned.

Got you.

The woman from the cemetery was Ana Rodriguez. She was an FBI agent.

His law enforcement sources in San Francisco and Houston had told him an agent with the FBI had been digging into the murders, asking to see the police files. The San Francisco police chief, a man on Carter's generous payroll, had shut that crap down immediately. He'd told the feds that it was a local case, and they could keep their noses out of it.

But the agent had threatened to go after the chief for the records, claiming that because Maria was a Columbian national, the agent would get the CIA involved, as well.

The chief had told Carter Barclay not to worry, and that he would keep him posted.

Now, the threads were coming together. He could handle both problems at once. Stop the prying by the agent and also use her as bait to draw Stella LaRosa out of hiding.

The first thing he'd realized was that LaRosa would do anything to keep this agent out of harm's way. Ana Rodriguez was the younger sister of that other agent, Carmen. His tech guy had dug deeper and found that LaRosa had gone to the grave every week since the FBI agent had been murdered.

He had been thinking about this long and hard.

The way to get to Stella LaRosa was through this woman, Ana Rodriguez.

Obviously, if LaRosa went to the grave every week, she felt some guilt.

Carter was counting on that guilt.

If Stella felt guilty about Carmen's death, she would do anything to stop the woman's sister from encountering the same fate.

Then his tech guy had come up with another little tidbit.

He'd sent a mugshot of a gang member who had recently been released from prison.

Carter had picked up the phone and called the man, asking, "Who am I looking at here?"

"Boss man, this is the FBI agent's ex-boyfriend," the hacker had replied. "He just got picked up in San Francisco for assault. He's on probation. He'll go back to prison if charges are filed. Or..."

"Or we can offer him a deal." Carter looked at the photo closer, noting the details of the prisoner. "Don't let her out of your sight. Let's send someone to visit this guy in jail and give him a get out of jail card."

"I'm on it."

An hour later, he got a call.

"She's at the airport."

"Do you have eyes on her?"

"Electronic ones, yes. But guess what, you'll be able to put eyes on her yourself real soon. Guess where she's heading?"

"Please say Texas."

"Bingo. Houston, baby."

Perfect.

"Expedite our deal with the con. I want him on a plane to Houston now. Hire a private jet. He needs to be waiting in the airport when she lands. That way we can orchestrate a little reunion."

"I'll handle it."

Ana was coming to him.

And he'd be waiting. With her ex-boyfriend to help out.

It was working out better than he could've imagined.

By the end of next week, his first mass transplant operation would be done. Once those were proven to have taken, he would open up the operation even larger. At some point, he hoped to legitimize it.

Ever since he'd found out about his son, he had thought a lot about his own mortality. He wanted to leave something behind. A grandchild with his DNA, yes. But also a legacy.

He was hoping his cloning and transplant operation would change the world.

In the future, he hoped they could even branch into immortality. What if he could perfect cloning to the point where when someone's body grew old, a new body could be created? Your same brain could be transplanted into a brand-new body, that of an eighteen-year-old. Repeat again when that body grew old.

That was his dream.

He wasn't sure it was possible within his lifetime, but that was what he was putting every penny into. He wanted his name to go down in the history of mankind as the man who made humans immortal.

Step one would be next week.

He had six patients flying to Mexico to be the guinea pigs. They were all billionaires on the edge of death. Without the transplants, they would die.

And one of them had something else he wanted besides money.

He picked up the phone.

"Where is your niece?"

"No clue," the man responded weakly. "Stella's off grid. Her mother said she's overseas, maybe Africa? Spain? Somewhere in those parts."

"Any chance she's in Texas?"

"Nah. Why would she be there?"

"I'm not sure, but an FBI agent from the San Francisco bureau is on her way here. An agent who knows your niece."

"Jesus. I'll make some calls."

"Good."

"Hey, I was worried when I saw your number you were calling about my, uh, donor. Everything still cool that way?"

"Everything is still on schedule. We will see you in Mexico soon."

"Great."

"One thing, though. we do require half the payment up front."

"I keep forgetting to arrange that."

"The deadline was two weeks ago."

"Bitcoin right?"

"Yes, please arrange that by the end of the day to save your spot."

"Consider it done."

Carter hung up.

He didn't like the fact that Dominic LaRosa hadn't known where his niece was, either.

27

STELLA HAD THOUGHT ABOUT IT AND DECIDED HER INSURANCE policy would be a story about what Carter Barclay was doing with the information that Maria had provided her. She spent the day in her hotel room writing the story.

This was going to be a bit different from her normal articles. This one was in first person. She began with the message from Maria Perez writing to her as a whistleblower. And how before they could meet, Maria was decapitated. Then she wrote about how another person sent her Maria's files and how they showed the bodies in the lab and the documents proving the illegal cloning and planned transplant operations to billionaires. Then how Carlos Mendoza had been murdered. How everything had led her to Houston.

She wrote about how she hoped one day detectives could prove that Barclay was responsible for the murders of Maria and Carlos, but she feared it would never happen.

"This article may be the only justice they receive. Just know they were both killed trying to do the right thing and expose Barclay's evil doings," she wrote.

Stella included her infiltration of the company and how she had been forced to leave for trying to enter the labs that held the giant test tubes and cloned people.

She ended the piece by saying:

The first step in Carter Barclay's plan to expand his cloning transplant operation is to transplant the first organs at a Mexican hospital next week.

Someone needs to stop this before then. I don't know how this will happen. He has connections with politicians in the nation's highest offices, with police chiefs and federal law enforcement agents, with organized crime leaders, you name it, someone is on his payroll. That is the only way he has escaped prosecution for this long. Someone needs to stop him. By bringing this to the public's attention, I'm asking for people in positions of power to investigate Carter Barclay before it is too late.

Stella stared at that last line.

Nobody would do anything.

Where was the power of the press nowadays?

With so many hacks claiming to be journalists, nobody believed anything anymore. Or worse, they believed everything they read or saw.

Nonetheless, she used a VPN to send the file to BL4D3 with a note.

Can you please encrypt this file and send it to Jack Garcia at the San Francisco Tribune. And maybe in a separate text to his phone send him instructions to open it?

Then Stella typed in Garcia's personal cell phone number. She needed to know that if something happened to her, the information she had wouldn't die with her.

Next, she used a VPN to log onto her newspaper email.

There was a message from Griffin. Her heart clenched. Emailing wasn't his jam. Had he tried to text her? Since she'd discarded her sim card for her personal cell phone in the airport bathroom, all texts or calls went into the ether.

She read through the email quickly and her face grew hot.

Ana Rodriguez just texted me to say she was heading to Houston to look into Maria Perez' homicide. She also said something about another man in Houston who worked with Maria also ending up dead.

Stella slammed her laptop shut and grabbed a burner phone, dialing Griffin. To her dismay, she realized his number was burned into the recesses of her memory.

"Griffin," he answered.

"It's Stella. Whatever you do, you need to stop Ana from coming here."

For a moment he was silent. "You're in Houston?"

Crap. If his phone was tapped, then she was screwed.

"Whatever you do stop her from getting on that plane. I don't care if you have to arrest her and lock her up. She can't come here. It's too dangerous. If Carter Barclay knows she's digging around, she's dead."

"Jesus, Stella."

"I'm dead serious, Griffin."

"She already left."

Stella swore through gritted teeth. "Do you have her phone number?"

"No, we only talk through email. You know how feds are weird that way."

"Can you get her cell through a supervisor? You need to warn her that she's going to step into a viper's pit here."

"I'll do my best."

"I'm on a burner phone, so it should be secure. Text me her flight number or airline at least, if you can get it. I'll try to find her at the airport to warn her."

"Stella, what are you into over there? What can I do to help?"

"It's best if you don't know anything."

Stella hung up before he could answer.

Shoving her laptop and gun into the tote bag, she hurried to her car, determined to get to the airport before Ana landed.

28

DETECTIVE ROB GRIFFIN SWORE AS STELLA HUNG UP ON HIM.

The waitress, Carla, raised an eyebrow.

"Girl problems?"

"Ha! I wish," he said jokingly.

"I'm sure you don't have any problems in that department," she said saucily.

Carla was probably eighty years old but flirted endlessly with every customer who walked into Maeve's Diner.

Griffin always tipped her twenty-five percent. She reminded him of his great aunt.

He dialed Ana's phone number and it went straight to voice mail.

Damn it. She was probably already on the plane.

"Refill?" Carla asked.

"Yes, ma'am!"

"Okay, none of that. I'm still a miss."

"Yes, Miss Carla."

She refilled his mug. He was sitting in his usual corner booth at the gritty diner, nestled in the heart of the Tenderloin district. The diner had the perfect amount of white noise for him to become lost in his own thoughts: the clatter of a spatula against a cast iron skillet, the murmur of working men's voices, and the sizzling sound of bacon on the griddle.

Sunlight filtered through the grimy windows, a rare occasion in San Francisco, that seemed to lift the mood of all the patrons.

Griffin took a long gulp of the bitter coffee. At home he had a fancy espresso machine, but nothing could beat the atmosphere at Maeve's Diner. He liked catching tidbits of the conversations of the other customers sometimes: the construction workers, cabbies, and warehouse guys who griped about bad bosses and unpaid overtime.

Here, he felt incognito. He'd been going there for years and yet nobody knew he was a cop, not even Carla. His badge hid in his pocket. His Glock in a holster beneath his windbreaker.

When his phone buzzed he glanced at it, hoping it was Stella, but it was a reminder that he had a dentist appointment.

He was annoyed she hung up on him.

That was so like her.

It was how she avoided, well, everything. That was why he knew it would never work with her. When he'd started falling hard for her, he realized she was out of his reach. She was fighting too many demons, and she was not ready to share the burden with him.

He had been heartbroken for a while. But after she continued to ignore his attempts to see or speak to her after she saved his life, he'd grown angry and resentful.

With her. And with himself.

How had he allowed himself to fall for an emotionally unavailable woman? He'd known better. His anger had faded eventually, and he'd become resigned to the fact that she wasn't a bad person. That she hadn't been able to help it. But it had still hurt to see and talk to her. For a while.

Until he'd met Carmen.

The new FBI agent had cast a spell on him.

Like Stella, she was powerful, independent, ambitious, and fierce.

And unlike Stella, she was able to be vulnerable, honest, and emotionally available.

They'd fallen hard for each other.

At first, Carmen had been a bit wary of Stella, but Griffin had reassured her that while Stella would always have a small piece of his heart, he was over her. That he was all in with Carmen.

Carmen, much like Stella, had a hard shell she had to wear when she was out in the world, dealing with the scum of the earth: the pedophiles, the mass murderers, the con artists preying on the innocent. But the difference was that Carmen had seen a therapist regularly and worked hard to shed her tough persona when she walked in the door at the end of the day.

That's when he saw the woman he'd fallen in love with. She was playful and spicy and a great cook. They would cook elaborate meals together and then watch football or movies in their pajamas, then make love before falling asleep in each other's arms.

Carmen had been the love of his life.

That's why when she was killed trying to help Stella, it had taken him a long time to accept that it hadn't been Stella's fault.

His phone rang. It showed an unknown number.

"Detective Griffin."

"Hello, Detective."

For a second, his breath caught in his throat. Carmen.

But Carmen was dead.

"You called?" It was Ana. Her voice was low and deep like her older sister's. For a second he was speechless, but then he got his act together.

"Stella LaRosa just called me. She said you need to stay put. You'll help the most if you stay in town." It was an utter lie. But he couldn't tell her the truth, she would scoff and think he was not confident in her skills. Or worse, that he was sexist.

The truth was that nobody, no matter how skilled, was a match for Carter Barclay and his endless sources of power.

"Too late," Ana said in a chipper voice. "Plane is already in the air."

"How are you on your cell?"

"I just held up my badge when my phone rang and the flight attendants sat back down and all the people around me understand. I mean this is official FBI business."

"When you land, turn around and get back on another flight."

"Hold up, Detective. last time I checked you didn't work for the bureau, and you most certainly were not my supervisor."

"I'm sorry," he said. "I'm just conveying a message. I truly believe your life is in danger if you go to Houston. I know you are perfectly capable of handling the worst of the worst, but the resources that this particular individual has and his ruthlessness, are a grave concern."

"I appreciate your consideration," Ana said. "But there is nothing that is going to stop me. This is my job. There is something wrong going on and it all started in Houston. It is all connected to Carter Barclay, and I aim to get to the bottom of it. We can't have people hired to cut off women's heads in our city."

"Ana, please think about what I'm saying. He knows you're coming. He has no qualms about eliminating federal agents. Or dignitaries, or even the president for that matter."

"Which makes me even more determined to stop him."

Griffin winced. She was as stubborn as her sister.

This was impossible. He was ready to beg.

But she spoke again, in a low, gentle voice. "I'm not Carmen."

He sighed. "I know."

"I know you wish you could've saved my sister. I know how that feels. But I also knew that woman for thirty years. Nobody—not me, not you, not her supervisor, not our parents, God bless their souls—could have stopped her."

He sat in silence for a minute, digesting that. It brought a lump into his throat. A strange mixture of relief, as if a giant weight had fallen off his shoulders, but also a powerful punch of grief. He choked back a sob.

"Rob," she said, using his name for the first time. "I miss her, too. When I get back, I'd love to get lunch with you. I want to thank you for making my sister the happiest I'd ever seen her."

"Ana," he said, his voice cracking. "If you want to thank me, come home today. Get on the next flight back. We'll do dinner. If something happened to you, it would destroy both me and Stella LaRosa."

Ana gave a long, loud sigh. "I guess I need to have this conversation with her again, as well. Listen, I have to go."

"Wait, Stella wants to meet you at the airport. At least do that. She can fill you in. Strength in numbers. All that. Flight number?"

"1772."

And then she hung up.

Griffin took several deep breaths, fighting back the ball of chaos rising in his chest and threatening to overwhelm him. Ana had told him he shouldn't feel guilty about Carmen's death. But he didn't have time for that kind of healing. Right now, he needed to call Stella back and tell her the flight number.

Relief and desperation fought for control of his emotions.

He couldn't stop Ana.

But finally, he acknowledged that neither he, nor Stella, could have stopped Carmen. That brought a strange, bittersweet relief. Even though he had initially blamed Stella, he also blamed himself. He had not warned Carmen about how dangerous Carter Barclay was. A small part of him believed that if he had, she might still be alive today.

But Ana didn't believe that. She believed that even if Carmen had known that she most likely would end up dead, she would have still charged into that building.

It was horrible to feel relief about that, but it also made him feel guilty for blaming Stella for so long.

But he'd have to deal with that another time. Right now, he had to call Stella and tell her it was up to her to stop Ana.

They both had to do anything in their power to make sure Ana didn't get hurt.

He owed that to Carmen.

And to himself.

29

ANA HUNG UP HER PHONE AND SAT BACK IN HER CHAIR closing her eyes, ignoring the woman beside her who rolled her eyes and sighed heavily. Ana had a job to do, plus she'd spoken as quietly as she could. She was surprised the airplane noise hadn't drowned out her soft-spoken tone.

What would Carmen have done?

She sure as hell wouldn't have turned around and taken the next flight back.

But then again, Carmen was dead.

Maybe Griffin was right. She wouldn't do anyone any good if she was six feet under.

That wouldn't be the best way to honor Carmen's memory. But running away from danger also wouldn't make her sister proud. Ana needed to find that middle ground.

She couldn't turn around. But she would be extremely careful.

Ana had packed her gun in her checked suitcase since she hadn't been able to meet with TSA officials to prove there was a need for her to fly with the weapon on her person. However, she had completed the "Law Enforcement Officers Flying Armed" training course, so she was certified to carry the unloaded weapon in her suitcase in a locked, hard-sided container.

Now, she wished she had taken the time to plead her case with TSA officials and carried the gun onboard.

A few minutes before Griffin called, she'd left her seat to use the restroom in the back of the plane and saw a man in a ballcap and red sweatshirt sitting near an exit door. A random image of him screaming and opening the door mid-flight raced through her head. She shook her head to get rid of the image, and he watched her as she grew closer. She locked eyes with him, wanting him to know she saw him. She knew he was up to no good. To her surprise, his lips curved into a small smirk. She didn't like it. It was cocky. It was confident. It was knowing.

She'd seen him earlier in the airport, near the gate. The ballcap was pulled low over his face, but he'd met her eyes briefly before shifting them away. Ana had gone to notify the attendants at the gate's desk, but they'd made the call for boarding. She'd sworn silently to herself and looked around for the man, but the crowd of people had swallowed him up.

Her eyes narrowed at him now, while a wave of unease rolled across her back.

She passed by him, heart pounding, and looked for a flight attendant at the rear of the plane near the bathroom. But the area was empty. The flight attendant was up toward the front, serving snacks.

When Ana came out of the bathroom and walked back down the aisle, she paused at the row where she had seen the man. Seat 27C. But the man's head was lolled back, and his eyes were closed as if he was sleeping.

After waiting a beat, Ana continued to her seat.

She'd been about to alert a flight attendant when her phone rang. Loudly.

The flight attendant was right at her seat about to say something when Ana pulled out her FBI badge on its lanyard and held it in front of her. The woman nodded, smiled, and moved on as Ana spoke to Griffin.

Now, she hit the button for the flight attendant. But a few seconds later, the pilot made the announcement that they were about to land and that the flight attendants should strap in. *Damn it.*

She'd deal with him on the ground.

After the plane landed, people stood and tried to rush the aisles as they do. Ana turned to glance behind her, searching for the man toward the back of the plane, but didn't see him through the mass of bodies.

She decided to wait at the gate for him to come through and then follow him. Or else she would alert the local authorities and let them deal with him.

Ana waited to merge into the aisle as the people in front of her surged forward seat by seat. Glancing behind her, she still couldn't find the guy. 27C was empty and she couldn't spot a guy with a worn blue baseball cap and red sweatshirt. Weird. Her gaze dropped, and she smiled over the seat back at the little girl behind her. The child had two bouncy pigtails and was clutching a small stuffed pink bear.

The mother smiled, too, and then yawned. "It's been a long day. We started our morning in Seattle at 4 a.m."

"Wow. She's very well behaved for having such an early start. What a sweetie."

The mother smiled again and muttered a thanks as she rubbed her daughter's back.

Ana turned to the front as the aisle began opening up. She stepped out from her seat when a commotion broke out behind her.

A man said, "Watch it, fella. We're all anxious to get off this plane."

"Some people!" a woman said.

The aisle in front of her was crowded, and she sighed, knowing it was useless to be in a hurry.

Then Ana heard a voice in her ear. "You're going to do exactly as I say, or the little girl gets a needle in her neck. What's in that needle will make it painless and quick and quiet. Don't turn around. Eyes straight ahead and do as I say. If you understand, nod your head."

Ana gave a slight nod.

"If you alert anyone, she's dead."

"Ow, you're hurting me." It was the little girl's voice.

Ana's hands clenched into fists. If it was just her and this guy, game over. But with a needle with God knows what in it pressed to a child's neck? She would do as he said.

"It's okay, Sadie. Just stay quiet and do as the nice man says." The mother's voice trembled. Ana didn't dare turn around.

"He's not nice."

"Sadie, please."

"Okay, Mama."

"Miss," the woman said to Ana, "please do what he says."

There was some commotion in the aisle and Ana had to step aside to let someone get a suitcase out from the overhead bin. As she did, she saw the man out of the corner of her eye. It was the same man from earlier except now the ballcap was gone. So was the red sweatshirt. He wore a black turtleneck and glasses. The little girl was pressed between them. He was holding his hand to the girl's head, his fingers wrapped around her neck under her hair.

Now the aisle was clear. It was their turn. The plane was empty in front of them. They moved quickly now, with the man whispering behind her. "Hurry. Hurry. Go! Go!"

Ana walked quickly, eyes darting, mind racing for a way to save the girl.

"I'm walking as fast as I can!" the girl said.

"Walk faster. You. Up in front," he said. "Don't try anything. Walk right past the cockpit and out that door to the jetway. Once you get into the airport, you're going to go to the right and go into the family bathroom. Leave it unlocked. You wait until I join you in there. If you speak to anyone or try to run, the girl dies. Nod if you understand."

Ana gave a short nod.

"Tell your kid to smile at the flight attendants and not say a word."

"Sadie...do you understand? Please listen to the man."

"I hate you!" she hissed.

"Do you want me to kill your mom?" the man threatened.

There was a slight pause. "No," the little girl said her voice barely a whisper.

Then do what I say."

Her heart was pounding as she walked down the aisle. As she passed the flight attendants saying goodbye at the plane's door, she avoided eye contact. She would follow his instructions to the letter. There was no way she'd risk a child's life to save her own.

Ana hesitated at the door where the flight attendants waited, saying goodbye.

"Oh, isn't she cute," one of them said.

The child didn't answer and then they were on the jetway.

"Keep going!" the man said. "You're doing great. In a few minutes, the girl and her mother will be free, and it will just be the two of us."

Great.

All she had to do was get into the bathroom. Once he came in, game over. She was trained in Muay Thai and wasn't worried about being able to take on this scrawny piece of crap.

Stepping onto the main walkway, she turned right. The family bathroom was a few feet down. She hesitated and turned. He was right behind her. He had picked up the little girl and had her hoisted on his hip. The girl looked shellshocked. Her mouth was trembling, eyes wide. The man held the child around her waist with one hand, Ana could see the needle in his other hand, his arm bent near the child's bare leg. The mother was behind him, tears streaming down her face.

He met Ana's eyes and nodded, jutting his chin slightly at the bathroom door. "Walk in backwards. Count to twenty and then you can come out and you are free."

No way, buddy. She was going to close the door for half a second to fool him and then open it and run after him and the kid.

Turning the handle, she opened the door and stepped into it backwards as instructed. The man watched her and nodded. Reluctantly, she closed the door.

She waited a beat with her hand still on the handle. She was going to open it and run after the man. But then she heard someone before she felt them. It was an exhale and a whoosh of air and then intense piercing pain to the back of her neck.

30

PEOPLE POURED OUT OF THE HOUSTON AIRPORT'S SECURITY clearance area in droves, heading for the baggage area or ground transportation, but there was no sign of Ana.

Wearing dark sunglasses and her hoodie pulled up over her head, Stella scanned the crowd for the petite, curly-haired woman.

Stella had been waiting for the past thirty minutes. The plane had touched down twenty minutes ago. She'd worried about being too late but had parked and was inside the American Airlines terminal a few minutes before the plane landed.

Instead of a steady flow of people, small groups walked in droves toward baggage claim and ground transportation. Thirty minutes after Ana's flight had landed, the crowds had thinned. Only a few people here and there still approached the security checkpoints from the other side. Stella approached a straggler as soon as he walked out of the secured area. A young man with a San Francisco Giants sweatshirt on.

"Were you on flight 1772?" she asked him.

The man wore a bored expression. "Yeah."

Stella frowned. "My friend was supposed to be on that flight. Was there a delay in getting to your gate?"

"Nah," he said. "I was one of the last people off. I was in line for coffee forever, though."

He held up a coffee cup.

"Okay, thanks," Stella said, but she was distracted looking over his shoulder. A blonde woman with a small child was being escorted by half a dozen police officers. Several other security personnel and TSA agents were rushing past Stella from her side, yelling.

A woman brushed by Stella heading toward baggage claim.

"What's going on?" Stella asked her.

"Some dude on our flight tried to kidnap a kid or something, I guess." The woman shook her head. "Nothing is safe nowadays."

Stella's heart dropped. "Did you come in from San Francisco?"

"Yes. They stopped and questioned me because I was sitting by the guy. He was fine during the flight. Just snored a little."

"What did he look like?"

"I don't know," the woman said, shrugging. "Average looking white guy. Baseball hat. Forty-niner sweatshirt. Average everything. Just like I told the cops."

"Okay, thanks."

The police had walked the woman and her child out of security but still surrounded her. Stella crept closer.

"My sister should be here any minute," the woman said, her voice sounding tearful.

"You sure you're okay by yourself?" an officer asked.

"I'll stay with her," a man with a security guard badge said.

Stella waited a beat until the police contingent left and then she stepped a bit closer.

A few seconds later, a woman in a beige trench coat raced over to the young mom and gave her a hug. "Oh my God. What happened? Are you guys okay?"

"It was awful," the mother responded. "A crazy guy held a needle to Sadie. It only lasted a few seconds. She's okay. Aren't you sweetie? You were so brave."

"Do you want me to escort you to your car?" asked the security guard.

"No thank you," the blonde woman said. "You've been wonderful."

The man nodded. "The detectives will be in touch."

The two women turned to walk away, and Stella approached them.

"Excuse me," Stella said, keeping her distance, but speaking loudly. "I'm so sorry to bother you. My friend Ana was on your flight and I can't find her. She had dark, curly hair. Petite."

The color drained from the blonde woman's face. She opened her mouth to respond, but her sister interrupted.

"Listen. My sister and niece have been through a very traumatic experience. I need to get them home."

"No, wait, Belinda," the blonde said and turned to Stella. "Your friend? Olive skin and really long eyelashes, right?"

"Yes, that sounds like her," Stella said evenly, but inside she was beginning to lose it.

"He held the needle to Sadie's throat and told the woman to do what he said, or he'd stab her." She gasped, putting her hand over her mouth and looking down at her daughter. The child had her face pressed against her mother's leg, clutching her hand.

"The airplane bathroom?" Stella asked.

"No, as we were deplaning. He made that woman go into a bathroom and then made us walk to another gate. He let us go and disappeared."

"Did they search the bathroom?"

She nodded. "Nobody was in there. Do you think they think I made it up?"

"Of course you didn't," Stella said, stepping closer. "I'm sure they believe you and are taking this with the utmost seriousness."

"But nobody was there when they opened the door. And the guy who did it was wearing glasses. But the woman he was sitting by said he had a red sweatshirt and baseball hat."

"He changed, of course."

The woman looked confused. "That had to be it."

"Listen, I'm sorry about your friend," the other woman said. "But I need to get my sister and niece out of here. They've been through enough already."

"I'm sorry," Stella said. "Thank you for your help."

Stella saw the police returning, heading their way. She turned and quickly walked toward the escalator for ground transportation. Once there, she hid in a bathroom for thirty minutes before leaving and making her way to her car. Just in case Carter Barclay had put out her description. His reach could never be underestimated.

He'd just proven it. He had to be behind Ana's disappearance.

There was no other explanation.

Stella carefully navigated the turns to get out of the airport and held her breath as she stuck one of her fake credit cards into the machine to get out of the parking garage. It worked.

Just how Barclay had managed to find out about Ana's last-minute flight and get a kidnapper on the same flight in time was terrifying. He had people everywhere. Cell phones? Check. CCTV cameras with video footage across the country? Check. The ability to run that footage through facial recognition software? Check.

Nothing was safe.

A burner phone and fake identity had worked well enough for Stella. But only for a while.

As she drove back to her hotel, she called Griffin. He didn't pick up. She'd have to leave a voicemail.

"They got her," she began and winced as her voice cracked.

She struggled to keep the distress out of her voice as she told the rest of the story and asked him to notify Ana's supervisor at the FBI and to ask him for help. She told him to insist on Ana's supervisor and not talk to anyone else.

"Trust nobody."

31

As soon as Ana felt the piercing pain in her neck, someone kicked her in the knees, and she collapsed to the bathroom floor. The door opened and feet rushed by her. Training as a black belt in karate launched her to her feet where she began punching and kicking wildly, spinning and ducking so fast that her attackers were a blur. However, her limbs soon grew heavy, and her thinking and vision became distorted. Before all her strength left her, she was able to jab an arm until it landed a punch in someone's eye socket before she collapsed on the floor again.

Her face was pressed to the floor and a foot on her back held her down. When she tried to turn her head, she couldn't move her neck. Each of her limbs went offline one by one, and she was unable to lift even a finger.

She was trapped inside her own body.

Bright light flooded the bathroom and someone hoisted her into a wheelchair. She tried to scream and fight back but couldn't utter a sound. Her thoughts were jumbled, but she tried to concentrate on what was happening.

Date rape drug.

Those three words kept streaming across her mind.

Still, it didn't track. Usually, the fastest acting date rape drug, GHB, took fifteen minutes for symptom onset. But she felt this immediately. Ketamine.

Her vision was a kaleidoscope. And the hallucinations had begun. Large velvety black bats swooped in from perches on the ceiling, flying in front of her and then disappearing in her peripheral vision. At the same time, an unprovoked sense of euphoria enveloped her in its warmth.

Distantly, where her brain still clung to reality, Ana knew she was in what was called the K-Hole. This sensation was why most people used the drug.

The K-Hole was a finicky beast. Many people took ketamine, or Special K, or Vitamin K, for the dreamlike hallucinations and overall sense of euphoria. But the K-Hole was highly unpredictable and could quickly turn into a horrific nightmare that could not be escaped.

Ana latched onto the word. *Ketamine.* It seemed crucial that she remember this word. It was her last grip on reality.

Her head lolled to one side. Someone jammed a large floppy hat onto her head. It slipped down low over her face and hid most of her view. She strained to see as a figure moved in front of her. A man with dark hair dressed in an airport uniform. Something about his hair and back was vaguely familiar, but she couldn't place him.

The man crouched in front of her and lifted her feet and legs so that her boots were placed on the wheelchair's footrest.

Look at me. Look at me. Look at me.

But the man stood just out of her line of sight.

A giant blanket was draped over her from behind. Hands tucked it in around her shoulders.

Then the door swung open and her wheelchair began to move.

It had all happened within about five minutes, if that.

She was being wheeled through the airport passing people, including police and security guards, and unable to scream or cry out for help.

The drugs had immobilized her.

The man pushing the chair was silent and walked quickly.

Soon, they had left the secured area and taken an elevator down. A few seconds later, she was in front of a large black van with dark windows. Two men jumped out as the first one wheeled her up. They lifted her into the back of the van, throwing her on the bench seat in the back. She lay sideways on the bench, hoping she didn't roll off and fall onto the floor. The doors slammed shut, and the van took off.

The van went around a corner too quickly and she rolled. Not off the bench seat, but onto her face. Panic flared. Her face was pressed into the leather. One nostril was sucking in as much air as it could, but she was slowly suffocating. She focused on calming herself. The van went veering around another corner and she rolled back to her previous position, air filled her lungs. Her abdomen cramped in intense pain. Even though she clocked the pain as an eight on a scale of one to ten, she was able to completely detach herself from it. She refused to let it infiltrate her overwhelming sense of intoxication. At the same time, an alarm was sounding in her head. The pain could lead to vomiting. If she threw up in that position she would surely choke on her vomit or aspirate.

She could feel the urge to vomit rising in her throat. She couldn't move, but she could feel that.

The van squealed around another corner, and she rolled back and forth a couple of times. She'd hoped the movement would keep her on her side, but when the van pulled to a sudden stop, she was jerked back onto her shoulder blades, staring up at the van's ceiling. If she strained her eyes, she could see the night filled with stars out the window near her feet.

But this wasn't a stop sign or traffic signal. This was a real stop. She heard voices. Then the van started again. A few minutes later, the night sky disappeared from the window across from her. The interior of the van was now filled with an orange glow. They were inside a garage.

The van stopped and the front seat passengers hopped out. The door near her head opened.

"She still can't move?" a voice asked.

A chill of mortal fear raced across her scalp. Who was that? Why was that voice so familiar?

"Use the wheelchair again." That voice she didn't recognize.

Her thinking still felt fuzzy. The voice. It evoked a strange mix of nostalgia and terror. What was going on? Was she still hallucinating? She had to be. It couldn't be him.

Someone opened the doors in the back of the van, and she heard a metal clattering. The wheelchair hitting the ground? Then she was lifted up. Someone had their hands under her armpits and her head and shoulders rested on the person's chest as they dragged her off the van's bench seat until her bottom was sitting on the seat and her torso was upright, pressed against the person holding her.

A familiar scent filled her nostrils. She blinked. And then was ecstatic that she could blink. Her ability to move must be coming back. She tried to speak but only managed a small exhalation sound combined with a guttural grunt.

The drug was wearing off. She was so excited she momentarily forgot about the person holding her. An old, nearly forgotten feeling, the tingling of chemistry and sexual attraction.

She was set down in the wheelchair and buckled in and then the dark-haired man moved in front of her..

"Ana, *mi amore*," he said. "I warned you that I would tell everyone your little secret if you didn't meet with me. They will learn about what you did. But you will not be around to defend yourself. I gave you so many chances. But you reject me. Over and over. And I can no longer deal with the pain of not having you. I'm keeping my promise. If I can't have you, then nobody can."

The man smiled at her. He was even more beautiful, now that he was older with gray flecks at his temples.

Angel Ruiz was the devil.

32

THAT MORNING WHEN CARTER BARCLAY HAD WOKEN UP, Stella had just been a nuisance. Someone he would eventually eliminate from the world.

The call he'd received at breakfast had changed everything.

He'd been seated at his large oak table eating his overnight oats, two strips of bacon from a hog raised on the ranch, and two hard-boiled eggs from his own chickens. As he ate, he leisurely perused his stock portfolios. In the background, he could hear the ranch hands rounding up the prized stallions. He had planned on going for a long ride in the meadow before work. That weekend he was leaving for Mexico and was planning on taking one of his thoroughbreds as a gift to the director of the hospital where the transplants were taking place. He'd already had ten million transferred into the man's personal account and was going to transfer the second ten million after the surgeries, but Carter Barclay knew how far a personal gift could go with a man like that.

He'd ride Jasper one last time. The horse was a beauty and worth millions himself. But when Barclay had heard the director, Diego Gonzalez, had a ranch, he knew it would be the right thing to do. He could afford to give away the horse to cement a friendship. Because if Barclay had his way, there would be dozens of transplants taking place over the next year or so until he could get the legislation through Congress making the cloning and transplant legal in the United States. People from around the world would travel to his country to experience this miraculous new medical technology. Getting the law passed was proving to be difficult, but he had ways to persuade the holdouts to agree with him.

As he thought of Jasper, his chief security officer appeared in the doorway. He hadn't even known the man was on site.

"Sir, you weren't answering your phone?"

Blinking, he looked around. Where was his damn phone? That was so unlike him. He must have left it in the bedroom.

"I flew in straight away. We figured out what files that woman, Maria Perez, had copied from the server. And we also have evidence that those files were sent to that reporter in San Francisco."

"Good God, man!" Carter Barclay exclaimed, standing up. "Get to the point. Quit beating around the bush. What were on the files?"

"Everything."

The word hung in silence.

"What do you mean everything?" Carter Barclay could feel his face turning purple, as it did when he lost his temper.

"All the data on the cloning transplants and photographs."

Impossible.

"Are you saying that Stella LaRosa has this information?"

"It appears so."

Barclay's plan had been to kidnap the FBI agent and use her as bait to draw Stella to him so he could kill her, but now he needed the agent to barter: the woman for the files.

It was a ruse, of course.

He couldn't trust Stella LaRosa to hand over the only copy of the files. She probably had already made copies or sent them to someone important.

The only way he could stop the files from becoming public was if he got his hands on LaRosa. He would torture her into telling him who had the copies, and then he would kill her once and for all.

A few hours later, Carter Barclay paced the prized room tucked away in his basement bunker, swirling the ice in his crystal tumbler. He kept his eyes on the three large monitors sitting on the big black desk. The dim lighting in the room made it easier to watch the activity on the screens.

As he leaned over to pour some more bourbon into his glass something caught his eye. Footage from flight 1772 showed passengers stepping out of the security clearance area toward baggage claim.

He'd been watching the little girl and mother that his man had used as leverage. Police had detained them and now, nearly forty minutes after the flight landed, they walked them out. A security guard remained until another woman ran up to the mother and child, hugging them both.

Then another woman, barely in the frame, caught his eye. All he could see was a glimpse.

It could be her.

She stood behind a large pillar. The way she stayed just out of the camera's view. He was certain.

It was Stella LaRosa.

He pressed a button and spoke. "Can you get me access to the video feed for ground transportation and baggage claim?"

"Give me twenty minutes."

"I need it now."

"I'll do my best."

"And then ping it for LaRosa's face. Search the cameras in the garage and freeways leaving the airport. I think we found her."

"Yes, sir."

Then his cell rang.

"We have the bird in the nest."

"Very good," he said. "Take her to the lab. I want three armed guards on her at all times. Keep her tied up. You can give her some water, but keep her hands bound."

"She's violent," the voice said. "She's already given one of our men a black eye and the other a broken arm."

"Jesus. What are your men? Boy Scouts? I thought I hired ex-Delta for this operation!"

"It just took them by surprise. Plus, with your directive not to injure her, it made it difficult to deflect her surprise attack."

"You are a bunch of pansies! A woman broke the arm of a special services man? Shameful. Don't ever let that man on any operation I'm involved in ever again. Do you understand?"

Carter slammed down the phone. What a joke. A woman who was no more than five foot two inches tall and 110 pounds, injured an ex-Delta man.

The woman was disposable. But not yet. He knew Stella would require proof of life.

Carter paced the dark room waiting for surveillance video to come through on his monitor. "Come on! Come on! Where is she?"

A few minutes later, the footage from the airport baggage claim popped up on his screen. He stared at Stella LaRosa in a bad disguise. He clicked the next file. Her face was hidden by the hat and large dark sunglasses as she checked out of the airport garage. Then there was footage of her vehicle leaving the airport and then another clip of her dark car pulling into a hotel on the outskirts of Houston.

Boom.

Carter Barclay rubbed his hands together.

"Got you."

33

STELLA WAS FRANTIC WITH FEAR AND ANXIETY AS SHE DROVE back to her hotel in the dark. Keeping her eyes on her rearview mirror, she took evasive action, driving in circles around the block or taking an unnecessary exit off the freeway in case someone was following her.

As far as she could tell, nobody was.

But Carter Barclay was more sophisticated than just putting a tail on her.

Her fear was not for herself.

She was terrified of what he was going to do to Ana.

Although Stella had convinced herself that Carmen's death was not her fault, that confidence was now thin and wavering. If someone disputed it, Stella would revert right back to feeling guilty for the other woman's death.

Now, Barclay had Carmen's little sister again, because of Stella's stupid decisions.

Pulling into the hotel parking, she turned off her headlights, and sat in the dark, watching for any cars to creep up on her or drive by the hotel. When she was convinced she hadn't been tailed, she quickly got out of her car and ran to her room. She kept the space dark, not wanting to alert anyone who might be spying on the window from the parking lot. Using a small penlight, she quickly packed up her belongings in her duffel bag and slipped out of the room, putting the "Do Not Disturb" sign on the door handle.

Before getting into the elevator, she looked out a window facing the parking lot.

Two large, dark vans had pulled in near the lobby on the far side of the building.

She shrank back from the window, but not before someone in the van peered back at her. He raised his arm toward her.

They were parked near her rental car. She'd have to escape on foot.

Bursting through the door to the stairs, she took them three at a time and flung herself out the emergency exit on the ground floor. Once outside, she ran across a small patch of grass and sprinted for the cluster of woods behind the building. As she entered the thicket, she heard shouting from the building behind her.

Tree branches scratched her face and arms as she ran. She plowed through the woods. An early recon of the hotel had showed that a large shopping mall lay on the other side of the trees. Running through the dark woods, darting through the trees, out of breath, she considered dumping the duffel bag since it was slowing her down, but she needed her laptop and gun. Without those, she was essentially a sitting duck in Houston.

The shouting grew closer. Someone crashed through the brush behind her, leaves and branches crunching underfoot.

Picking up the pace, she burst through the other side of the woods and into the parking lot of a movie theater attached to the mall. The lot was full, and people streamed toward the entrance.

Instead of joining the crowd and trying to get lost in it, Stella quickly veered left and ducked, crouching as she ran between the cars. At the far side of the parking lot, she slowed and began trying door handles, one after the other, keeping her body low and hoping that whoever was following her had headed into the mall and theater.

Her thighs burned from walking at such a low crouch through the rows of cars and her ears pricked for any sound of someone following her. She tried handle after handle. Then, when she was only two rows away from the end of the parking lot, a door opened. She froze for a second, half-expecting a car alarm to start blaring, but there was nothing.

She opened the back door of the Blazer, only wide enough to slip inside the crack. Once inside, she reached to the front and locked all four doors, keeping her head lower than the seat. It took all her willpower not to look around for her pursuers. Once the door locks engaged, she lay in the wheel well of the back seat. Her duffel bag rested on top of her, and she rummaged through it until she found the cold, hard metal of her gun. She scolded herself for not having it on her person the entire time. Lying in the dark, she held the gun on her chest and watched the back window opposite.

After a few minutes, she heard the distant sound of gunshots and screams. Again, she fought her instinct to sit up. When the shouts drew nearer to her, she had to sit up and look.

Cursing that she had never learned to hotwire a car, Stella allowed herself to peer out the bottom portion of the window. People were running out of the mall and movie theater. *Damn it.* The owner of this vehicle was most likely heading her way. She didn't dare get out. She would be seen for sure.

People screamed and ran to their cars, tires squealing as they left the parking lot. Horns honked. Children cried. And voices were raised.

Stella remained in the wheel well clutching her gun, hoping against hope that no children would be opening the back door of the car.

Then she heard a voice close by. "Come on," a man said. "Let's get out of here."

Stella's heart stopped for a second as she heard the click of the locks disengaging. Her muscles tensed. The front passenger door opened. And then the driver's.

She waited, frozen, trying to barely breathe. Then the engine started, soft music began to play, and the back doors remained closed.

She was filled with relief.

"What do you think was going on?" a woman's voice said. "Someone said they heard gunshots. If I wasn't with you, I'd be terrified."

"You don't have to worry when you're with me."

For a second, fear shot through Stella. What if they looked back and saw her? Did the man have a gun? This was Texas, after all.

"I know. One look at your big muscles and any gunman would run."

The man chuckled. "I don't know about that, but I wouldn't let anything happen to you. You know that."

"I do," the woman said. "But I'm a little shaken up. I mean what if someone was hurt?"

"I'm sure it's fine. Why don't we stop and get ice cream? Will that cheer you up?"

"You are trying to ruin my diet, aren't you, honey?" a woman's voice said in a teasing tone.

"You know I like my women with a little meat on the bones, darlin'."

The woman giggled.

Stella rolled her eyes. It was torture to listen to these two. She wondered how long she could get away with her hiding spot. She didn't want to startle the driver and make him crash. But she was worried they would hear her or sense her back there. Keeping her breathing slow and easy, she concentrated on staying as still as possible, even though every gentle turn of the vehicle rocked her and her bag from side to side.

"Here we are," the man said, stopping the vehicle. "Drive-thru or park and go inside?"

Stella held her breath, waiting for the woman to answer.

"Let's go inside," she said, sighing. "I want a banana split and that's too messy to eat in the car or at home."

The man chuckled. "Sounds good."

As soon as the couple got out of the car, Stella sat up and peeked out the front window. They had their backs to her. As quietly as possible, she opened the back door and squeezed out of as little a space as possible. She crouched to the ground and slung the duffel over her shoulder, rounding the car until she was behind it.

She stood, looking around, and saw she was in a strip mall with a coffee shop. Pulling her baseball cap low, she also tugged the hood up on her sweatshirt and put on her dark glasses. It was a subtle disguise, but hopefully it was enough to stump any facial recognition software.

Once inside the coffee shop, and after scanning for cameras around the establishment, she ordered a double espresso and tucked herself away in a corner table facing the door. She glanced at her burner phone. It had several missed calls. All from Griffin. She was reluctant to call him back without any information on Ana. More than reluctant. She was dreading that conversation with her entire being.

Unearthing her laptop, she logged onto the Dark Web using a VPN on the coffee shop's Wi-Fi. She needed BL4D3's help. However, when she tried to message him through the usual channel she was told "user unavailable."

He had been spooked by what the file had contained. That was the only explanation. It was unfathomable that Barclay had gotten to him as well.

During her years on the Headway team, she'd set up a website for random messages for Black Rose. She opened that website to see if the hacker had reached out to her there.

He hadn't.

But there was one message.

From Carter Barclay. Of course he knew her as Black Rose. He had known all about Headway and had been close to Senator Walker who had started the covert overseas operation.

Even so, Stella had never expected him to reach out to her there.

Dread raced over her as she clicked to open the message.

A photo slowly loaded, and her anxiety increased, peaking as the picture loaded. It was Ana, bound to a chair by her wrists and ankles. Her mouth was gagged. Her neck appeared to be strapped to the chair.

She was alive.

At least in the photo. Stella knew of serial killers who had sewed the eyelids of their dead victims open as proof of life for photos.

Underneath the photo were five words.

The files for her life.

That was it.

He knew she had the files. This wasn't a simple ransom note.

The demand was too casual, too succinct.

Her hand hovered over her keyboard for just a moment and then typed, "Proof of life."

Then she hit send.

A few seconds later, there was a reply. She opened it. It was a video.

Ana's head lolled slightly to one side. She was drugged.

A voice off camera said, "It's 9 p.m." A boot nudged Ana. She looked directly into the camera and said, "Stella, don't do a thing they say."

Then it ended.

Stella looked at her watch. It was 9:03 p.m.

Ana was alive.

"Where? When?" she wrote and hit send.

1 a.m. Near the Space Center. Will message exact location at 12:50 a.m.

That meant that they would have her at a location no further than ten minutes away from the Space Center. That wasn't great info, but it was better than nothing.

However, Stella was not waiting for the meet.

She was going to go get Ana before that.

Stella watched as a woman got up from her laptop and headed to the bathroom. She had left her purse on the bench before her.

Stella walked by, slipping her hand in the bag and gripping the woman's car keys. she hit the alarm release button before she was outside. The beep came from a small Honda. Perfect.

Hopping in, she peeled out.

Ana was clearly being held at the lab.

The eerie blue light surrounding her was a dead giveaway.

34

Angel and the others had left the room. He was the last to leave, so easily turning away from her without a backward glance. The door slammed shut behind him.

Ana sat there in the cold, dimly lit room shivering, her wrists, ankles, and neck strapped to the wheelchair. Still unable to turn her head, but what she saw from her peripheral vision was horrifying.

Life-sized test tubes containing ghost white naked human beings, suspended in air. Hairless beings with tubes attached to parts of their bodies. She strained her peripheral vision, wishing desperately to see if they were watching her. To see if they were alive, or unconsciously floating in formaldehyde.

She couldn't turn her head, but she could blink. Her eyelids felt like sandpaper scraping against her dried-out eyeballs. As she blinked, her eyes began to moisten, and tears rolled down her cheek. She moved her tongue just barely to taste the salt of the tears on her lips.

Her little secret.

Of course, Angel would threaten to expose that.

She'd regretted ever telling him, ever trusting him with her secrets, and with her heart.

One night, not long after they'd met, he had said he was going to break up with her because she was too good for him, and he would ruin her life.

"You are too pure and good for me. I've broken the first commandment. I have confessed to Father Luis, but I am still going to hell."

Ana met his eyes. They shimmered with love and vulnerability. She loved this man with her entire soul.

"*Mi amore*," she began, and then exhaled loudly. "I am not pure."

It was time to share herself with him fully. She took a deep breath and began.

Ana had gone into the city with friends to go dancing.

They were in the bathroom at the nightclub. The music just outside the door was like a pulse pounding in Ana's body, caressing her, drawing her in. She loved, loved, loved to dance.

The attention from the boys was a bonus.

Leaning over the porcelain sink, she reapplied her apple red lipstick, pressing her lips together. Her best friend Margarita leaned against the spraypainted wall, taking a hit off her vape.

They met each other's eyes through the mirror. Margarita lifted a brow and held the vape out to Ana.

"Nah, I'm good." Ana would take a toke off a joint every now and then, but she was too paranoid to use a vape. The chemicals inside them had messed up too many people, at least according to her sister, Carmen. Ana pretended not to take her big sister's advice, but ninety-nine percent of the time, she actually did listen.

"You look fire, *chica*," Margarita said, admiring Ana's tight black skirt and silver lame halter top.

"You do too, girl." She turned to face her friend.

"That cute military guy wants you bad."

"Not interested."

"I'll take him then."

"All yours, girl."

"You still sad about Matt?"

Ana shrugged. "Maybe. I'm just not ready to date right now."

The truth was, when her high school boyfriend had left for college in Vermont, he'd taken a chunk of her heart with him. Although she wasn't still pining for Matt, she was also gun-shy about falling for another guy. It hurt too much when it ended.

The two young women went back to the dance floor. Margarita and the military guy hit it off and he never looked back. After a while, Margarita winked at Ana and walked off toward the exit holding the boy's hand.

"Text me," Ana mouthed.

She was always worried when Margarita went home with a guy from a club. It was dangerous.

Having an FBI agent sister meant Ana could never be careless like that. But she also couldn't stop her friend. She'd tried in the past and failed. The most she could do was ask her friend to keep her posted and track her on Life 360. At least Margarita had agreed to do that much.

Without her friend there, Ana was bored. It was late, she was yawning. She'd take a ride share to the train station and then BART back to the East Bay.

Pulling up the app on her phone, she ordered a car. When she was notified it was out front, she slipped out the front door. Checking the app, she saw the license plate on the SUV was the right one. The driver rolled down the window.

"Ana?"

"Yup."

She approached the vehicle and glanced inside. As her hand rested on the handle to get in, a tremor of apprehension rolled across her spine. She shook it off. He was an official ride share driver. That meant he'd passed certain criteria, right? And that his movements were tracked?

At least that's what she thought.

As she opened the back door and slid in, she glanced up front again. The driver kept his eyes in front of him.

"How are you tonight?" she asked as she shut the door.

He didn't answer. The door automatically locked.

Unease rolled through her and she pulled on the door handle to no avail. "Unlock the door," she said. "I've changed my mind."

The man stayed silent.

About a dozen people milled around on the sidewalk a few feet away, talking and smoking.

Ana tried to unlock the door herself, but it wouldn't budge. Child locks were activated.

She screamed. "Unlock the goddamn door right now!"

But the driver pulled into the road.

Ana began pounding on the window, screaming, hoping someone on the sidewalk would notice her. But nobody even looked her way. Her fists pounded the glass, and she was screaming at the driver.

"Let me out right now!"

"My sister is a cop."

"You'll regret this."

But he ignored everything she said.

She reached forward to punch him in the head, but he caught her wrist and twisted it.

Howling in pain, she crouched on the footwell until he released it.

"You cooperate," he said in a hoarse voice, "and I'll let you live."

She shouted a stream of expletives at him. But then as they passed under a streetlight she saw his eyes in the rearview mirror. They glowed red.

That couldn't be right. She had to be hallucinating.

He drove her to a deserted road down by the water. Leaping out of the vehicle, he opened the back door. Before she could escape, he forced her down onto the back seat.

She fought, clawing at his eyes and mouth, trying to knee him, but he was preternaturally strong and held a knife to her throat until she stopped fighting, tears streaming down her face on each side. Then she remembered. Another piece of advice she'd taken from Carmen. She reached down slowly, her hand creeping lower to her waist and inside the pocket of her skirt, where she felt her own knife. Then it was in her hand. In one fluid motion, she brought it up and stuck it in the side of his neck.

He froze as a wide arc of blood spurted out of him like a sprinkler, then he collapsed. Frantically gulping for air, she pushed the dead weight of his body off her and reached for her phone before she clawed at the door and fell out of the backseat.

She dialed 911, but her phone wasn't working.

She ran toward the top of the road, not bothering to look back at the dead man or the stalled vehicle he lay in.

When she reached the road, she punched in Carmen's number.

This time the phone worked.

"Hey baby girl, what's up?"

"I killed him, Carmen," she said, her voice shaking.

Carmen was silent for a moment. "Don't move. I'm on my way."

Carmen was there in ten minutes. Ana led her to the scene and Carmen helped her cover it up, no questions asked. Ana never asked why they didn't report it to the police. Instead, Carmen drove Ana to her apartment in the Marina District and dropped her off. But first she grabbed Ana's phone and ripped the sim card out before handing it back.

"Go inside with my code. Then grab the gun out of my nightstand, take it in the bathroom with you, take a hot bath. Don't talk to anybody until I get back."

Shivering and sobbing, Ana nodded.

Carmen never told her how she'd cleaned up her little sister's mess. Ana looked for reports about a dead body in the news, but never found any. The one time she asked about it, Carmen said, "I have no idea what you're talking about. And neither do you."

35

STELLA PARKED A FEW YARDS FROM THE FRONT GATE OF Barclay's compound. She made sure she was far enough away that surveillance cameras along the perimeter would not alert security to her presence.

She was dressed all in black: hoodie, baseball hat, military fatigue pants, and steel-toed combat boots. The deep pockets of her pants held her knife and gun.

Turning off her headlights, she crouched low in her seat and reached for her burner phone. Punching in Patrick Barclay's personal cell phone number, she exhaled loudly.

It would be risky, but Stella needed to try to turn him. Otherwise, she wouldn't be able to access the Barclay compound and rescue Ana.

"Hello?"

"Patrick, please don't hang up. It's a matter of life and death."

Such a trite, cliché phrase, but when she had seconds to convince him to hear her out, it would have to do.

He was silent for a moment before responding, "I'm so glad you called."

Stella paused, wary. She wanted to ask why, but she needed to tell him what was going on first.

"Whether or not you believe me about your father, please believe me when I tell you he's kidnapped an FBI agent and unless I cooperate, she dies."

"What?"

"I think she's in the lab at ImmortalGen. At least, that's what it looked like in the video he sent me. Her name is Ana Rodriguez. Time is of the essence, and we need to get to her—"

"I believe you," he said. "I found something after you left."

Stella didn't wait for him to continue.

"I need access to the compound now. I'm parked outside."

"Give me five minutes to call the gate and then head inside. The access code for the lab changes every night, so I'll get that to you in ten. I'll meet you there in twenty."

"Better to stay out of it. Please call this San Francisco Detective. His name is Griffin. Tell him where I am. Ask him to send backup." She reeled off Griffin's cell number and then hung up.

Glancing at the clock, she waited five minutes and then headed for the guard house.

As she turned the ignition on the stolen car, Stella wondered what Patrick had found that changed his mind. She didn't have time to worry about that. Her entire focus needed to be on rescuing Ana Rodriguez.

Stella slipped her pistol into the kangaroo pocket of her hoodie, tucked the switchblade into her boot, and pulled out onto the main road.

She didn't want to hurt anyone, but she had to protect herself if it came to that. If her name and ID were flagged and the guard drew a gun on her, she'd pull out her own. She had no plans to fire it, only to use it to keep herself out of Barclay's clutches. In other words, to keep herself on this side of the grave. If Barclay got ahold of her, she knew what her fate would be.

They'd danced around it for far too long.

Before she even pulled up to the guard house, two guards armed with pistols in their hands at waist level and AK47's hanging by straps on their shoulders stepped in front of the gate. Her headlights shone on them, but they didn't even blink. Another guard stepped out of the shack. He held his gun loosely at his side.

He took a few steps toward her, still keeping his distance. She watched his finger wrap around the trigger as he grew closer.

"Stella LaRosa," she said, keeping her right hand in her hoodie's pouch and her finger off the trigger.

He crouched down slightly, and his eyes met hers. He was still about five feet away. She held her breath. His hand was on his pistol, but it remained pointing down. He would either let her pass or he would try to take her into custody, or worse. She kept her eyes on his gun instead of his face.

Please don't make me shoot you.

"Good evening, Miss LaRosa. Mr. Barclay called ahead. You have clearance to proceed."

Tension whooshed from her body. He nodded, and the two guards stepped aside as the gate swung open.

Just then a phone rang loudly. Stella jumped in her seat but proceeded forward.

The guard half-turned back toward the shack. A guard inside stuck his head out and said something. Stella drove through the open gate, controlling the urge to stomp the accelerator.

Keeping an eye on the rearview mirror, she saw the guards step out of the shack and watch on as the gates closed behind her. One of them locked eyes with her through the rearview mirror.

As soon as she rounded a corner out of sight of the guard shack, she stepped on the gas, squealing around the curves as she raced to the main compound.

She parked crookedly in front of the main door and grabbed her old access pass. Patrick had said he would reinstate her card and give her the access code within ten minutes. It had been nine minutes since they'd spoken. When she tried her pass, it worked.

Rushing inside, she punched the elevator button. When she saw it was on the nineteenth floor, she headed for the stairwell and raced up the four floors to the skyway. Bursting out of the door, she swiped her card at the skyway entrance. The light turned green, and she pulled open the door wide enough to squeeze through and raced through the skyway, glancing down at the ground below to see if anyone had followed her. No one had.

Slowing as she approached the entrance to the lab, she swiped her card and gaining access to the main hallway. The lab was at the other end. That's where she would have to enter the access code. But Patrick hadn't texted it yet.

Pausing to catch her breath, she glanced at her phone again. Still nothing.

Someone else had called the guards as she'd headed inside the compound. She knew someone was after her. She hoped Patrick would hurry.

It was best to assume that Carter Barclay had been alerted to her presence and he would try to stop her. Time was of the essence. The sooner she got in and out with Ana, the better. Her phone screen remained blank.

It had been eleven minutes.

36

SITTING IN THE BLUE-LIT ROOM, STRAPPED INTO A wheelchair, Ana realized she didn't care about anything except making Carter Barclay pay for what he had done to these people hanging in the ether in this nightmarish room.

The ability to move was slowly coming back. Her fingers could bend, and she was finally able to turn her head. Craning her neck, she gained clearer views of the several life-sized test tubes suspended around her. She couldn't see behind her, though. There may be even more.

Then the door opened, and the bright light of the hall momentarily blinded her. Three dark silhouettes entered. Angel was not among them. She would recognize his gait anywhere. Two men came forward. One stood back, his figure illuminated by the light of the hallway behind him.

Carter Barclay.

"You bastard!" she said. Her words came out slurred and garbled, but she was pretty sure he got the gist of them.

Thank God her voice was back.

He laughed. "I've been called much worse than that honey. That the best you got?"

"Don't you call me honey, you *pendejo*!" Again, the words jumbled together in a strange drunken-sounding sequence.

"We're just sending proof of life," Barclay said. "Smile pretty."

The brightness of a flash momentarily blinded her. She blinked until the dark spots had vanished from her vision.

Then all three men stood there silently. She could tell Barclay had his head bowed over something in his hands. She saw the screen light up. It was a cell phone.

"Your new bestie Stella LaRosa wants a video. She is smart, but not smarter than me. She, like you, will die tonight. But first she's going to give me the files that she has."

Ana swore at him. This time the words came out crystal clear. Good.

Barclay chuckled. "You are a fiery one. Like your dear dead sister, right?"

Ana growled and fought wildly against her restraints. Her legs and arms were numb and tingly as if they had fallen asleep, but she could move them.

That meant she had a chance to escape.

Barclay stepped closer. "You're going to say what I want you to say and maybe in return I'll give you a little sip of water. I bet you're wildly thirsty right about now."

Saliva filled Ana's mouth. She would kill for a glass of water. But not for the price of doing what this monster wanted.

"Beg her to do as I ask, saying otherwise I'm going to kill you."

Ana glared at him. He ignored it.

"Lights, camera, action." Barclay pressed a button on the phone and said, "It's 9 p.m."

A boot nudged Ana. She looked directly into the camera and said, "Stella, don't do a thing they say."

A few seconds later, the man closest to her leaned over and punched her in the side of the head. A flash of pain coursed through her skull as it jerked away from her neck. She wanted to scream, but she bit her lip to prevent herself from crying out. Her ears were ringing, and her vision went blurry for a few seconds.

"Next time you don't do exactly as I say he cuts off a finger."

Ana glared at the dark silhouette in the doorway. "There's not going to be a next time."

He surprised her by chuckling. "We can definitely arrange that."

"You'll have to kill me before I do anything you want."

"I see you mean that."

"I do. I'm not afraid to die."

"Good to know," the man said. "We can shift direction then. If you aren't afraid to die, you most certainly don't want to lose your beloved job, do you?"

Ana's heart clenched. Angel had squealed. Of course he had.

This man had seen into her soul. She wasn't afraid of death, but she was afraid of dishonor. She was horrified at the thought that she would tarnish her family's name, the legacy she carried on for them. That what she had done so long ago in darkness would be brought to light.

This man. He knew that.

As if he could read her mind, Barclay said, "Yes. He told us. Everything."

"What do you want from me?" she said through gritted teeth.

"I think we might be able to arrange something where your past stays buried," he said, stepping in closer. She could almost distinguish his features in the bluish light.

"I don't believe you."

"How bad do you want your secret kept?"

"Screw you!"

Smirking, he leaned forward, and plunged a knife into the center of her hand. She howled as it twisted, causing excruciating pain and blood oozed out.

"That's what's going to happen every time you are disrespectful. I've had a lifetime of disrespect from women. I no longer tolerate it."

"Are you an incel?"

He stared at her wide eyed and then sliced into her forearm. This time she didn't cry out, only winced.

"You will speak when spoken to. If your own pain isn't a concern, then maybe we can torture that journalist in front of you. You two seemed very cozy at the cemetery."

Ana hid her emotions, keeping a blank expression. How long had they been watching her? And how had she failed to know about it? Instead of responding to his words, she shrugged. The last thing she wanted him to know was that she was concerned about Stella LaRosa. It would be another weapon in his arsenal. Ana wasn't stupid. She knew that she was the bait, not the reporter. She had nothing worthwhile for him except her life. He had kidnapped her to lure Stella LaRosa into his lair.

Barclay turned to one of the men beside him. "I think we need a more sophisticated form of torture besides the Russian mob style of breaking bones and chopping off body parts. I think this woman is more worried about her brain than her body. We don't have time to experiment. Hook her up to the lie-detector."

Ana burst into laughter. "You think that works?"

He stared at her with his cold, hollow eyes. "The one I have does."

A man in a white coat stepped forward from the shadows with something Stella had never seen before. A skull cap with wires and lights.

She fought him placing it on her head, whipping her head from side to side and spitting on him until another man came forward and grabbed her skull by the back, his fingers digging into her hair, holding her head immobile.

"Put it on now," the man behind her said.

The cap went on and a chin strap was pulled tight, restricting oxygen to her throat. Then the men used trailing wires to stick electrodes near her carotid artery, elbows, and wrists. A second later, Ana felt a prick in the side of her neck. Bastards.

Then the men withdrew.

"Let's give the serum a few minutes to work. It's barbiturate sodium pentothal—used by the CIA overseas. I doubt you locals in the FBI will know about it. It's a little bit controversial. It will keep your mind crystal clear but also impel you to spout the truth."

“Whatever,” she said.

He paused and glared. “That’s bordering on disrespect, Agent Rodriguez.”

She kept a neutral expression.

“While it’s kicking in, allow me to tell you about the device on your head,” Barclay said. “The beauty of this machine is it’s from the Department of Defense. You lie, you get shocked. It’s much like the electroshock therapy of the fifties. We will just shock parts of your brain, and you will have convulsions, seizures, memory loss, and even in some cases, broken limbs or dislocated bones.” His wide smile was demonic in the blue light, his gums purple.

Terror zipped through Ana. The memory loss was her biggest concern. She could handle pain. But anything that affected her brain function was not okay.

She’d cooperate and tell the truth unless it was something crucial. She’d save her resistance for the important items.

The door behind him opened, and a man wheeled in a cart with a monitor on top of it. It appeared to show Ana’s vitals, plus some other aspects she couldn’t identify.

“First question will be easy.”

She glared at him.

“Did LaRosa give you the files she stole from me?”

“No.”

Nothing happened.

“Good girl.”

“Don’t call me that, old man,” she spat out.

He chuckled. “Next question. Also, an easy one. Why did you fly out here?”

“To investigate the deaths of two of your employees in the hopes of nailing you for good this time.”

“I like your spirit,” he said.

“My spirit hates you.”

He glanced at the monitor. “Your honesty and bluntness are refreshing.”

"I have nothing to hide from you," she said. "Especially my hatred."

"Any chance you'd come over to the dark side?"

He glanced at the monitor.

"Is that an official question?"

"Sure, why not."

"I'd come over to the dark side..."

He lifted an eyebrow and glanced at the monitor. "Be careful now. You're about to lose muscle memory and gross motor skills. You do like to walk, don't you?"

Ignoring him, she continued. "I'd come over to the dark side long enough to get close to you and stab a knife through your heart."

He burst into laughter this time. The monitor stayed silent. "Another truthful answer. I like that. A stake through the heart like Dracula?"

"I said a knife, but a stake would work. I'm starting to think that's the only way to take you down."

The monitor beeped.

"Lie," he said. "You must think there's another way."

"Correct," she said. "Plus, you know those things aren't reliable anyway."

He ignored her comment.

"What files does Stella have anyway?" she said. "Must be something good to freak you out like this." Barclay's expression dropped. She had him. "You're right, Stella is smart. Even if she turned the files over to you, you know she's given someone else a copy. And you'd have to work to track them down too." She paused for a moment, her eyes narrowing at the man. "You are going down regardless."

Ana made one last ditch effort to save the reporter's life. Even though they would both most likely die at Barclay's hands.

"You are too smart for your own good," he said with a smirk. "I didn't want you to know that Stella will die regardless, but you already did, didn't you? The same as you know that you will also die. Regardless."

"Like I said, I'm not afraid to die." Then she gave a slow smile. "And neither is Stella LaRosa."

Barclay's face contorted in the blue light, making him look sinister.

"Kill her if she tries to escape," he said to the two gunmen in the corner and stormed out of the room.

37

THE HALLWAY TO THE LABORATORY WAS DARK, LIT ONLY BY A few small, dim white lights along the floor, placed every ten feet. It was meant to be dark and covert, Stella realized.

Stella's phone lit up the black hallway.

The access code. Finally.

She was about to punch it in when she heard a voice.

Dipping into an alcove, she froze, heart pounding as the laboratory door opened. Her hand snaked into her hoodie pouch. She wrapped her palm around the gun, her finger resting on the trigger. She pressed her back against the wall. The doorway was deep, at least two feet from the actual hallway. But that wouldn't matter if the men emerging from the lab looked to the side or went to enter the room behind her.

Two men passed by. Her heart raced as she recognized Carter Barclay. They paused just out of her line of sight.

"What do you want me to do?" one of the men asked. His voice was familiar.

"As soon as we get eyes on LaRosa," he said, "kill her."

"Gladly."

"Why do you want the woman you love dead so badly?" Barclay asked.

"There is a thin line between love and hate, my friend," the man said.

Carter Barclay chuckled.

Stella felt her hands clench into fists. Her body was tense, ready to spring.

"If you handle this right, I think I might keep you on for other projects."

"It would be my honor," the man said and then walked past Stella's hiding place again, making her shrink even deeper into the shadows.

Bluish light emerged as the other man opened the door to the lab again. Stella held her breath, listening as the door to the lab clicked closed. She strained to hear whether Barclay had walked away. She could hear nothing. Did he know she was there? Was he taunting her?

The sound of him clearing his throat nearby startled her so much she slightly jumped.

The gun was now out of her pouch and aiming toward the open hallway.

Then she heard footsteps retreating. A few seconds later, a door clicked open and closed.

Creeping out of the alcove, with her gun leading the way, Stella glanced down the dark hallway in the direction Barclay had gone. The space glowed red from the emergency exit light. It was enough for Stella to see the hallway was empty.

Quickly, she tapped the keypad, entering the access code. The light turned green. She had seconds to enter the room. She slipped into the laboratory like a shadow blending into the deep blue glow that bathed the room. Tense and alert, she waited for an attack, but it was silent and dark, save the hum and eerie glow of medical research machines droning around her. Her eyes narrowed as she scanned the space. Giant glass tubes lined the walls, each one filled with a floating, naked, unconscious body. Pale ghosts suspended in time.

At the center of the room, bound tightly to a wheelchair, was Ana —her face pale, eyes wide with terror as she caught sight of Stella. Several gunmen stood behind Ana, their expressions in the dim light a mix of boredom and vigilance. Then one of them spotted Stella. He raised his weapon, but she was already moving, charging toward them.

The others followed the first gunman, closing in. She ducked low and dodged left while still racing toward them. As soon as she was close to the man leading the charge, she swung out her leg and swept him to the ground, catching his wrist and twisting until he cried out, his gun falling from his grip. She slammed his face into the floor. Hard.

She spun around, rising in time to meet the second attacker.

Reaching down, she slipped her knife out of her boot, slicing through the air as she prepared for his attack. He managed to squeeze off a round that grazed her shoulder, but not before Stella spun and lunged toward him, driving her knife into his knee. He screamed and fell to the floor.

Before she could finish him off, the butt of a gun came out of nowhere and slammed into her eye. She howled in pain. Before she could react, there was another blow—this one to her lip—the stinging was accompanied by a metallic taste.

Stella wiped the blood off her mouth with the back of her hand and launched herself. She twisted and aimed her boot toward his ribs. He grunted in pain. While he was bent over, she slammed her palm down on his wrist. He dropped the gun, and it went skidding across the floor out of his reach.

Within seconds, another gunman raised his pistol with a shout and squeezed the trigger, but Stella spun the first man's body and put it between her and the gunman. His body jumped as bullets hit it. Continuing to use it as a shield, she moved toward the gunshots swiftly until she was close enough to wrench the gun out of the man's hand with a sharp twist.

The movement sent him reeling forward, and he staggered, just in time for his face to meet Stella's knee. She followed with a series of uppercuts, striking him hard in the gut. He raised his forearm in defense and landed a jab in her abdomen. It sent her reeling, gasping for air.

For a second, neither one moved—then Stella lunged forward in one fluid motion, her leg extended in a powerful spinning back kick aimed at his ankles. After connecting her heel to his leg with a solid crack, she stepped back and reset. Then, while he was still off balance, she sprang with her other leg in a roundhouse kick that swept his legs out from under him. He hit the ground hard, his head landing with a loud crack, and didn't get up.

She was already racing for Ana.

"Stella!" Ana's voice was a breathless mix of relief and urgency. "Barclay is coming back."

"Let's get you free first," Stella said, her fingers working quickly at the straps that bound Ana's arms and legs. "Can you stand?"

Stella kept her eyes trained on the door and turned back to Ana. "Is there another entrance?"

The other woman shook her head. "I don't know."

Stella gripped the knife in her hand and cut the ties on Ana's ankles and wrists, pulling her up from the chair. Ana turned, her eyes darting at the suspended glass tubes.

"Was this what you were trying to stop?" she asked.

Stella nodded.

"They'll kill both of us. Without question."

"We're not letting that happen." Stella glanced over her shoulder. The sound of footsteps echoed from down the hall. Reinforcements.

As Ana struggled to her feet, Stella turned back to the door, adrenaline pounding through her bloodstream. Her gaze swept over the lab and settled on a rack of large glass vials.

"Stay behind me," she whispered to Ana.

With Ana on her heels, the two women raced toward the door.

As they neared the exit, Stella could almost feel the eyes of the cloned bodies floating in their liquid prisons. She still needed to come back and save them. But she had to get Ana safe first.

With one last swift kick, she kicked open the laboratory door.

She drew up short.

The hallway outside was eerily black. The bluish light from the lab seeped into the hallway, creating a small rectangle on the floor. As that door closed with a whoosh behind them, Stella reached for the walls with one hand to guide her toward the skyway.

Within seconds, they burst through and were met by more darkness.

Stella drew up short and pressed her body against the wall. Ana mimicked her, staying close.

It took a few seconds for her eyes to adjust and all she saw through the glass skyway walls was more shades of dark. All the lights in the compound had gone out.

The entire complex was enveloped in black.

The lab clearly had a back-up generator or else the power outage was orchestrated, so only other areas outside the lab were without power. If the power was out, she wondered if the keycards would still work, allowing her to open the door on the other end of the skyway and escape to the ground floor.

It was time to find out.

"Let's go," she whispered.

With Ana on her heels, she ran through the skyway, only able to distinguish the walls because they were a slightly lighter gray. At the other end, she lifted her keycard and groped for the entry pad. It shone green and there was a small click. She pushed through the door and toward the elevator bank, but at the last minute, headed to the stairs.

Pushing open the door, she reached behind her and Ana squeezed her hand. Holding onto the rail, the two women ran down the four flights of stairs. At the bottom, Ana pushed hard on the door's bar, and they burst into the night.

As they stepped outside, they were startled when a blinding spotlight shone on them and someone yelled through a megaphone for them to put their hands up.

They did.

Stella could tell the light was coming from three places. Two headlights and then a spotlight perched on the back of a pickup truck.

Squinting, she tried to make out how many people were near the truck. Maybe two.

Ana was right behind her, still against the door.

"We're going to send someone over to frisk you," a southern voice drawled. "Don't make any funny moves. We got a sharpshooter on you."

"If they capture us, we're dead," Ana whispered.

Stella gave the slightest nod.

"Is the door behind you closed all the way?" Ana asked, her voice barely an audible level.

"Nope. My heel is keeping it propped. On three, we back in and run."

"One. Two. Three."

Without turning around, both women rushed backward into the doorway and then slammed it shut. They heard shouting.

"Can we barricade it?"

"No." Stella yelled. "We have to run."

Racing back up the stairs, they'd made it to the third floor when someone burst through the ground floor door, followed by shouting and footsteps.

"Here."

Stella opened the third-floor door and waited for Ana to slip inside before she silently shut it. They were in the hallway with elevators. A red exit sign cast an eerie glow.

Stella had a keycard that would give her access to the penthouse. It was their only chance. It was unlikely the guards could follow them without their own keycard.

She punched the elevator and shifted anxiously, waiting for it to arrive.

The door opened and they stepped inside. The lights were on in the elevator. Stella pressed her keycard to the keypad and hit the button for the penthouse. It lit up green, and the elevator started to rise.

Both women stared at each other, wide-eyed.

This was it.

38

PATRICK BARCLAY HADN'T EXPECTED TO FIND HIS FATHER waiting for him in the penthouse office when he arrived at the compound.

Carter was sitting in the dark in the leather chair behind his desk. Patrick flipped on the lights and jumped and swore loudly when he saw his father.

"A bit early for work, isn't it, son?" Carter's ice blue eyes glittered dangerously. "Were you looking for me in my office?"

Patrick had planned on rummaging through his father's desk and files to see if he could gather proof of the cloning operation. He had decided taking it to the police was the right thing to do.

Theo was waiting for him in the car.

"I heard we were having some security issues again, so I headed straight over."

The other man smirked. "And you thought you could help by coming into my office?"

"I wanted to make sure nothing was disturbed up here."

His father reached out and tapped on his computer mouse.

"The only security issue I'm concerned about right now is you accessing some information that really isn't part of your job description."

Patrick swallowed. "Isn't it my job to know everything we do here?"

"Son, don't make me do it."

Patrick felt a zing of alarm.

"Do what, Dad?"

"You choose," he replied. "Me or her."

He shook his head. "Who?"

"Stella LaRosa."

His father reached over and turned the large computer monitor until it faced Patrick.

It showed camera footage of Stella and another woman racing through a hallway.

Patrick realized the time to feign innocence was past.

"It's not a choice," Patrick said and straightened his shoulders. "It's about right and wrong."

"I see your mind is made up." Carter's voice was filled with sorrow. "I had hoped for you to carry my legacy. To be the one who continued our family name."

"I'm gay, Dad. How am I going to continue our family name the way you want?"

"I was going to have you impregnate a woman, you imbecile."

Patrick ignored the name calling. He had to stay calm, cool, and collected to get out of this situation. And to keep Stella safe.

"It doesn't have to be like this. You can abandon this line of research," Patrick said carefully. "Nobody will be the wiser. We can carry on doing the highest-level stem-cell research that is critical to the future of mankind."

"It's not like that, son," Carter said. "Anyone can do that type of research. I'm going deeper. What you don't seem to understand is that I'm going to become God. I'm going to make man immortal."Patrick tried to hide the horror threatening to show in his expression. "It can be done a different way. Secretly cloning people and keeping them in a comatose state is treating them as subhuman."

"This is the way!" his father said, slamming his hand on the desk. "I've studied this for years. I have the best of the best working for me."

"I can no longer have anything to do with you if you continue this line of research."

A strange surge of exhilaration rushed through Patrick for standing up to his powerful father.

Carter stared at him for a few long seconds. He stood up from the desk and let out a lifeless chuckle. "What you don't realize, son, is that I can clone you, too." He paused and looked directly into Patrick's eyes. "In fact, I already have."

His words hung in the sudden silence.

Patrick internally winced but kept his expression neutral. "Why would you do that? I don't even think you like me."

"That sample you gave me when you began? I've used it to clone you and will mate the specimen with a woman, and then I will get my grandchild, my legacy."

"You're insane," Patrick said, his voice wobbly. Tears threatened to spill from his eyes. A scream was lurking somewhere inside of him, but he kept that tucked away. Rage boiled beneath the surface.

Some father he had. No wonder his mother kept the secret until her death.

"Whatever," his father said and waved a dismissive hand. "They thought Galileo, Charles Darwin, Anton Johannson, and Nikola Tesla were all insane. People who change the history of the world are often misunderstood and labeled. History proves they were geniuses."

Patrick watched the monitor as Stella and the other woman stepped into an elevator. It closed and the changing number above the door began to increase. Were they heading for the penthouse? He was banking on his father keeping the monitor facing him so he wouldn't know of the women's arrival.

Maybe Patrick would have time to distract his father.

"Okay, fine, you're a genius," he said in a weary voice. "Just let Stella go,"

Carter tapped his chin in mock thought, and then shook his head. "Not possible."

The elevator bell dinged in the outside room.

Stella and the other woman.

Patrick kept his eyes glued on his father as he heard footsteps and then the door opened.

"Patrick?"

No! It was Theo.

Patrick whirled to see his partner standing there and watched in horror as Theo threw up his hands. His breaths were coming short and shallow, eyes widening. "Don't shoot," he said.

Turning back around, he saw that his father had a gun pointed at Theo.

"Over here, boy."

"No!"

Patrick's voice came out as a screech. Every inch of his body was shaking. He was worried he was going to pass out from the fear. "Let him go! He has nothing to do with it. I'll do anything you say. Just let him go."

Carter released the safety. "Get over here, boy, or I'll shoot you right now. See this thing here? It's called a silencer. I'll kill you both and be gone before anyone is the wiser. And then we will blame it on Stella LaRosa."

Theo walked over to Carter.

They all froze as the elevator bell dinged again.

39

STELLA STEPPED OUT OF THE ELEVATOR HOLDING HER switchblade and drew back in horror.

Ana was right behind her, keeping a few feet back.

The penthouse office was dimly lit from an antique, green-shaded lamp on a large Mahogany desk.

Carter Barclay stood in front of the light with a gun to a man's head.

Stella had only seen the man in photos on her boss's desk. It was Theo, Patrick's partner. One of Barclay's hands wrapped tightly around the man's shoulder, the other held the gun.

Patrick was a few feet away, his face ashen, eyes darting toward Stella and Ana.

"Let him go, Barclay!" Stella pointed the knife in front of her. "I'm damn good at knife throwing."

"Drop the knife," Barclay replied, "or he's a dead man."

Stella threw her hands up. As soon as she did, Carter Barclay smiled and aimed the gun at her.

"That was your first and last mistake."

Before Stella could react, the FBI agent sprang forward. She had grabbed Stella's gun out of her waistband and had it pointing at Barclay.

"FBI!" Ana screamed. "Put your weapon down!"

Immediately, Carter pointed the gun back at the blond man.

"Dad, please," Patrick said, his tone begging. "Let him go. I'll do whatever you want. I promise."

"No, son, you have already broken my trust and my heart. That ship has sailed."

"In case you're unclear about what's going on here," Ana said, "I have reinforcements on their way. You may control this town, or this state, but you don't control this country."

Then Barclay cocked his head. They all heard it at the same time.

A helicopter.

Ana smirked.

"You're not a very good liar, Ms. Rodriguez." Carter Barclay smiled. "That helicopter is for me. Your sister was a much better agent than you."

He was trying to provoke her. Stella watched the emotion roll over Ana's face, but when she spoke again, her words were ice. "This is your last chance to release him."

"Here's what's going to happen," he said. "I'm going to walk backward to the door to the roof. None of you will move and once the helicopter leaves with me and my son's gay lover, you will go on with your pathetic little lives. If you try to stop me, this one"—he nudged Theo's head with the gun—"dies."

Stella stepped forward. "Let him go and we won't try to stop you."

"I'm coming with you," Patrick said and walked slowly toward his father with his hands up in the air. "You need me, Dad. Let Theo go. We can spin this. Let's just leave before anyone gets hurt. We can figure this out."

Barclay's forehead wrinkled and his eyebrows knit together. Then his lips parted, and a dangerous smirk appeared.

"Okay, son. You go first. Go up to the roof. I'll meet you there."

Patrick opened the door. A staircase was behind it.

"Don't do it, Patrick!" Stella said.

He was standing behind his father now, and he winked at her. She closed her eyes. He was going to get himself and his partner killed.

Before she could do or say anything else, Patrick disappeared up the staircase.

Barclay took a few steps back and backed into the doorway keeping Theo in front of him as a shield. The door slammed shut.

Ana and Stella ran for the door.

Before they could open it, the sound of a gunshot filled the air.

Stella wrenched the door open.

Theo was slumped at the foot of the stairs. Blood pooled around him. He'd been shot in the abdomen.

Patrick's screams sounded above them, and a door slammed shut.

40

"GO AFTER HIM!" ANA SCREAMED AND THRUST THE GUN AT Stella. "I've got Theo."

As Stella disappeared up the stairs, Ana leaned over and lifted Theo's shirt. He was bleeding profusely. The bullet appeared to have gone into his side and exited the back.

"How bad is it?" Theo asked through labored breaths.

"It could be worse. Let's get you downstairs."

Ana ripped off her sweatshirt and used the sleeves to create a large bandage around Theo's torso, pulling the knot tight. Then she took out her phone and called 911.

"There's been a shooting at ImmortalGen. We need emergency workers asap."

She turned to Theo.

"Can you stand?"

He nodded and said, "I need to get Patrick."

"No time for that. Stella will help him."

"He's going to kill them both."

Ana shook her head. "Don't worry about her."

As she helped him up, he tilted for a second, reaching for her arm, but then steadied himself.

"Sorry. I feel a little woozy."

"Normal. Let's get you downstairs. An ambulance is on its way. Probably a few stitches and you'll be good."

Her voice was firm, but she was still worried. Her job was to get him to a hospital ASAP.

They had just made it out of the penthouse when the elevator door whooshed open in front of them.

Ana stepped back, her breath catching in her chest.

Angel was alone. He stepped out of the elevator, his expression unreadable, and began to reach behind him. She knew he was going for a gun.

Letting go of Theo, Ana gave a banshee type yell and charged.

She had trained for this day for years. Every punch she gave the bag. Every kick she gave her opponent. Every jab, cross, hook, uppercut; every knee strike; every spinning hook kick—through all of them, she had imagined Angel's face receiving the blow

It was as if she was acting out a role she had studied for years.

The elevator beside her opened and she shouted to Theo.

"Meet me downstairs," she said.

Leaping into the elevator with Angel, she punched the first floor, staring defiantly at him.

He gave her a slow smile.

"Your coffin," he said.

Ana inhaled sharply as the elevator doors closed, sealing her inside the mirrored box with Angel. Looming over her, a sneer twisting his mouth, she could see his confidence and knew that would be his downfall.

He moved first, lunging with a wild swing.

Ana pivoted, letting his fist cut through empty space. Her left leg snapped up in a roundhouse kick right into his ribs. Angel staggered, hissing with pain.

"Is that all you got?" he said, but his hand instinctively went to his side where she had landed her blow.

She answered with a smirk, raising her fists to her face, her elbows tight at her side.

He charged again, and she sidestepped his blow, grabbing his wrist and yanking him off balance. As he stumbled forward, she drove her knee into his solar plexus.

Air exploded from his lungs in a strangled gasp.

He doubled over. Slipping behind him, Ana wrenched his shoulder, driving him back until he hit the wall of the elevator. Her fists came up and her right one connected with his jaw, a quick jab that snapped his head to the side. She followed it with a right hook that smashed into his cheekbone. He reeled back and his reflexes were sluggish: his fist came up and then fell back down to his side.

Before he could recover, Ana struck with a side kick to his knee, which buckled inward. He howled and dropped, catching himself on one knee, dazed. His eyes filled with desperation, the rage dissipating into confusion.

She wasn't his punching bag anymore.

Ana finished him with a sharp back kick to his chest, knocking him onto the floor. He landed with a painful grunt, clutching his ribs and glaring up at her.

Standing over him, she gave a slow smile. "Not your little bitch anymore, am I?"

He chuckled softly, his gums lined with blood. "You're always my bitch."

Her boot came down hard on his fingers. She heard the crunch of bones breaking beneath his howl of pain.

"You're lucky I don't stomp your head in," she said. "But I'd rather see you back in prison, rotting for the rest of your life."

He spit, a bloody mess that dribbled down his cheek.

"If you ever threaten me again, I will kill you," she said. "Consider this your one and only warning."

The elevator doors slid open to reveal the lobby, and Ana stepped over him, leaving him sprawled on the polished tiles.

Theo was leaning against the wall, panting. Blood was staining the sweatshirt wrapped around his waist. He jutted his chin at Ana. "What was that?"

"My ex."

41

Stella took the stairs to the roof two at a time.

Leading with her gun, she burst through the door.

There was no helicopter on the landing pad ringed by green lights.

Instead, Barclay stood in the center of the pad with his gun jabbed into Patrick's side. Both men faced her.

For a second, his words were drowned out by the distinctive siren of an ambulance on the ground below. The sound grew closer before it stopped. She also heard the squealing of tires on the pavement and shouting. Good. Theo would get treated.

The thudding of an approaching helicopter filled the air.

"Go away, Stella LaRosa," Barclay said. "I've grown weary of you and the nuisance you've been in my life."

"I'm not going anywhere until you let Patrick go."

"Go on, Stella," Patrick said, his eyes filled with sorrow. "I'm going with my Dad."

"Actually, son, you're not going anywhere." He raised the gun to his son's temple. "You have disappointed me."

He locked eyes with Stella's. "Dare me?"

For a long moment, their gazes remained locked—Carter's laced with fury and something darker, and Stella's filled with an unbreakable resolve.

Stella took a steady step forward. "I'm not here for a showdown, Carter. Let your son go. I'll come with you."

Carter smirked, pressing the barrel harder against Patrick's temple.

"Bold words, but you're out of your league. You think I'll get out of here alive if I hand him over to you?"

"I think that there is zero chance of you getting out of here alive if you touch a hair on his head," Stella said coolly as she edged closer.

Barclay's face hardened, but Stella could see a flash of something—hesitation, maybe even regret.

She capitalized on it.

"Lower the gun," she said, her own gun steady in her hands. "You're only destroying the one person who still believes you have a soul worth saving."

Something flashed across Barclay's face, and his grip on the gun loosened.

Stella seized the moment. "Patrick, drop to the ground!"

In the instant Barclay flinched, she fired.

Her shot was fast and precise, hitting his shoulder with a crack that echoed through the night.

Barclay staggered back, his face twisted in pain, but he kept his grip on Patrick and even as he fought to regain his balance, he lifted the gun toward Patrick again.

But Patrick had turned and leaped onto his father.

"You shot my husband, you monster!" Patrick screamed as he threw a punch at his father that landed in the man's side.

Instead of recoiling, Barclay lunged toward his son and pressed the gun hard into Patrick's stomach.

Before he could squeeze the trigger, Stella fired again. The bullet whizzed over Patrick's shoulder and into Carter Barclay's forehead.

Patrick sidestepped his father's falling body and ran for the stairwell.

"Theo!" he shouted as he disappeared.

Stella slowly walked over to Barclay. She was wary, circling him before leaning down and pressing her fingers to his neck to feel for a pulse.

There was none.

His ice blue eyes stared straight up into the endless night sky, seeing nothing.

Stella straightened and stared into the dark. Standing over the lifeless body of her mortal enemy. No matter how hard she searched herself to feel something, anything—rage, relief, sorrow, joy—she felt nothing. Absolutely nothing.

Then the helicopter was directly above her, the thudding of its rotors vibrating throughout her limbs, its fierce winds lashing at her body, bringing sensation where there had been none. Blinded by the hair whipping around her face, she turned her back on the body beneath her and walked away.

42

Standing in Patrick Barclay's office, Stella looked out the window at the scene below.

Several black sedans were parked helter skelter. Feds?

Only two marked squad cars were off to one side.

Three ambulances were pulled up close to the building.

She could see Theo, Patrick, and Ana in the back of one of them. Theo was on the stretcher, Ana and Patrick sitting on each side of him as EMT's worked on him.

She watched as they helped Theo sit up.

He would be okay.

Heading for the elevators, Stella decided she would make a brief appearance and try to slip away before they found Barclay's body. She would admit to it, but didn't trust the Houston police.

Carter Barclay had everyone on his payroll.

Stepping out of the building into the night lit up with red and blue lights, she nearly ran into Ana who was standing near the entrance speaking on a cell phone. She noticed Stella and held up her finger.

Stella saw the ambulance door close with Patrick and Theo inside.

Ana followed Stella's gaze and held her hand up to her phone. "He's going to be okay. They think the bullet went in and out through flesh only, but they are going to take him in to make sure."

Stella smiled with relief.

"Hey, Griffin, I got Stella here." Ana thrust the phone at Stella and stepped a few feet away.

Stella took a deep breath. "Hey," she said warily.

"Guess you're not going to make the ceremony in the morning. I'm sure Mazzy will understand."

"Damn it." Stella looked around. Everybody was busy. Nobody was watching her. "I've got an idea. Do me a favor, and I'll pay you back. Book me the next flight out of Houston. I don't want to be questioned here right now."

"Questioned?

"Barclay. He's dead."

"Jesus, Stella."

"He was going to kill Patrick."

Ana's eyes grew wide.

Stella shook her head.

"You shot him? Dead?" Griffin said. "I can't believe the local authorities have even let you out of their sight."

"I don't think they've found his body yet."

"They will in a minute."

"That's why I have to leave. Now."

"Nobody is going to be able to leave. Active crime scene."

Ana chimed in, clearly catching the tone of the conversation. "I'll tell the other agents from San Francisco to let her pass."

"Are they all here?" Stella asked.

"They came after Griffin told them I was kidnapped."

"You'll get in trouble by letting me leave."

"I'm not worried," Ana said. "Let's get you out of here."

"Ana is paving the way for my getaway," Stella said into the phone. "Text me my flight info."

She hung up when she saw an EMT walking toward her.

The stolen car was around the corner. She could cut through the building to get to it.

"I'm out of here," Stella said to Ana and ran back inside, using her key card to access the building.

Once inside, she was in the clear. As far as she knew, none of the police or federal agents or emergency workers had key cards. She raced through the first floor and flung herself out the back door where the car was parked. She'd have to drive past all the emergency vehicles to leave, but she might get away with it. Especially if Ana held up her end.

They hadn't even put up crime scene tape yet. The good news was, they apparently weren't actively searching for suspects.

Stella was the suspect. But they didn't know that yet.

Rounding the corner of the building, she took some deep breaths as she slowly drove past the vehicles with strobing blue and red lights, keeping her gaze straight ahead.

A uniformed officer spotted her car and started to move toward her to block her way, but a man in a suit—clearly FBI—touched the cop's sleeve and said something. The cop stopped and scowled at Stella as she drove past.

It wasn't until she drove out past the abandoned gate house that she breathed a sigh of relief.

As soon as she was on the main road, she floored it. She needed to make that red eye flight to San Francisco.

* * *

Stella ignored the stares of the passengers as she hunched over her laptop at the airport bar, punching the keyboard. Finally, the feeling of being watched was gone. She'd never figured out why she had felt that way, but it must have had to do with Carter Barclay. Maybe she had a sixth sense about him keeping tabs on her all this time? Either way, she could see who was watching her now: Every person she walked past or encountered. They were all staring at her prizefighter face.

Her left eye was an angry purple and blue shade and was completely swollen shut. She debated pulling on her dark sunglasses just so people would stop staring, but didn't want to pause from her writing to root around in her bag for them. There may or may not still be blood spattered on her. She wasn't sure. She had run her hands under the sink in the airport bathroom and slicked back her hair. When she'd run her hands back under the warm water, the sink had turned pink with blood.

Her lip was swollen and cut, giving her a strange lopsided appearance if she tried to smile. Which she only did once when the bartender made a crack about her being a boxer in town for the MMA tournament. It wasn't a genuine smile, and it hurt like hell to even attempt it.

Garcia needed the story thirty minutes ago.

She'd called him on the drive to the airport and he said the best way to protect herself was to get the true, full story in print ASAP.

Head bowed over her laptop; she wrote like the wind.

Her flight was scheduled to leave in thirty minutes, which meant boarding could happen at any time. She was told the flight wouldn't have Wi-Fi, so she needed to file her story before she boarded.

Finally, after writing furiously, she realized she had told the entire story. She had begun with the email from Maria Perez and ended with Barclay's death.

It was a rather odd story for a journalist to write. She had been trained to write objectively, telling a story that she was observing. But for this one, Garcia had told her to write from first person, telling the story through her eyes, what she had seen and done.

It felt wrong. It was not traditional by her field's standards. But after giving her first draft a quick read, Stella realized there really was no other way to tell it.

She had only done this once or twice before in her career.

Garcia and she had also discussed the importance of publishing the photos from the lab that Maria Perez had given her. He wasn't sure who the photo credits would belong to.

Stella argued she had seen the lab and oversized test tubes with the bodies in them herself, so she could vouch for their authenticity.

Just then, the final boarding announcement was made. Stella called Garcia as she frantically packed up her things, realizing she hadn't even heard the first call for boarding.

"Sending you the story now! What's the call on the photos?"

"Let's just get the story online without photos and then figure it out for the print edition," he said. "I'm having a Zoom call with the publisher and the president of the hedge fund about publishing the photos."

"Gross," Stella said, shoving her laptop into her bag. "When does the president get involved? What happened to free and independent journalism?"

"Preaching to the choir, Collins."

Stella pushed down the frustration and tried to keep her voice calm as she slung her bag over her shoulder. "You know what they're going to say. Kill the photos."

"Um, yeah." He sounded distracted.

"What's their concern? We need to be prepared to argue our case. The pics are legit. I saw the lab. I was there," Stella said as she half-ran through the crowded aisle toward her gate.

"Their concern is…" he paused. "They say it's an extremely disturbing photo. At the very least, we need to put a warning that it might upset some readers. They are saying that Aunt Ethel over in Walnut Creek isn't going to want to unfold the morning paper tomorrow and choke on her Grape Nuts when she sees the photo."

Stella scowled. Damn it. Garcia was right. But still, it was important to print the photos so people could see just how horrific Carter Barclay's operation truly had been.

As she approached her gate, she saw an employee start to close the door to the jetway.

"Wait!" Stella yelled. The employee turned.

"What?" Garcia said in her ear.

"Do what you can. My plane is leaving."

"I'll fight for it," he said, "but no guarantees."

43

THICK FOG CAUSED A TRAFFIC JAM AT THE SAN FRANCISCO airport. Stella's plane circled the starry skies above the murkiness for a half hour before it was cleared to land, slicing through thick soupy gray skies hugging the ground.

The sky to the east had turned a brilliant orange and pink. But as they descended into the thick fog, the sunrise was blotted out.

It was dreary as only a San Francisco summer can be, with bone-chilling cold and biting wind. Stella shivered as she waited for a rideshare on the curb, half-heartedly missing the heat of Texas.

All these delays meant Stella was going to be late to the 8 a.m. ceremony at City Hall.

As soon as she hopped into the car, she texted Mazzoli she was on her way. Late, but coming.

Leaning forward from the back seat, she kept her eyes glued on the window and silently cursed the traffic that was slowing her driver down.

Once they turned onto Market Street and were two blocks away from City Hall, traffic came to a dead stop. After sixty seconds of this and no sign of traffic clearing in front of them, Stella reached for the door.

"I'm good. I'll take it from here!"

Jumping out of the Uber, she grabbed her things, and ran the last two blocks to the front door of City Hall.

The judge was going to marry Mazzoli and Carol in five minutes.

When she got into the huge building, she grabbed a man's arm.

"Where do people get married?"

He made a face at her, staring at her hand on his sleeve, then he jutted his chin toward another staircase. Good Lord. Not more stairs.

Rushing up the stairs two at a time, she reached the top only to find four people staring at her. A person who looked like the judge. Mazzoli. Carol. And damn it all—Griffin.

"You made it," the judge said wryly. "We were about to ask my law clerk to stand in for you."

"I just flew in. My landing was delayed. There was—" Stella stopped and looked at the faces around her. None of that mattered. "Let's do this!"

Ignoring Griffin, she smiled at Mazzoli and Carol the entire time as the judge performed a simple ten-minute ceremony. Afterwards, Griffin and Stella were pulled aside to sign the certificate as witnesses. Mazzoli and Carol acted like the lovey-dovey newlyweds they were.

Mazzoli walked up to Stella while Carol and Griffin chatted.

"Hey, LaRosa," he said, smiling. "Cut it a little close there."

"Tell me about it."

"Hope you worked up an appetite. We're all going to Ruth Chris Steak House to celebrate for lunch. They're opening up special for us. Me and the manager go way back."

Stella looked at a clock on the wall. "It's 9 in the morning."

Mazzoli blinked at her. "Is that a problem?"

She laughed. "I guess not. I like steak and eggs for breakfast."

"Exactly!"

Then she thought about what he had said. *We're all going*. Ugh. Didn't Griffin have to go to work or something?

But Stella smiled. "Wouldn't miss it for anything."

. . .

An hour later, they'd already demolished three bottles of Veuve Clicquot between the four of them. They were starting in on a fourth bottle when Stella turned to Griffin.

"Clearly you don't have a shift today," she said.

"Hell no. It's not every day my best bud gets married."

Best bud? Stella fumed. Mazzoli was her friend first.

By noon, it was clear the server was eager to kick them out of the empty restaurant and go about his day. He lingered around and filled their water glasses unnecessarily.

Mazzoli pushed back his chair and put his arm around Carol.

"Thanks for coming," he said to Stella and Griffin.

Carol nodded, cheeks pink from the Champagne. "It means a lot."

Mazzoli pushed back his chair to stand. "Suppose we should let this fella have a break before they reopen in a few hours."

As they filed out of the restaurant, Griffin stepped aside to let Stella go before him. As he did, he placed his hand on her lower back. It sent a wave of desire through her. And then the hand was gone.

As the four of them stood on the Market Street sidewalk waiting for ride shares, Stella found she was longing for Griffin's touch again. It had to be all the alcohol. Day drinking was dangerous.

A car came for Mazzoli and Carol first.

"We're heading on our honeymoon!" Carol said. "Don't wait up!"

Stella kissed both of them goodbye and then the car was gone.

She and Griffin stood awkwardly on the sidewalk.

Then the car Griffin had ordered pulled up. He paused with the door open.

"I'm not leaving you here," he said. "Get in."

Stella did. She liked this bossy side of him. Or maybe it was the alcohol.

He gave the driver her address.

In the backseat, Griffin put his hand on her knee. Then her thigh. Soon she had unlatched her seatbelt and was pressed up beside him, her own hand on his leg. Her head turned, and they were kissing.

The car came to a stop. Stella scooted toward the door, but then turned and reached for Griffin's hand. She pulled him out of the car and into her apartment building, up the stairs, through her living room, and into her bed.

* * *

When Stella woke, he was gone.

Thinking back to the first night they had ever slept together, she smiled. She'd told him not to stay the night and woken with him beside her. They had argued over it later—how he hadn't listened to her and left that night. He'd claimed he'd been too drunk to drive.

Her smile grew wider as she remembered the day that had turned into night. They hadn't fallen asleep until dawn. Then they had stayed in bed and talked in the dark. Spilling secrets, revealing the difficulties in staying apart from one another, digging into the misunderstandings.

But Stella had kept some things close to her chest. He could never know about the lives she had taken besides Nick's, who she'd only killed to save Griffin.

Being with Griffin had somehow healed her in so many ways.

But it had also marked the closing of a door that she had unknowingly left cracked.

She dug his hoodie out of her closet and put it on, inhaling deeply. She frowned. It didn't smell like him anymore.

Her phone rang. It was him.

She answered immediately. "I still have that hoodie you loaned me. I should've given it to you before you left."

"When can I see you again?"

Stella paused before answering and thought carefully about what she wanted to say. "Last night was one of the best nights of my life. And I don't want to spoil that."

"How would it be spoiled?"

"There are parts of me I haven't shared. Things that will make you hate me and hate yourself for being with me."

"I doubt it," he said, but his voice sounded uncertain.

A wave of sadness washed over Stella.

"I'm glad you stayed over," she said. "I'm glad that we were so honest with each other. But I think it's best if we stick to being friends."

Stella felt a pang of regret as she spoke. Her words would hurt him. But she couldn't lie to him.

For a second, he was quiet.

"Let me know if you change your mind," he said, almost whispering, and hung up.

An hour later, the buzzer for her apartment chimed. She wasn't expecting anyone. She peeked out her window. She saw three men on the street below her. Two were uniformed San Francisco police officers, and the third looked like a detective.

Just then, her phone dinged.

She didn't recognize the number, but the message was clear.

It was from Griffin. *Houston detective in town. They have an arrest warrant for you. For the murder of Carter Barclay.*

44

STELLA HAD NO CHOICE BUT TO TURN HERSELF IN. SHE WAS booked. Fingerprints. Mugshots. The entire nine yards. In Griffin's hoodie. Which unfortunately said, "SFPD" on the back and had his name on the front.

It would not look good for him.

But that was the least of her worries right then.

Carter Barclay's murder had made international news.

They left her alone in the cell for what felt like forever. Nobody came to speak to her. The rest of the jail seemed empty. Eventually, she curled up in a ball on the blanket and took a nap. All the flight-or-fight adrenaline had drained, and she was exhausted.

Waking up after an hour, nothing had changed.

Thirty minutes later, a deputy came and unlocked her cell door.

"Time to go."

"What's going on?"

"No clue, lady."

When she stepped out of the police station, she was blinded by flash bulbs. Dozens of reporters were gathered outside, shouting questions at her.

Turning on her heel, she fled back into the lobby, the door swinging shut on the shouts of the journalists outside.

She rapped on the plexiglass window separating the lobby from the rest of the office, trying to get the receptionist's attention. The woman was pointedly ignoring her and talking on the phone.

"Please. Can I make a call? I need to get a ride."

The reporters and photographers had pressed up against the glass windows of the lobby and she saw camera lenses pointed her way.

Stella wasn't going to call her parents. The last thing they needed was to deal with this scene. She wasn't sure if Ana was back in town. She couldn't call Mazzy. He'd left for his honeymoon right from the restaurant. He was somewhere in the Maldives off grid.

Having no other choice, she called Griffin.

"I'm sprung. Not sure why. But I'm trapped in the lobby by paparazzi."

"I heard. Someone pulled some strings. I'll send someone to rescue you. Call me when you get in a car."

A few seconds later, a young cop with red hair stepped out of the door to the back. She smiled at Stella. "Come this way. I heard you need a getaway car."

"Boy, do I ever."

The police officer, a woman named Sherry Smith, pulled her squad car out of the lot and several cars followed them.

"I should've laid down in the back seat," Stella joked.

"Don't worry," Smith said. "I'm trained in evasive driving. This should be fun."

The cop sped around the corners and put her lights on to run through the red stoplights, and soon they were clear.

Stella dialed Griffin. "Smith drives like a beast. We are home free. Have you heard why I was released without bail being set?"

"They say you've been released pending further investigation."

"Is that good?"

"No clue. But you might not want to head back to your place."

"Why is that?"

“There’s a circus parked out front. Journalists from around the world.”

“Because I was arrested for Barclay’s murder?”

“No,” he said. “Because of your story in the paper.”

Stella had nearly forgotten what with racing to Mazzy’s wedding, sleeping with Griffin and then getting arrested.

Stella turned toward Officer Smith. “Do you think you could drop me at the Union Square BART station?”

“Of course.”

She gave her attention back to Griffin.

“I’ll be at my folks’ house if you need me.”

“Mum’s the word. I’ll keep you posted. Right now, there are two hotshot detectives in Houston saying that Patrick Barclay’s version of events is a lie. That he was in with you on murdering his dad so he could inherit the man’s fortune.”

“Good grief.”

“These crooked detectives are saying they were eyewitnesses.”

“There were only three of us on that roof.”

“I believe you.”

“Thanks, Griffin.”

45

STELLA WAS GOING STIR CRAZY.

Not only was she forced to hide out at her parents' house, but the newspaper had placed her on unpaid leave. Garcia had told her he was sorry but that it was the newspaper's policy: any employee under criminal investigation was on unpaid leave until the results of that investigation were completed. She had not specified who had shot Carter Barclay in her article. She had written that he had been shot dead in a flurry of gunfire. She didn't write that the bullets had come from her own gun.

Stella was bored out of her mind, but this way she avoided the swarm of international reporters who wanted to interview her.

The fate of the cloned bodies had sparked an international debate. And more.

Stella kept the news off.

Nobody knew what to do with the cloned bodies.

It had become one of the largest ethical dilemmas the world had seen.

In America, which had jurisdiction, Homeland Security, NASA, the FBI, the CDC, and various other agencies had convened a special task force to determine what to do with them as the world watched breathlessly and the subject was debated on every talk show, podcast, and radio station.

Stella had turned down dozens of interview requests, saying her story stood alone, and they could quote from that if they needed more information.

Worldwide, other organizations had been formed to try to resolve the question of whether the cloned bodies were actually people.

Protests had been held in every country.

It was a mess.

Stella tried to block it all out. Her parents were supportive and didn't ask any questions. God bless them. But she was chomping at the bit to get back in the newsroom.

The only release had been the gym. She'd spent long hours there weightlifting, kickboxing, and practicing martial arts. Honing her body into a lethal weapon. But after her throwdowns in the blue-lit lab, she realized she had become soft. She'd barely made it out of there alive.

Never again would she allow herself to be in that position.

In addition, she spent an hour every day at the shooting range out in the East Bay near her parents' house. She ended up having to stay there for two weeks.

The past few years, she had quickly discovered that being a daily newspaper reporter was definitely not without risk. At least for her.

After an hour of shooting each afternoon, she headed back to her parents' house for dinner, only three miles from the indoor range.

Her mother was delighted to have Stella home. Even if it was only temporary.

"I know the circumstances aren't ideal for you, but I'm just thrilled we get to see you so much, Stella!"

"Yeah, not ideal at all. I'm so bored."

"I know you had to kill that awful man in self-defense and that everybody is going to realize that" her mother said. "But you don't have to worry. They would never find you guilty."

"Thanks, Ma."

Some mornings, she would help her mother in the garden. She was always in awe of the energy her mother had. And the optimism. Stella hoped one day she would be like her mother. Or at least age like her.

The woman was less than five feet tall and still had the same figure she'd had as a high school cheerleader. Besides a few lovely smile lines around her eyes, her mother didn't look her age. She kept her bleached blonde hair pulled back in a neat ponytail unless she was going to a formal event and then she went into Oakland and had her hair "did."

Stella adored her mother. And tried to relish her time spent living there.

In the back of her mind, she was terrified that by some unfair fluke she'd be convicted of murdering Barclay and be sent to prison for life. The worst part would be not being able to spend time with her mother like she was doing right now. So despite being antsy, she tried to savor her time in the East Bay.

One night she returned from the range and the house was empty.

Stella checked her messages. Her phone had two missed calls and a voicemail from her mother.

"Your uncle has taken a turn for the worse. Can you please meet us at the hospital? For me, please, Stella. He said he wants to see you."

Stella closed her eyes. The last thing she wanted to do was see her uncle. She would not cry when he was underground. But she also felt a sliver of guilt. Her uncle had been one of the wealthy patrons who had been scheduled to receive a transplant from the cloned bodies.

Of course, all the transplants had been canceled with the exposure of Barclay's operation.

* * *

Heart thudding in her chest, Stella pushed open the door of the hospital room.

It was dimly lit, but the first thing she noticed was her uncle's mustard yellow skin. Every inch she could see was the ghastly color: his face, neck, arms, hands.

A fear she hadn't felt since she was a child crawled up her scalp.

The second thing she noticed was that her parents were nowhere to be seen. It was only her and her Uncle Dominic.

She stood in the doorway paralyzed.

He looked like a toddler. The short, fat man with the perpetual five o'clock shadow and thick head of brushed back dark hair usually had a cigar hanging out the side of his mouth and wore three-piece suits.

This man now wore a hospital gown, had a shaved head, and obviously no cigar.

"Why did you shave your head?" she asked.

Ignoring her question, he said, "Come in. Don't just stand there like a *un pantofolaio.*" A couch potato.

Inhaling sharply, Stella took the first step. When she saw she actually could move and wasn't under some weird Italian spell, she walked over to a chair that had been pulled up beside the bed and sat down on the edge, keeping her torso partly turned toward the door.

"Your mama went to the cafeteria to eat. Your papa had to go do some business for me. God bless him."

"Who is taking over for you?" Stella asked, arching an eyebrow.

Her Uncle Dominic chuckled. "Why? Now that I'm on my deathbed, you want in?"

Stella stopped herself from spitting on the ground. Instead, she stared at him, daring him to piss her off more.

He sighed heavily. "I asked you here not to anger you, but to ask your forgiveness."

"Really?" Stella said in a cold tone.

"I should never have meddled in your life."

"You're right. You should've stayed out of it. You didn't answer my question. Who is taking over for you?"

He shrugged. "I'm still deciding."

"You better decide fast."

"You always were a feisty one."

"Is that why you never liked me?"

He was silent for a moment. "I'm considering turning the family business over to your brother, Christopher."

Stella's heart sank.

"What about Al and Jack?"

They were Dominic's sons, her cousins.

"Those boys aren't leaders. Good boys, but they can't lead a family."

"Christopher can't either."

If it had been anyone else, she could have expected the same abuse she'd been receiving her entire life, but Chris would let her live peacefully.

That didn't help her heartbreak.

Because by having Chris take over, Stella knew she'd lost another family member to the mafia. Chris would become hard and consumed. It was his personality. He didn't do anything halfway.

Her uncle waved his hand, dismissing her protest.

"Sure, he can."

Stella frowned.

"Do I have it?" her uncle asked. "Your forgiveness."

She stared at him for a long moment.

"Yes. I forgive you. Not for you. For me. I'm sick of carrying such hatred and rage around for you."

He bowed his head as if receiving a blessing from a priest at communion. "Thank you."

Stella snapped. "Since you are atoning for your sins, I'm surprised there's not a line out the door of people you are asking forgiveness from."

Her uncle laughed. "Oh Stella, there are not enough years left for me on this earth to do that. I am only asking for yours."

She blinked and then scowled, despite herself. "I don't get it."

"You are blood."

"Did it take you dying to remember that? What about Uncle Joe and Aunt Kathy? They were blood. They are dead because of you."

To her surprise, her uncle let out a choked sob. He pressed his lips together tightly and his face contorted. After a few seconds, he inhaled sharply. "That is my only regret in this life. I could not protect them from my enemies. But you need to know that I made their killer pay and every single person up the line who was involved. They all died horribly."

"Good for you," Stella said in a dull voice.

"Stella, the reason I was so hard on you. The real reason is because you were the only one who knew it was my fault that Joseph and Katherine died. Well, everybody knew. But you were the only one who wanted me held accountable for it. Everybody else was too afraid. That's why I wanted you in the business. You would keep people straight and accountable."

"Whatever," Stella said trying to make her voice sound bored. But inside, her heart was racing. He knew he was responsible. He had finally admitted it.

"Does it help that I pulled some strings and got you out of jail the other day?"

She just glared at him. She didn't want to be grateful to him for anything. And she certainly didn't want to have to thank him for anything.

Just then her mother walked in. "I didn't know you were here, Stella. I can leave. Do you want me to leave?"

Stella turned toward her mother. "We've just finished up."

She turned without looking at her uncle and walked out of the room, letting the door slam behind her.

46

THE POLICE INVESTIGATION WAS OVER.

The murder of Carter Barclay had been ruled self-defense.

Although she tried to tamp down her anxiety about the investigation by pushing herself to the limits physically, in the gym, in the range, running along the trails in the East Bay, she had been worried.

The call came early one morning, two weeks after Barclay's death.

It was Griffin.

"Self-defense."

That was all he said when she answered the phone. It was enough.

She burst into tears.

"You did it, Stella. You stopped him. And you dismantled all the webs he has woven. His kid is taking over and issued a statement about the charges being dropped and his goal to right all the wrongs his father spent a lifetime doing."

"Unbelievable," Stella said, swiping at her tears. "Are you sure I'm not dreaming?"

Griffin laughed.

"Tell me more," she said.

He told her that Patrick Barclay's witness account of the shooting had prevailed despite conflicting reports from the detectives who ended up being on Barclay's payroll.

With him dead and no more money coming their way, they recanted their initial accounts of the shooting under oath.

Griffin told her they had done so under a plea deal: Tell the truth or face criminal aiding and abetting.

"There was a surveillance camera. Backed what you and the kid said."

"Thank God."

The police chief and the district attorney had held a press conference saying that not only was the shooting self-defense, but that personnel in both departments were under internal investigation for wrongdoing.

"I thought those two were beholden to Barclay?"

"Apparently not, but most of their employees were."

"Of course."

"Guess who prompted the internal affairs investigations?" he asked.

"No clue."

"Ana Rodriguez. The director of the FBI reached out to her and promoted her. Put her in charge of the whole shebang. All because of your article."

Stella's heart soared for her new friend. They'd made it out alive, and Ana had gotten a promotion from it.

It was the victory that Stella had never thought she'd live to see.

"Thanks for letting me know."

"You did it," he repeated. "You finally stopped him."

"Yeah," she said in a quiet voice, and then hung up the phone. It was anti-climactic. Somehow, she'd expected to feel differently. But she still felt hollow and empty and numb. His death did not bring back all the lives he had taken. It did not bring justice for all the wrong he'd done in the world.

Within hours, she had clearance to return to work.

Although she'd only been gone a few weeks, she felt like a newbie walking back into the newsroom.

The room was the same. The people the same.

But she was different.

It felt like she'd been gone a year.

Like she always did, she stopped at Garcia's desk first on her way to her own.

Looking up, he grinned. "I've got good news!"

"They said I killed in self-defense?" she said ironically even though they'd already discussed it earlier that day.

"Ha! Was there ever a doubt?"

Stella just smiled. When it came to corrupt people in places of power, there would always be a doubt.

"No," he said, "my good news is that Sontag was replaced."

"Oh?" Stella said, not sure how to react. Most likely they had just put another greedy hedge fund employee in the spot.

"The new publisher is a newspaper man of the best sort. Used to work at the New York Post. Won them a Pulitzer. He's going to have our back on everything we do."

"That is fantastic news. Except couldn't they find another woman?"

Garcia grinned. "I thought the same thing, but this guy seems all right."

"We'll see."

A few hours later, Stella had barely caught up on her emails from while she was gone when Garcia called her desk phone. When she saw who it was calling, she said, "Too much work to walk over here?"

Her head swiveled to see his reaction.

Ana Rodriguez was standing near his desk.

Standing up, her smile grew even wider.

47

"LET'S TAKE A WALK," ANA SAID WHEN STELLA WAVED HER over.

"Perfect."

The two women didn't speak much in the elevator. It wasn't until they settled into a café across the street with coffees that they really spoke.

"It's good to see you," Ana said, taking a sip of her mocha.

"Same."

"I just wanted to thank you for everything."

"And I want to thank you for stopping a murder rap."

They both laughed.

"We did it," Ana said and smiled.

"We did."

"I don't know about you, but I finally feel that justice has been served."

"Same girl, same," Stella said.

They had both lost people they loved because of one man.

"What now?" Ana asked.

Stella shrugged. "Life goes on. I guess I'm going to have to learn how to let go of all the rage I felt toward that man. I thought it would disappear when he was dead, but I still feel it at times."

"I do, too," Ana said in a quiet voice.

The two women sat there for a few moments in silence, sipping their coffees.

"I have an idea that might work for both of us," Stella said.

"What's that?"

"You've got this cool new promotion that gives you the ability to pick and choose what you go after, right?"

"Yeah?"

"And I can go after whomever I want, as well."

"Okay."

"So we should team up to stop all the bastards out there still hurting people."

Ana's face lit up in a huge smile. She held up her coffee cup and clinked it with Stella's.

"Deal."

The two women sat quietly again for a moment.

Stella had something on her heart that she needed to say. But it wouldn't be easy.

"I still can't help but feel responsible for your sister's death," she said quietly, staring at the tablecloth in front of her and then looking up to meet Ana's eyes.

For a second, Ana didn't answer, and Stella's heart clenched in her chest, unable to breathe.

But then very solemnly Ana nodded.

"Thank you for sharing that with me and making yourself vulnerable with your honesty," Ana said. "I won't lie. At first, I thought it might be your fault, too. And don't be mad at him, but it was because of what Detective Griffin told me."

Stella's mouth was wicked of all moisture. She wasn't sure she was ready for this.

"And what was that?" she managed.

Ana took a deep breath. "He said that the assassin was after you and that Carmen was trying to save you."

Nodding her head slowly, Stella exhaled. "Yeah. That's true."

"But I also know my sister. And she would have died to save you. Even if—" Ana paused. "Even if she didn't like you."

Looking away, Stella shook her head. Staring out the café window, she said, "We didn't have a great start."

"Carmen is...was...a force of nature. She was beautiful and brilliant and single-minded and so brave, but she wasn't a girl's girl." She wore a sheepish smile and looked down at her coffee cup. "I'm kind of a girl's girl. I always had all the girlfriends, and she was a loner, intent on doing well in school and building her career. As you know, she was a beast when it came to her job. Her goal in life was to take killers down."

"It wasn't that" Stella said, shaking her head. "It was because Griffin is my ex-lover."

It wasn't a lie, Stella told herself. One night of passion did not make them lovers again.

Ana's eyes widened.

"I can assume by the look on your face you didn't know that."

"No, but that makes sense."

Again, silence filled the air.

"Even if you pushed her in front of you and the guy with the gun fired, it's still not your fault. I know that's an exaggeration but what I'm trying to say is you couldn't keep Carmen out of a situation like that even if you begged her."

"I seem to recall someone begging you not to go to Texas," Stella said, smirking. "Maybe you are more alike than you think."

Ana nodded. "Or maybe I'm learning from the example she left on how to be selfless when going after the bad guys."

"That's what it was," Stella said. "She was selfless."

"To a fault, maybe."

"Maybe."

"Can you tell me what happened that night?"

Stella nodded and told her how she and Carmen had made a deal. Before an inmate had been murdered, he had sent a letter to Stella. Carmen had asked to know what the letter contained, and Stella had agreed to tell her. The letter said an assassin was in town to kill Stella and then kill the president. When Stella found out where the assassin was staying in San Francisco, she told Carmen she was heading that way.

"I should never have told her."

"She was probably parked outside your house ready to tail you," Ana joked.

"I begged her not to go inside with me, but she didn't listen." Swallowing hard, Stella continued. "He had me cornered. I was a goner. He was about to fire when your sister showed up. He turned and fired at her instead. They killed each other."

Ana's face crumpled a little, and she pressed her lips together hard.

"We had a moment. I nearly forgot. For some reason, talking to you reminded me. We were about to go in and she asked me a question. She asked me why I did what I did."

"What did you say?" Ana asked.

"I said someone had to do it because these killers think they are invincible and we have to stop them. She told me that she got it and that it was the same reason she did it."

"You would've become friends if she'd lived," Ana said in a matter-of-fact voice.

"I think you're right."

Ana stood. "I need to get back to work."

"Me too," Stella said.

Outside the café, the women paused, and Ana reached forward and hugged Stella.

Stella awkwardly hugged her back.

When the FBI agent pulled away, she said, "Stella LaRosa, I think we're gonna be friends."

Watching as the other woman walked down the sidewalk, Stella was filled with a sense of lightness and gratefulness. Ana Rodriguez had taken away a giant burden.

Finally, Stella was at peace with Carmen's death.

48

HER UNCLE WAS DEAD.

The call came in the middle of the night.

"I wasn't with him," her mother said and began to weep. "I had just gone down to get a cup of coffee in the cafeteria. They told me that it had just started and would take a few hours."

Stella was quiet for a moment, letting her mother cry.

"Ma, do you remember I did that story about the mom and dad who died within twenty-four hours of one another? How he died of a broken heart they said?"

"Yes," her mother answered and sniffled.

"One thing the kids were broken up about was that, when the mother was dying, they were told the same thing, that they had a few hours. The kids all went in the hall to talk about what they wanted to do and how they wanted to act and what they wanted to say to their mother while she could potentially still hear them, right?"

"Yes?"

"Their mother passed while they were in the hall. And you know what the hospice nurse said? Most of the time, even if it seems like your loved one is not aware or is in and out of consciousness, most of the time, they won't want to cross over with you in the room. Most people wait until they are alone."

Her mother let out a wail. "All alone? Why would anyone want to die all alone?"

Stella winced. Hoping to comfort her mother, it didn't seem to be working.

After a few seconds, her mother spoke again, still sniffling. "Okay. Yes. I guess that makes sense. I would want to spare you that."

"Oh God, mom, don't even mention something like that."

"Stella, you know it's going to happen one day."

"Stop."

Her mother sniffled again. "Okay."

"Are you still at the hospital?"

"No, they sent us home. Me and your dad. He's in his office making all the calls."

"Dad is?" Stella frowned. Usually, her mom did everything. Her dad was the one in the background, holding her up and supporting her, but not active in much.

"Of course he is, Stella." Her mother's voice was a little sharp.

"Okay, mom, I didn't mean to upset you."

"It's okay." She let out a deep breath. "Why don't you come over in the morning?"

"I can't," Stella said. "I have to go into the newsroom early tomorrow. I can come now?"

"It's okay, honey."

"Can I help with the arrangements?"

"Your uncle had it all pre-arranged. All you have to do is show up."

"Tell me when and where and I'll be there early. And call me if you need me before that, okay?"

"I'll be fine, honey. I'll keep you posted."

Stella had one last nagging question.

"Hey, Ma, is Christopher back in town?"

"No, he's flying in tomorrow. Your dad called him right away."

"Okay. Love you. Call me if you need anything. If it's important, I'll take off from work."

"It will be fine, Stella."

After hanging up Stella sat in the dark in her bed.

Her uncle's reign of terror was over.

She didn't hate him, but she still didn't like him, either. She most certainly wasn't going to shed a tear over his death. Blood is thicker than water didn't apply to him, despite his half-hearted attempt at an apology.

What his death did mean to her was hope.

If she could somehow talk to Christopher, maybe the family could escape from the organized crime life her uncle had created. She had kept so far away from it, she didn't know much about the details.

Her two brothers sometimes did some dealings with the family business, but for the most part, kept clean with their work as attorneys. Her father ran one of her uncle's legitimate businesses. It could work.

At least her immediate family could break free.

Her cousins? Maybe not. But one of them could take it over.

The thing she had hoped and dreamed about her entire life—to be free of a mafia family—could be realized now with her uncle's death.

Stella had turned out her light and laid back down in her bed when her cell rang again.

She was surprised to see it was Griffin.

"Hey," she said.

"I hope I didn't wake you."

"Nah, I just got off the phone with my mother. Were you at the hospital or what?"

"Actually, I was."

"Why?"

"I'm sorry about your loss."

"Don't be."

"No love lost?"

"Nope," she said. "Now, why were you at the hospital?"

"I was assigned a security detail there."

Stella laughed. "Were you worried someone was going to try to kill my uncle on his death bed or were you worried the people watching him die would incite a riot?"

"Very funny."

"My uncle lived his entire life walking around this town without a security detail, so why would he need it on his deathbed?"

"Just some rumblings I heard."

Stella sat up in her bed. "Spill it, Griffin."

"Nothing for sure, but I did hear some chatter about violence against the LaRosa family."

"That's absurd."

"I have a security detail in front of your apartment and am going to have someone there until the funeral. And maybe after."

"Oh my God. Who would want to kill me?" She laughed. "Well, you know, besides the usual suspects."

Griffin didn't answer and suddenly a chill ran across Stella's back.

"What about my mom?"

"I sent a security detail out there, too. At least until the funeral. Or until we figure out who was making these threats."

"Actual threats?" She reached over and turned on the light on her nightstand.

"Worse. This is partly why I'm calling."

"Talk about burying the lede. Spit it out." Stella was pissed. It seemed like Griffin could never, not once in his damn life, get straight to the point. It drove her crazy.

"Your cousin, Johnny LaRosa? He was found stabbed to death in Oakland last night."

"Jesus."

Stella never got along with Johnny, and they weren't close at all. He never once went to a family gathering, but that didn't mean she wanted him dead.

"This looked like a professional hit."

"That's too bad, but Johnny was living the life. When you are playing with fire, you can expect to get burned."

"We think it's because he's the successor to your uncle."

"But he's not."

Griffin paused. "He wasn't?"

"Not from what my uncle hinted at."

"Just stay safe," Griffin replied. "We'll get to the bottom of this. I'm assigning a team to do some investigating."

"Okay. Thanks, Griffin. But take my security detail off and put it on my mom, please."

He laughed. "It doesn't work that way."

"The hell it doesn't."

"Stay safe, Stella."

He hung up.

Stella threw off the bed covers, fuming.

Who would go after her family? She stomped into the kitchen and ground some espresso beans, loading her maker before she called her mom. The call went to voicemail.

She tried another eight times until her mother answered.

"Good grief, Stella, I've been talking to your aunt. Did you hear? Poor little Johnny is dead. This is bad. What more can this family stand?"

"Ma, I just got a call from SFPD."

"Was it that good looking detective?" her mother said, interrupting.

"Yes. But that's not the point. He said he heard something about someone going after people in our family."

"That's ridiculous," her mother said.

"Why is that ridiculous?"

Her mother's voice became low. "A long time ago, your uncle made a deal, a truce, to keep our family safe."

"Safe? From everyone in the city?"

"People know not to mess with us. That kind of deal. Anyone who did would be risking everything."

"Does his death change that?"

"No." Her mother scoffed. "A deal is a deal."

"Okay, Ma, but please be careful and safe, okay?"

"Okay, honey. I got to call your aunt back."

Stella hung up.

A deal? To keep the family safe?

49

ONE LONG, SHINY BLACK CAR AFTER ANOTHER PULLED UP IN front of Saints Peter and Paul Church in North Beach.

The fog had lifted slightly from earlier in the day, but not high enough to let the sun in. Everything was coated in a gray mist.

The hearse was parked at the foot of the steps.

Each time the back door of the cars opened, another group of men in black suits emerged. In addition, the sidewalks were filled with people swarming toward the church steps.

Then there were the cops.

Stella hadn't seen so many San Francisco cops since the Saint Patrick's Day parade.

There were dozens. In uniform. Standing guard.

That's when Stella realized that they were worried about violence.

For some reason, it irritated her. Did they think people in the mafia just killed each other all the time? At a funeral? As far as Stella knew, her uncle had no enemies. Unlike mafia bosses in the movies or on the east coast, he never traveled with bodyguards. He walked freely through the city at all times and had done so her entire life.

Looking around at the people going into the church, she saw some of the most prominent men *were* flanked by armed bodyguards. A sliver of alarm raced down her spine. She hadn't seen Christopher yet. She felt a sudden urge to go find him.

They hadn't discussed him taking over the family business.

As soon as she had him alone, she was going to try to talk him out of it. He was too soft.

He probably had never killed anyone in his life. Thank God. She wouldn't wish that on anyone. It messed with her mental health every day.

And to be honest, it was keeping her from falling head over heels in love with Griffin.

She was a killer. He was a cop. End of story.

Stella was confident if she sat down with her brother, she could convince him that nobody had to run the family business. She would explain that with Uncle Dominic dead, the family could be free of its criminal enterprises. They would walk away. They could live like a normal family. Eventually, his children, and maybe one day hers, would no longer have the stigma of the mafia attached to them. They wouldn't grow up having relatives murdered and finding the bloody bodies like Stella had as a child.

It was their chance to be free.

Christopher was a father. He had mostly kept out of the family business. Stella was certain she could convince him to free their family from the tyranny of organized crime. He was making a great living on his own without his uncle's interference.

Stepping inside the church to look for her brother, Stella thought that her uncle's funeral was over-the-top. The altar was practically buried in flowers.

Everybody who was anybody had sent their condolences.

Earlier in the morning, Stella had helped her mother keep track of the arrival of flowers.

Her mother had been frantic trying to write down who sent what.

"Who cares?" Stella had said. "Get someone else to do this."

"It's my job," her mother had hissed. "Your father told me to do it."

Stella had made a face and stepped back. "Since when he is your boss?"

"When is *he* my *boss*?" her mother said and scowled. "Don't you dare speak disrespectfully about your father."

"I didn't mean it that way, I just thought..."

"Don't think. Help me write down the names on the cards."

Stella really hadn't meant it disrespectfully, but her father barely said boo to anybody. He was the most mild-mannered, easy-going man she knew. He deferred to her uncle and mother in all matters. One of the things that had always broken Stella's heart was that her father would never stand up to her uncle for her. And now he was telling her mother what to do?

Weird.

Confused, Stella had done as her mother asked without arguing. Maybe her mother was taking the death of her brother harder than she was letting on. That's the only reason Stella could think of that her normally sweet mother would be snarky to Stella.

Now, making her way through the throng of mourners inside the church, Stella nodded as people offered condolences, but kept her eyes on the front, where her mother talked to Christopher's wife. She searched the crowd but couldn't spot her brother's head in the sea of men in black suits.

By the time she got to the front of the church, the music started. Her mother pulled her down onto the pew as everyone else settled into the seating.

It was crazy how packed Uncle Dominic's funeral was.

For most of her life, Stella had been shielded from the enormous power the LaRosa crime organization wielded.

Now it was obvious.

As the priest began to speak, Stella noticed that her father wasn't sitting with them. Her head swiveled, and then she found him across the aisle. He was sitting with a bunch of men she didn't recognize. Her brothers sat on each side of her father.

For a second, she saw him from the perspective of an outsider, rather than his daughter. He was in his sixties, but still tall and strong. He wore his black hair short but not too short and had a little goatee that Stella thought was cute and made him look a little like an Italian Javier Bardem.

But why wasn't he sitting with her mother? And his daughter?

Instead, he sat with her brothers and her jerk cousins, Alfredo and Giacomo—Al and Jack. What kind of patriarchal crap was this?

Her eyes narrowed. What was going on?

After the funeral mass ended, everybody stood.

That's when Stella noticed something odd.

Everybody was filing toward the front and, instead of coming over to hug or greet her mother, they were veering to the left and heading straight for her father.

Not Christopher.

Her father.

And one by one, they were speaking to him, all being deferential.

She stared at him until he met her eyes.

When he did, he gave her a look and she didn't recognize him as her own father.

Her mother tugged at her arm. "Come on, Stella."

She allowed her mother to drag her out of the church but kept turning to look at the mass of people surrounding her father, watching in horror.

Toward the back of the church, she saw Griffin. He wore a dark suit that made him look like a movie star.

Turning again, she looked at her father in the front of the church and then turned back toward Griffin raising an eyebrow.

He gave her a sad smile.

That's when she realized. Her father was now the new LaRosa family mafia boss.

* * *

Stella LaRosa returns in *White Lies*, coming soon. Continue for a sample or get your copy now:

https://www.amazon.com/dp/B0DW96Y87X

Join the LT Ryan reader family & receive a free copy of the Rachel Hatch story, *Fractured*. Click the link below to get started: https://ltryan.com/rachel-hatch-newsletter-signup-1

White Lies: Prologue

City of Souls

A long procession of shiny black Cadillacs trailed the hearse as it glided into the Italian Cemetery, a small city of 80,000 dead nestled beneath a series of rolling hills south of San Francisco.

Sitting in the backseat of one of those cars, Stella LaRosa thought it was eerie that a cloak of thick fog blotted out the blue sky just as the caravan reached the necropolis.

The "City of Souls" was said to be second largest city in California —if you didn't count the fact that most of the residents—1.5 million— were dead.

The Italian Cemetery, one of 17 cemeteries in the city, was the one Stella was the most familiar with, having been to several graveside services for family and friends of the family over the years. It was dotted with palm, Eucalyptus, and olive trees but not much grass as most of the crypts were under concrete slabs.

Stella's car drove slowly past ornate family vaults, adorned with stunning marble monuments: Michael the Archangel standing tall with his sword, his boot on Satan's distorted face; a stone angel folded face-down over a headstone in grief, her wings akimbo; a majestic Virgin Mary holding a crowned baby Jesus up high in one hand.

And then there was the row of dead babies: a seemingly endless row of marble pillars each topped with a small cherub-cheeked angel.

But none of the beauty registered with Stella. Her mind was racing with anxiety. Not over the death of her uncle, whose body was in the hearse. No, it was because at the church she had discovered that her mild-mannered, salt-of-the-earth family was now head of the LaRosa Mafia Family.

With the death of her Uncle Dominic, Stella had harbored hopes that her family, at least her immediate family, could leave that life behind.

That dream was shattered when she saw the most powerful men in San Francisco paying homage to her father at the front of the Catholic church.

Before she could question her mother, Celeste LaRosa was ushered away by Stella's brothers. Her mother tried to reach for Stella, but the crowd of mourners leaving the church came between them. Outside the church, she found that the hearse and several of the Cadillac's had already pulled away.

A man she had never seen before quickly escorted her to one of the black cars and as soon as the door was shut, the driver sped up to catch up with the procession.

She'd never felt so alone.

Something was going on and nobody had told her.

She felt abandoned, not just physically but emotionally.

For her entire life, she'd been able to count on her mother, but suddenly her mother seemed like a pawn in the LaRosa family.

It was hard to swallow that her mother had left the church without insisting that Stella be with her.

It was a punch in the gut.

When her car, apparently the last one in the procession, arrived at the grave site, her mother rushed over to the door.

"Oh honey, I'm so sorry," she said as Stella stepped out. "It was a little chaotic at the church. I told them to wait for you. But your Dad said you'd be taken care of and that we couldn't wait since we were in the lead car."

Stella stared at her.

The explanation didn't make her feel any better.

Looking over her mother's shoulder, she saw her dad standing near the open family vault, flanked by two dark heads—her brothers.

The slab of concrete marking the LaRosa family vault was the size of two king-sized beds side-by-side. But the crypts beneath went six deep. As many as 12 family members could be buried there. Right now, it only contained Aunt Cora. Now, Dominic would join his wife. The monument on top of the vault was a direct slap to the second LaRosa family vault just across the stone path. That one was topped with a sorrowful angel that had seemingly thrown himself on top of the crypt as if he were lying in bed, wings spread and a palm clasped across his face in eternal grief.

Never one to be bested, before his wife Cora had died, Dominic had commissioned the monument for their family vault. No matter who else was buried there, it would always be a shrine to Dominic and Cora because he had statues carved of both of them. The likenesses of the couple stood on either side of a larger-than-life angel who was smiling down on them benevolently.

It was utterly grotesque, Stella thought, and made a mental note to beg her parents to never bury her in the family vault where Dominic's effigy would lord over her for eternity. Then again, he probably had already forbid her burial there anyway. Problem solved.

Caught up in counting how many crypts were left compared to LaRosa family members left, Stella didn't notice a commotion near the cemetery entrance until heads turned that way.

Several men dressed in suits were blocking a man from entering. The man, dressed in coveralls was wielding what looked like hedge trimmers and speaking in an Italian dialect that Stella didn't recognize. He began to push his way in, his face growing red. The bodyguards tried to grab him but he began wildly swinging the sharp tool in an arc.

The gunmen surrounding her father began to run toward the man.

Stella turned toward her father to see what his reaction was.

As she did, she heard three short pops and then horrific screaming. In seemingly slow motion, she watched the horror unfolding before her as if she were high above.

The violence etched into her brain in snapshots: her father's body jerking spasmodically; blood blooming on her father's white shirt and somehow coating a wing of the stone angel; her father slumping to the ground so hard his head bounced off the hard concrete; her mother falling to her knees and sprawling across her father's body, a keening wail coming from her open mouth; her two brother's reaching for their guns and turning toward a chapel-sized mausoleum where a man in a ski mask was scrambling off the rooftop with a sniper rifle slung on his shoulder.

White Lies: Chapter 1

Out of nowhere, bodies surrounded her and hustled her to a car where she was thrown in the backseat and told to lie face down on the floorboard.

She struggled to sit up but felt a strong palm on her back. "Please stay down, miss."

"Get me Detective Griffin now!" she shouted through gritted teeth.

There was no time for tears. She was in shock.

A few seconds later, she heard the detective's voice.

"Let her up! For God's sakes, let her up."

"Sorry, ma'am," another voice said and she was lifted to a seated position.

There was a strange piercing noise she couldn't identify. It sounded like a continuous caterwaul.

Griffin was in the back seat with her, the door open behind him. He took her by the shoulders and looked directly in her eyes. "Are you okay? You might be in shock."

Realizing she was hyperventilating, Stella tried to speak but nothing came out. Finally her breath came back, filling her air passage and she managed to squeak out two words: "My father?"

"I'm sorry."

"Where's my mother?" she said her voice wobbling. She arched her back to see over his shoulder. Her mother was lying across her father's body. She tore at her hair with one hand and clung to him with the other as a terrible, heart wrenching noise streamed out of her mouth. She was the sound.

.

It was the most horrific thing Stella had ever seen.

Even worse, if possible, than watching her father's body jerk from the impact of bullets.

Then Griffin's voice filled the space.

"We can't get her to leave. The scene is safe. Your brother's caught the shooter."

The shooter.

Her mind reeled.

Then Griffin added after a pause. "He's dead."

"They killed him?"

Now Christopher and Michael would got to prison for life. There was no way chasing down a sniper and murdering him could be viewed as self-defense. Even though in Stella's eyes it would be 100 percent justified.

"No, actually. They cornered him and he put a handgun in his mouth."

"What?"

"Do you want to go see if you can get your mother to come with you? We need to take you both down to the station for questioning."

Fury filled Stella.

"Right now? Right now?"

Griffin looked down. "I'm sorry. It's standard procedure."

"I don't give a flying you know what about standard procedure, Griffin. My mom isn't going to be in any state to talk to anyone. Look at her for Christ's sakes."

The sound of sirens from ambulances, fire trucks and police cars racing into the cemetery drowned out Griffin's response. He got out of the car and as she scooted to get out, as well, she saw her mother being half-carried by two police officers over to the car.

She stood and met her mother, who threw herself into Stella's arms.

"Stella. Stella. Stella."

"I got you, mama. Let's get in the car."

Her mother stared straight ahead toward where her father's body lay behind a sea of uniformed people. She was clutching something black and soft. It was her father's winter scarf. It had small stains on it. Blood?

"Let me have that, mama."

Her mother violently jerked it away from Stella. "No!"

"Okay. You can keep it."

"They are making me leave him. I can't leave him."

She was like a child.

Suddenly, her mother darted away at a sprint, trying to make an escape back toward the murder scene.

Griffin caught her and met Stella's eyes over her mother's shoulders.

"Mrs. LaRosa, we're going to take you home, now."

"I can't leave him."

"They are going to take care of him, mama."

"Nobody can take care of him now."

Stella didn't answer.

She helped her mother get into the back of the car and then turned to Griffin who was standing there with a stricken look on his face.

"You can send a detective to question us later."

"I think it can wait until tomorrow," he said and swallowed.

Stella gave him a curt nod and then slipped inside the Cadillac, holding her mother in her arms.

White Lies: Chapter 2

When they got home, escorted by three squad cars, the police searched the house before they let them enter.

Stella stayed in the back of the car with her mother, who was staring straight ahead.

When the all clear was given, Griffin came over.

Her mother got out of the car like a zombie and walked into the house.

Eyes on her mother's back, Stella stayed back to speak to the detective.

"I'm assigning two patrol cars to stay here. I've also taken the liberty to hire four bodyguards. Two will be inside the house with you. Two will be at the foot of the driveway."

At first it seemed like overkill and Stella was about to protest, but then changed her mind.

"Thank you."

"I'll be back in the morning unless you need me to stay."

His black eyes met hers.

More than anything, she wanted him to take her in his arms and hold her all night. He seemed the only person who could make her feel safe right then. Of course that was not an option.

Theirs was a love that would never be realized. At least not in this lifetime.

But still that bond remained.

"Thank you. We'll be fine."

When Stella got into the house she called for her mother. There was no answer.

One of the bodyguards, a man she'd never seen before, spoke in a low voice.

"Upstairs."

Stella went to her mother's bedroom. Her mother was not there. She looked in the en suite but it was also empty. After checking the other bedrooms and not finding her mother, she walked into the only room left—her childhood room.

Her mother was curled up on the bedspread in the fetal position, clutching her father's scarf with one hand and holding her dog, Tino, with the other. The dog whined and wagged its tail when it saw Stella but did not run to her like it normally did.

Stella closed and locked the door and climbed in bed with her mother, wrapping her arms around her.

The next day, her mother refused to speak or get out of bed, although in the night, Stella had had least convinced her to get under the covers, but her mother would not change it a nightgown stella had offered.

After a shower, Stella tried again.

"Mama?"

Her mother shook her head violently and buried her face in a pillow.

Leaving her mother, she went downstairs to meet Griffin.

He took a statement from her. She told him what she had seen: her father's body jerking from bullets, then a man in a ski mask with a gun scrambling off the roof the yellow mausoleum and her brothers pursuing him. End of story.

That was it.

"Thank you," he said and then cleared his throat. "is your mother...?"

Sadly Stella shook her head.

"I can call you when she's not ..." She didn't know what that word was. When her mother was not grieving? That wouldn't happen.

"I'm so sorry."

Stella swallowed the ball of grief welling up in her throat.

"If we're done, I'm going to go check on her."

Griffin stood. He moved toward her, his hand outstretched but then it fell to his side and he stopped a foot away.

He looked like he was about to say something. He looked away and then said,

"Your brothers are in the other room."

"Oh."

She turned and walked back up the stairs.

"Mama?" she said. "You have to get up."

Her mother shook her head violently.

Stella sighed. "Okay. Fine."

Pulling aside the curtain, Stella watched as her brothers walked Griffin to his car. The driveway was filled with cars. A few police cars and some other cars she didn't recognize. She waited and then after a few minutes they both got into their vehicles and drove away. Two squad cars pulled behind them. They had a detail on them, as well.

It made sense.

"Are you going to answer the phone?"

Stella turned. Her mother was sitting up in bed, the black scarf draped over one shoulder.

It was the first time her mother had spoken since they got home.

The phone had been ringing off the hook since they got home the day before. It had become background noise to Stella.

"Do you want me to answer it?"

Her other shook her head sadly.

"I'm going to go find something for us to eat. You have to eat and drink Mama, okay?"

Her mother didn't answer, but later Stella was able to get her mother to drink a glass of water and half a grilled cheese sandwich by holding it up to her mother's mouth and telling her to take a bite.

That afternoon, she heard a car pull up. Her brothers were back. In one vehicle this time.

A few minutes later there was a knock on the door. They tried the handle but it was locked.

"Stella? Ma? Let us in."

She unlocked the door and her brothers brushed past her to rush to her mother's side.

"Oh my God. You look awful, Ma," Christopher said.

Stella glared at him.

"What? You just letting her lay her all day?" Michael said.

"Letting her? Screw you. You finally come to check on her two days later and that's what you have to say?"

Stella stormed out of the room.

She was making an espresso when they both came down.

"Sorry, Stell," Christopher said. "It was just a shock seeing Ma like that."

She ignored his apology.

Instead she turned toward her brothers, leaning her back against the counter.

"Why? Why Dad? Who did it? Who was the shooter?"

Her brothers exchanged a look.

"That's why we've been MIA. We tracked down who did it."

"Who did it?" Stella said and slammed her coffee cup down on the counter.

"A guy from the Emerald Legion."

"What on earth is that? Speak English."

"You're going to have to ask Ma about it."

"You're kidding?" Stella was incredulous. "She's catatonic if you haven't noticed."

"She'll tell you."

White Lies: Chapter 3

Two days later her mother got out of bed.

Stella woke to bright sunlight streaming through her window.

The curtain was wide open and her mother was gone.

Stumbling into the kitchen bleary-eyed, Stella found her mother making her regular breakfast, oatmeal with dried fruit. There was a fresh pot of coffee on the stove.

"How are you feeling?" she asked her mother in a tentative voice.

"WE have a funeral to plan," she answered, pressing her lips tightly together.

"Okay." Stella stared at her mother waiting for the catatonic toddler to reappear.

Stella poured herself a cup of coffee and seated herself opposite her mother at the dining room table.

A wave of sadness threatened to overwhelm her, but she resolved to keep it at bay until she was alone. Breaking down right then would not help her mother. Even if all she wanted was her mother to comfort her.

She also wanted—needed—answers.

"Who are the Emerald Legion?"

Her mother exhaled loudly.

"I suppose it's time you knew."

An hour later, Stella sat at the table still, stunned by her mother's revelations.

Everything she knew about her father had been a lie.

He was half Italian and half Irish.

Stella had never questioned why her mother had kept the LaRosa name and given it to her children. She and her brothers had always been told that this was the way they did it in Italy.

Her father's last name was Costello. She'd always thought that name was Italian. It was not.

Stella had pretty much forgotten about that since everybody called him Mr. LaRosa.

Jake Costello had been the head of an Irish crime family in San Francisco called the Emerald Legion. He had fallen in love with Celeste LaRosa, a member of the legion's bitter enemies, the LaRosa Crime Family.

He loved her so much he defected from the Emerald Legion, a decision that nearly started a violent gang war. Celeste's powerful brother, Dominic, engineered a truce: he would allow the Emerald Legion to continue to operate in San Francisco as long as they left the LaRosa family alone.

"You lied to me my whole life?"

"We didn't lie. You never asked."

Rage filled Stella. "Asked what? I wouldn't even know to ask anything?"

"You never asked about your father's family."

"You told me they were dead."

"Well, that's true."

"What does that have to do with dad's murder?"

Her mother looked at her, eyes red and swollen. "With your uncle's death, Luke White has decided the truce is over. He sent that message by killing your father."

"Luke White? That's the head of the Emerald Legion?"

Her mother nodded.

"Noted."

"Stella," her mother's voice held a warning.

Stella stood abruptly nearly knocking over her chair.

"I'll kill him, Ma. I'll kill him."

"Stella! The last thing I need is to lose you, too."

She began crying but Stella turned and walked out.

Nothing would stop her. Not her mother's tears. Not the danger of her own death.

Nothing.

White Lies: Chapter 4

The funeral was held secretly at a small chapel in the Oakland Hills. There were more bodyguards and police than mourners.

Less than twenty people were there: her mother, brothers, a few aunts and uncles, some cousins. Not Dominic's lecherous sons, though.

Good riddance, Stella thought. She was happy to never see them again for as long as she lived.

Police had said family attending the graveside service was a bad idea.

Stella nearly choked with laughter on the irony. You think? Why? Because my father was murdered at a graveside service. But her laughter quickly turned to tears.

So after the mass, everyone said goodbye one by one by approaching the closed casket.

Stella kneeled down and put her hand on the shiny dark wood.

"I love you, papa."

She had meant to say something profound, but it was all she could do not to fall apart right there.

She stood and walked out without saying goodbye to her mother.

Near the back of the church, her younger cousin, Ruby, made eye contact from a pew. Stella gave her a wan smile. She hadn't seen the girl in years. In fact, Ruby was no longer a girl. She was a young woman. Instead of messy hair in a ponytail, she wore her sleek black hair in a chic bob and wore a vintage-looking black lace dress. Her round face and full cheeks were porcelain instead of the normal LaRosa burnished olive skin. Her full lips were painted red, but her eyes were ringed with dark shadows.

Ruby quickly reached over and grabbed Stella's arm tightly.

"I need to talk to you."

Stella's eyes narrowed.

"I don't have—" time she was about to say, but then her mother began calling her from the front of the church.

Pulling away from Ruby, she merged back into the heavy crowd of mourners filing out of the church, hoping to leave before her mother caught up but through the cacophony of other voices, she heard Ruby say, "They're coming for us. You're next."

Whirling, she tried to fight her way back into the church, but a bodyguard planted his bulky frame in front of her.

"We've got to keep moving for safety reasons, miss."

Standing on tiptoe, she looked over his shoulder for Ruby's dark head, but the young woman had disappeared. The church was nearly empty. Ruby was nowhere to be seen. What Stella did see was her mother barreling down the center aisle toward her.

"Stella!" her mother cried.

Without answering, Stella turned and headed toward her bike, barked at the foot of the church stairs. She yanked the black motorcycle helmet off the back of her bike just as her mother caught up to her.

"I'm sorry, ma, I just need some time."

"I told you. It was to protect you. That's why we never said anything."

"I believe you," Stella said sincerely. "I just need some time to process all of this."

"Please don't leave without saying goodbye to me. No matter how angry you are," her mother said, eyes filling with tears.

Stella's heart softened and the rage she had boiling inside for the past few days slowly seeped away. She hugged her mom tightly.

"Mama, I love you. I believe you. But I'm still processing all this. Are you going to be okay?" she said as she drew back and met her mother's eyes.

"Your Aunt Rosalie will take good care of me."

Her mother was being escorted to the airport and then had a bodyguard who was going to fly with her to where her older sister lived in Southern Italy. The bodyguard would stay with her mother indefinitely and family in Italy had vowed to keep her mother safe.

Otherwise Stella would have gone with her.

"Please come with me, Stella."

"I can't."

Her brothers came out of the church carrying the coffin with the pallbearers. They glanced at Stella but then looked away.

Like her boy cousins, Al and Jack, she was done with them, too. They had never been close and Stella was okay with that right now.

Her mother gave her a long look. "God keep you safe."

Stella nodded and yanked on her helmet. She slung her leg over the seat of her Kawasaki Ninja 400 and revved the engine before roaring away.

The bike had been a godsend. Hounded by paparazzi and worried that she would be ambushed in her vehicle and assassinated, Stella bought a fast bike that was okay for beginners and spent two days taking lessons from the best instructor in the Bay Area.

She dared any assassin to try to follow her on that bike.

On Detective Griffin's advice, she'd also moved.

Now she was staying in a secure building with an underground garage.

Even so, she was careful. She often took circuitous routes to and from the newspaper building and her home. If a vehicle had been behind her for more than a block, she would detour until she lost it before going to either location.

It wasn't an ideal way to live, but she'd been taught well during her time overseas with the covert Headway team. Her teammates had taught her evasive driving, counter surveillance, psychological warfare —and how to kill.

The only times she'd killed in her life, less than a handful, had always been either in self-defense (to save her own life) or to save someone else's. She knew she should go to therapy for it. Her own form of therapy over the years had been drinking herself senseless every night, sleeping around, and now, extreme workouts.

If she missed a day in her building's gym, she was haunted by the ghosts of those she had killed. Only by running, practicing martial arts, and lifting weights to exhaustion was she able to tamp the specters down. But now, she had one more horror that kept surfacing despite her workouts: the memory of her father being shot dead right in front of her and the nightmarish sound of her mother's weeping and wailing as she clung to his dead body.

Now she woke up each night in stark terror, sometimes waking herself with her screams, wondering if her new neighbors thought she was being murdered over and over.

The only thing that kept her sane was her resolve to find whoever had ordered the hit on her father and make them pay.

* * *

Also by L.T. Ryan

Find All of L.T. Ryan's Books on Amazon Today!

The Jack Noble Series

The Recruit (free)

The First Deception (Prequel 1)

Noble Beginnings

A Deadly Distance

Ripple Effect (Bear Logan)

Thin Line

Noble Intentions

When Dead in Greece

Noble Retribution

Noble Betrayal

Never Go Home

Beyond Betrayal (Clarissa Abbot)

Noble Judgment

Never Cry Mercy

Deadline

End Game

Noble Ultimatum

Noble Legend

Noble Revenge

Never Look Back (Coming Soon)

Bear Logan Series

Ripple Effect

Blowback

Take Down

Deep State

Bear & Mandy Logan Series

Close to Home

Under the Surface

The Last Stop

Over the Edge

Between the Lies

Caught in the Web (Coming Soon)

Rachel Hatch Series

Drift

Downburst

Fever Burn

Smoke Signal

Firewalk

Whitewater

Aftershock

Whirlwind

Tsunami

Fastrope

Sidewinder (Coming Soon)

Mitch Tanner Series

The Depth of Darkness

Into The Darkness

Deliver Us From Darkness

Cassie Quinn Series

Path of Bones

Whisper of Bones

Symphony of Bones

Etched in Shadow

Concealed in Shadow

Betrayed in Shadow

Born from Ashes

Return to Ashes (Coming Soon)

Blake Brier Series

Unmasked

Unleashed

Uncharted

Drawpoint

Contrail

Detachment

Clear

Quarry (Coming Soon)

Dalton Savage Series

Savage Grounds

Scorched Earth

Cold Sky

The Frost Killer

Crimson Moon (Coming Soon)

Maddie Castle Series

The Handler

Tracking Justice

Hunting Grounds

Vanished Trails

Smoldering Lies (Coming Soon)

Affliction Z Series

Affliction Z: Patient Zero

Affliction Z: Abandoned Hope

Affliction Z: Descended in Blood

Affliction Z : Fractured Part 1

Affliction Z: Fractured Part 2 (Fall 2021)

About the Authors

L.T. RYAN is a *Wall Street Journal* and *USA Today* bestselling author, renowned for crafting pulse-pounding thrillers that keep readers on the edge of their seats. Known for creating gripping, character-driven stories, Ryan is the author of the *Jack Noble* series, the *Rachel Hatch* series, and more. With a knack for blending action, intrigue, and emotional depth, Ryan's books have captivated millions of fans worldwide.

Whether it's the shadowy world of covert operatives or the relentless pursuit of justice, Ryan's stories feature unforgettable characters and high-stakes plots that resonate with fans of Lee Child, Robert Ludlum, and Michael Connelly.

When not writing, Ryan enjoys crafting new ideas with coauthors, running a thriving publishing company, and connecting with readers. Discover the next story that will keep you turning pages late into the night.

Connect with L.T. Ryan
Sign up for his newsletter to hear the latest goings on and receive some free content
➜ https://ltryan.com/jack-noble-newsletter-signup-1

Join the private readers' group
➜ https://www.facebook.com/groups/1727449564174357

Instagram ➜ @ltryanauthor
Visit the website ➜ https://ltryan.com
Send an email ➜ contact@ltryan.com

***

Kristi Belcamino is a USA Today bestseller, an Agatha, Anthony, Barry & Macavity finalist, and an Italian Mama who bakes a tasty biscotti.

Her books feature strong, kickass, independent women facing unspeakable evil in order to seek justice for those unable to do so themselves.

In her former life, as an award-winning crime reporter at newspapers in California, she flew over Big Sur in an FA-18 jet with the Blue Angels, raced a Dodge Viper at Laguna Seca, attended barbecues at the morgue, and conversed with serial killers.

During her decade covering crime, Belcamino wrote and reported about many high-profile cases including the Laci Peterson murder and Chandra Levy disappearance. She has appeared on *Inside Edition* and local television shows. She now writes fiction and works part-time as a reporter covering the police beat for the St. Paul *Pioneer Press*.

Her work has appeared in such prominent publications as *Salon*, the *Miami Herald*, *San Jose Mercury News,* and *Chicago Tribune*.

Instagram ➜ Instagram.com/kristibelcaminobooks
Facebook ➜ facebook.com/kristibelcaminobooks